ONE DEAD HEN

Published by AmazonEncore
P.O. Box 400818
Las Vegas, NV 89140

ISBN-13: 9781935597506
ISBN-10: 1935597507

CHARLIE WILLIAMS

ONE DEAD HEN

PUBLISHED BY

amazon encore

1

'Someone in here lookin' for you, not four hours ago.'

This were Doug the shopkeeper talking. I were in his shop, see, peering into his freezer at the little frozen chicken in there and wondering if I shouldn't get it for me tea. Besides me and him the place were empty. I liked it that way. I didn't like it when them others was in there, cos it meant they'd be looking at us funny or even trying to talk to us. No good ever came from that, and I preferred it if they'd all just leave us on me todd, ta very much.

'Who were lookin' for us?' I says.

'They never said who. Just asked did you still live in that there house. And she wanted a packet of Camels, which I don't do.'

'Why?'

Doug sucked a lot of air and shook his head slow. 'Because they don't sell. I tried em once and flogged only one unit. *One* blinkin' unit. And that were to Mrs Garside up the road, who were having mental problems at the time. Thirty year ago, it were, and—'

'No, I mean why'd she wanna know where I lived?'

'Oh, well…she never gave a reason for that.'

I slid open the freezer and got the chicken out. It really were quite a small one and wouldn't cost us more than a couple of quid, like as not. I'd bought some vittles already but nothing of this quality. Maybe I ought to treat meself, I were thinking. Of late I'd been denying myself the finer things in life, it seemed to me, and maybe it were time I stopped that.

'Didn't you ask her?' I said.

'Course I did. But she never said.'

'Well…what'd she look like?'

'I'd say she looked very nice. Not quite as respectable as she might be, but very nice nonetheless. Well turned out. And polite. You know how I'd call her? I'd call her *a cut above*. The overall effect, you know. You could tell she weren't from Mangel.'

'How?'

'Like I say, the overall effect.'

I turned the chicken over, trying to picture this posh bird who were after me. 'She have nice tits?'

'Hoy, I won't have womenfolk spoke of like that in my shop.'

'Did she, though?'

'A bit on the large side, aye.'

'And what did you tell her?'

'Nuthin'.'

'Eh?'

'I refused to answer her questions.'

'*Why*, fuck sake?'

'Because I don't divulge that information regarding my customers. You never do know who she might be.'

'But she's a fuckin' bird, Doug. And you says she were polite and a bit of a sort and that.'

'It don't make no odds—you never do know who yer talkin' to. She could be workin' for someone else, see. She could be dressed up like a nice lady so she can get all manner of information about honest working folks, and then pass it on to her cohorts, them being nasty criminals.'

'Doug…'

I didn't know what to say to him. I just stood there, shaking my head at the chicken and wondering at the shite luck I'd been getting of late in the area of romance. But after a bit me swede stopped shaking, and Doug's words started seeping through and making emselves heard proper, and I saw that they was indeed wise ones. Especially that about cohorts and them being nasty criminals. You just cannot trust folks these days. Not even nice-looking birds with big tits.

'You buying that bird or what?' says Doug. 'Only she'll start thawing in a minute, you keep pawing her like that.'

I put the chicken back and went home.

I couldn't afford it anyway.

THE EVIL THAT CANNOT BE CAUGHT

Editorial by Malcolm Pigg

Mangel has always been prone to a certain type of murder. Ever since I started as a young reporter, bodies have been found. Sometimes they've not been found, and go up on the missing persons chart (although we all know what most likely came of them). These kind of murders are what I call reasonable murders. Killings where there is something to be achieved. Maybe it's a simple revenge murder, or a crime of passion, or the removal of a dangerous criminal by another dangerous criminal, for business reasons.

These kind of murders are the ebb and flow of community life in our town, and we should applaud them. They root out the bad eggs and give us all a reminder of what can happen if you play at cowboys and Indians. They are the natural expression of a human urge, and they have come to pass since the earliest days of man, when Cain and Abel were some of the only people living in the Mangel area. The people who commit these killings live and walk among us. We might know them, or be related to them. We wring our hands and shake our heads but forgive them for it—because if they weren't committing these reasonable murders, someone else would.

But now we share our town with a new type of killer, one whose many crimes seem to hail from a place far beyond the realms of normal human nature…a place more akin to hell itself. This is a man who murders and mutilates our women. Not once or twice, but four times so far. The Reaper, they call him, and who knows when he will strike again? The only thing we know for certain is that he will. You know it and I know it. Our bones tell us and they do not lie. The police know it, too.

And that's about all they do know.

The list of things they don't know, on the other hand, runs to a few pages. Here's some highlights:

- Who is the murderer?
- Why is he doing it?
- What has he done with the victims' heads?
- How many more of our womenfolk will die before they catch him?

I can tell them the answer to the last one: Too many. Just like there are too many officers in that police station who don't know what they're doing, besides drawing a wage against our taxes.

2

I went for a stroll down the main road. Not cos I were off somewhere, but because I wanted a think. So I yanked me collars up
against the parky autumn elementals and set me swede off thinking in the direction I wanted it to.

And that direction were romance and birds.

Like I already noted to you just there, that side of me life
seemed to have winded down a bit of late. And when I says a bit,
I means all the fucking way. And by that I means I hadn't had a
shag in fuck knowed how long. Nor a blowjob neither, nor any
other kind of joint effort in the groin area. As for copping a feel,
you can forget that and all. I couldn't even recall what a breast
were like to the touch. Unless you means a chicken one. I knew
what one of them were like, but I couldn't see your human version
feeling like that. Especially not the ones Doug flogs you, which
are always frozen (even after you cooks em). But in all honesty I
didn't know, maybe they did feel like that. I just plain could not
recall. You could blindfold us and put a pair of coconuts on the
one side and a woman's chest on the other, and I'd find my arse
and shout bingo.

Mind you, it weren't cos I couldn't pull no more. If I wanted
to, I could walk into town and get meself paired off with a proper
cracker before you can run across the park. But I chose not to do
that. Not cos I didn't want to cop off, but because I didn't want
to go downtown. I didn't want no part of that no more. It had all
changed, town had, and not for the better.

I'd come to see the world as it truly were, see. And in particular how shite it can be at times. It's down to folks, I'd come to realise. The things they does to each other—how they carries on in such a bastard of a way for no good reason other than they got an itch up their arse—you can see that they just ain't no fucking good. I'd seen it all, pal, and I'd come to realise how it's the same the world over. And getting worser by the fucking minute.

But Mangel's where you got your highest concentration, in terms of shiteness. Downtown in particular. You just gotta trust us on that one. And if you don't trust us, you can fuck off right now.

Go on.

'Hiya, mister.'

I almost dropped me bag. There were a bird stood there, just outside that alley halfway between Clench Road and my street. I plain hadn't seed her, which were odd, considering how there were no one else around and she were a bit of all right, if a mite on the young side.

'Oh, all right,' I says, pulling meself together and looking her over. I'd put her at twenty, although she were that sort who could be twelve if you ain't careful. She had a red bomber on and tight jeans, and they didn't half work on her. I could tell she didn't mind having my eyes on her. She did the same right back to us and I could tell she liked that and all, which I weren't surprised about. I'd been looking after meself of late, losing a bit of weight and doing the press-ups and that. Also a bit of jogging on the spot.

'Can you help us, mister?' she says, her voice surprisingly sweet and fragile, considering how she looked like a young prostitute. 'I'm scared, and I...'

She put a trembling white paw to her gob and looked behind her up the alley.

I felt ashamed. There and then I could see how I'd been wrong to judge her on her appearance. Me of all folks, learning all about how we as human beings is liable to look at the surface and not at the soul beyond. This girl here were in need of my help. You could see it all over her, once you got beyond the tits and eyes and lips and hips.

'What is it, love?' I says, stepping forward in a protective, non-sexual manner. 'Summat shite you up, did it? I'm here now, s'all right.'

'I'm sorry to bother you, mister, it's just that I need to go down there to get me bike, to go to me friend's house and do me homework, only...' She looked down the alley and bit her lip.

'What? Come on, love.'

'Only I think there's someone down there. A man. He's round that corner there and he's waitin' for us. I don't mean to be such a little girl, mister, only me mam says I shouldn't take no chances, what with the Reaper at large. The way me mam goes on, you'd think all men is bad.'

'Not all men, babe. Your mam is right to warn you like that, but some men is all right. You'll learn em apart when you gets older.'

She smiled and held onto me arm, pulling us up the alley all gentle. Up close I could smell her perfume and feel the heat of her soft hip against mine. As I looked down at her pretty face and smiled, and she smiled back with her lovely white teeth, I felt a bit guilty again.

'I'm probably just bein' silly, ain't I? I bet there's no one there. I can't help it, mister. I think it's cos I ain't got a boyfriend. It's nice to have a man to hold onto, you know? Especially with all the horrible stuff goin' on just now.'

She gave me arm a squeeze.

Pulling meself together, I had a quick scout around. It were one of them high-walled alleys running between the houses, and at the end it joined another alley running behind em. From there you had a little network of alleys, if I recalls em right from me burgling days, leading you all the way back to them lock-up garages off Myrtle Crescent. And the bird were correct in her caution: it were a right dangerous place for one such as her to be knocking about.

'Where's yer bike, love?' I says.

'What?'

'Yer bike. In one o' the lock-ups, is it?'

'Bike? Oh, yeah. Yes, it's in them lock-ups. Erm, I keeps it there. Yeah.'

'Oh aye?'

'Yeah. You don't believe us?'

'Eh? Course I do. Why would you lie?'

'Lie? Me?'

I felt a bit awkward now. All I'd meant to do were find out where the bike were and I'd ended up offending her. In the old days I could charm the bra and knickers off a bird just by asking her the time, but I do admit that I found it hard to make meself plain, just now. You can blame that on all the learning I'd been doing, which makes you a bit rusty in the charm department after a while.

'So, erm,' I says, 'this feller…round that corner there, you say?'

We was right atop said corner and sailing into it, her leading me on like I were the scared one and her the hero. 'No, no,' she says. 'It's the next one. Down there, see?'

It were quiet. Too fucking quiet. All them back gardens just a fence-width away, you'd think there'd be some noise. But no, not even the tweet of a thrush or the yap of a Jack Russell. You could see the corner she were referring to up yonder, about twenty yard off. Between that and here the alley were all spilt dustbins, burst bin bags, and rotting old wooden gates, some of em hanging open. A few poles of scaffolding lay rusting to the one side with nettles growing up between em. There were summat black next to an old wooden crate, and I think it were a dead crow.

'I'm really glad you came with me down here. You're such a big strong man, I feel safe with you. Come on...'

We walked on. Her dragging us, more like. I don't wanna sound like a ponce but summat weren't right here. I sensed danger. Do you know what I mean? I ain't a chicken nor nothing but it ain't clever to go looking for it. And here I were, waltzing down a dark alley with a strange lass who had summat of the gypsy about her.

'Come on,' she says, yanking on me arm. 'It's just round this corner. I mean—'

'Look,' I says, digging me heels in, 'maybe we ought to—'

'Come on. You ain't a chicken, is yer?'

'Fuck off. Course I ain't.'

'You *is*, ain't yer?' she says, poking me ribs. 'Here chicky chick, here—'

'*Fuck off*, you dirty fuckin' slag,' I says, batting her away.

'You what?'

'You heard.'

'You callin' us a slag?'

'Too right I fuckin' is. Pickin' up strange fellers on street corners and leadin' em down back alleys for a shag? Woss that if it
ain't a fuckin' slag?'

'You cheeky bastard,' she yells, turning them filthy eyes on us.
They was burning now, pure raging at us. And I do love that in
a woman. Suddenly I weren't so irate at her calling us a chicken.
Quite the opposite. So opposite, in fact, that I had to pop a paw in
me pocket and adjust meself sideways.

'What right you got to say that?' she says. 'You ain't got no
right. I got a fuckin' *boy*friend. *No* one calls us a slag. You really
thought I'd shag *you*? Don't make me laugh. Look at yer…What
are you, a beggar or summat? You're fuckin' dreamin', mate.
And if—'

'Aw, Trish…you *fucked* it up.'

I didn't know where this new voice were coming from.
Sounded like behind us, but when I turned that way there were
no one.

'You fucked it up *again*,' it went on. 'Yer meant to lure em
down here and keep em sweet, and then me and Nige jumps out
an'—'

'Fuckin' *shush* it, you twat.' This were another voice, just as
hard to place in terms of where it were. Mind you, I could hear
some rustling and twig-snapping behind that fence there. And
the way them overhanging saplings was swaying didn't look natural.

'*Fuck off*,' the bird were yelling in that direction. 'Weren't my
fault he—'

I grabbed her and stoppered her gob with a paw, holding
her firm around the middle. Then I stood stock-still and harked,
watching the little holes in that fence. The bird were struggling

under me arm so I pulled her tighter until she squeaked like a dog's toy, then went still and quiet like a good girl. I were glad she'd got the message. There were summat going on here and I needed me wits about us. I might have knowed this would happen. I should have gone straight home after leaving Doug's, like normal. Or when the bird had stopped us back there on the street—I should have known there and then that you don't wanna be going down dark alleys. There's danger in the world these days. Every fucking direction you turns in, there's folks wanting to rob you and hurt you. And if yer a bird, they wants to rape you and all. Even some fellers gets raped, so I heard. Mind you, my own arse is a one-way street. A doctor tried showing me different once and I elbowed him out cold. Dirty fucking bastard.

But I should have telled this bird here about the dangers.

Me ticker were going fast, and I could feel meself getting ready to turn and peg it like billy-o. I weren't meant to be down here, were I? So I didn't really have to stand and fight like I normally would. I'd been tricked down here, you see, by this lass here, so she could look after her own arse. The selfish fucking slag.

Just about then I felt her lashes fluttering next to me face, like two black butterflies caught on flypaper. Her soft lips struggled against the palm of me paw, crushed there like two warm slugs. My other arm were clamped around her chest, and I could feel her fragile ribcage trembling under the twin pillows of her tits, which felt a lot bigger than you'd think em to look at. A girl like that, she needed looking after.

I picked her up and walked on down the path, the bag of vittles hanging off me arm and swinging to and fro, knocking on me legs. It takes more than one spilt egg to make a chicken, though, and two of them's worth one in the bush, long as you don't count em. I turned the corner, whispering: 'You was right, girl, there is trouble there. Two of em behind that fence back there. Aye, them's who you must of heard. Tell you what, we'll get you to yer bike and you can fuck off out of it, nice and safe. And, erm…soz about callin' you a slag, eh? No hard feelin's.'

I had her in me arms like a babby, face tucked into me shoulder with the relief and emotion of it all, me saving her from them nasty fellers. I couldn't blame her for not wanting to look us in the peepers. She felt ashamed, like as not. She'd called us fifteen types of cunt just now, and I'd gone on to save her life. But I didn't give a shite about that. Long as she showed her gratitude when I got her to a safe and private place, I were all right.

I stopped at a little crossroads. To the left you had the alley leading out towards Higgis Wharf, and the other way you could see the back of them lock-ups. I checked behind us and then struck out to the right. She were a slim young lass despite carrying a lot chest-wise, but she weren't no sprog and it weren't natural to carry her like one. Felt like holding a dumbell semi-loaded at half curl, and walking around like that for a few minutes. Me biceps was starting to burn like two haystacks in August, and I knew that if I didn't set her down soon they'd pop open.

I sort of jogged the final few yards, holding her up to me face now. One of the up-and-overs were up but not over, being at half-mast, so I kicked him home and went inside, almost dropping the bird on the bare concrete. She weren't going on her feet but I couldn't fret over that just then, and I set her on her back, the bag of vittles next to her.

The lock-up were empty but for a few dusty boxes on the one side, an old chest of drawers in the corner, and some filthy rags lying around.

'Hey, love,' I says, swinging me arms and trying to get the ache out. I scraped me knuckles on the ceiling and soon stopped that. 'Hey, you all right? Yer safe now. You wanna get up, love?'

She didn't answer.

'Listen, if you wants to give us a special thank you, in a way that only a woman can, now's the time. I'm here for yer. It'll only take about a minute, and…Hey, where's yer bike?'

She still weren't answering. I had a quick look in the boxes, giving her a moment to pull herself together. Just old tools and a few tiles and the like, covered in dust and cobwebs and no use to no one in their current state. I picked up an old saw and tapped it, watching the rust float groundward like brown snow. In one of the drawers I found a blonde wig, which raised a little chuckle inside us. It were quite a nice one actually, although some varmint had been living in it and chewing some of the lining away. I shook the droppings out and put it on me head. Not cos I likes wearing birds' wigs, but because I thought it might raise a smile in the young lass here when she come to. A gasp behind us and I turned, seeing the bird moving slightly. She gasped again and moaned a bit, and generally didn't sound too rosy. I went and knelt beside her, putting down the rusty saw. She seemed to be having trouble breathing, and her cheeks was all red. I touched her face and it were hot and damp. Behind us I heard a noise. I looked up and clocked a woman stood there in her apron, holding an old broom. She screamed and pegged it away, still screaming.

I sat watching the place where she'd been stood, wondering if I might have imagined it.

'Ah…' the young lass said. 'What the…'

She were sat up now, scratching her swede and everything. Actually she were rubbing the back of it and grimacing. She took her paw away and looked at it, and it had red on it. I must have laid her down on the hard stuff a bit too sharpish for her.

'You all right, love?' I says. 'You must of fainted.'

'Where am I?'

'Them lock-ups. Where's yer bike?'

'What bike? Where's Ian? And Nige?'

'Ian and Nige? Yer a bit disori…dis…Yer in a bit of a tizz, love. It's me here, Blakey. You asked us to walk you down here just now, cos—'

'Oh, is it you still? Fuckin' hell…Look, I'll be all right, you can leave us now.'

'No, you don't understand, darlin'. I fuckin' *saved* you. You was correct—there is a feller hidin' up there. Two of em, to be precise. So really you ought to be a bit more gratef—'

'I said I'd be *all right*, all right? Thanks an' all but just *leave* us now. Jesus…'

I stood looking at her for a bit, shaking me swede.

'Are you still here?' she says. '*Fuck off.*'

I truly couldn't believe the way youngsters went about their business these days, thinking like they'm the only ones in the world. I didn't understand em, pure and simple. There were summat wrong with em, and I didn't want no part of it. Not even this one here, who were quite fit.

'You'll come a cropper, you will, with that attitude,' I says. Then I fucked off before she had chance to reply.

Coming out onto Myrtle Crescent, I walked past a feller and nodded hello to him without thinking about it. It's cos I clocked him as a kindred spirit, him wearing a white shirt and dickie-bow, and that being the formal regalia of the door industry. I walked homeward, swinging me bag of vittles and wondering if I oughtn't to get back into the world of work meself.

MANGEL TODAY—PUBS

Russell Pank

Mangel's pubs are renowned throughout the whole of Mangel. From trendy wine bars to Irish theme pubs to the spit 'n sawdust saloons of yesteryear, Mangel has them all. I took some time to sample their wares and soak up the unique ambience of Mangel by night. Over the new few days I will lay out my findings, starting today with Tubthumpers on the High Street.

Tubthumpers is fast becoming Mangel's premier nightspot. A cavernous former church decked out tastefully in orange and chrome, it is packed out nightly with the more image-conscious of Mangel's youth. A wide selection of beers, wines, and spirits is on offer from the fast-moving bar, with an emphasis on alcopops and bottled lager. There is a medium-sized dance floor to one side, plenty of seating and tables, and a polite and attractive staff. Tubthumpers is open until 2 a.m. nightly. There is an entrance fee on weekends, although women get in free.

I asked manager David Ogilvy what the enigmatic name "Tubthumpers" meant. 'It means people who thump tubs.' Asked how business was bearing up, he ignored me. I told him who I was and showed him my press card, upon which his manner warmed considerably and he offered me my choice from the bar menu. 'I just want to tell your readers about the new minibus service we've got, for women. We've got two buses running every night, four at weekends. We take the safety of our female customers very seriously here. No woman who comes to Tubthumpers need worry about how she's getting home. With the horrible things going on in Mangel lately, we feel this is the only responsible thing to do.'

I had a half-pound Aberdeen Angus steak burger, Swiss cheese, lettuce, salsa, spring onions, and mayo—served with my choice of skinny fries or wedges. I chose wedges.

Next week: The Shamrock.

3

I were well pissed-off when I got home. I don't mind breaking an egg or two, like I says, but all six of em had popped. I scraped em into a pan and spent a while picking the bits of shell out, then dropped some lard in and fried the lot up with the rashers and bangers and mushies. There weren't no room for the bread so I had to stick that in the toaster. A few minutes later and I had a couple of nice plates of scran and a cup of tea. I took em downstairs to the cellar on a tray, perching the second plate atop the mug. It were a well hairy way to carry stuff, especially halfway down when I almost tripped on a varmint, but I made it down without too much bother, besides a few beans falling in me tea. I flicked the telly on and fished the beans out, popping em in me gob. They didn't taste too bad with the tea on em, actually, so I left the rest in the mug and sat down to eat me dinner and watch the telly.

I used to watch a lot of telly in them times. You could say that telly had become my job. But in a good way. You see, I were in a unique position in the Mangel area. I had access to shite like no other person had, in terms of telly watching. And it weren't just crap and boring shite, like *Coronation Street* and the like. I'm talking important shite. Shite that makes a man wise.

This is what I were touching on back there, about finding out about the world, and how plain dire it were getting, strait-wise.

See, one day, about a year prior, I were queuing up at the dole office. I were half dead on me feet from the sheer not knowing much about the world around us. It's the same for everyone at the dole office, although I never knowed it at the time. That's how come they ain't got jobs—cos they're so thick and dunno how to do nothing. All except meself, who were just down on his luck at that time. No one would give us a job, see, cos the papers had dragged my name through the slurry so many times over the years that you couldn't even read it. Anyhow, one of them thick lads in the dole office taps us on the shoulder, and when I turns around I finds it to be Johnny Bengel, who is a good mate of mine from me burgling days.

'You all right, Blakey?'

'All right, John.'

'Here, you want a satellite?'

'A what?'

'A satellite. You know, one of them dish things for watchin' telly.'

'I knows what a fuckin' satellite is.'

'Oh aye? Why's you askin', then?'

'I never fuckin' asked. I'm just sayin'.'

'Sayin' what?'

'You startin' on us, John?'

'Take it easy, Blakey—I'm just joshin'. So you got one, have yer? A satellite.'

'Don't need one.'

'Everyone needs one, Blakey.'

'Not me. I don't watch much telly. Got me vids, see.'

'Vids is all right, but you gotta have a satellite. You know what sort of channels they got abroad? Dirty ones, Blake. Fuckin' filthy—shaggin' and dick-blowin' and the lot of it, mate.'

'Nah.'

'Aye.'

'But they don't work right, them channels,' I says. 'Gerry Furlong down the Volley told us. You can get em up on the screen but they'm all blurry.'

'Scrambled.'

'Aye, scrambled. And in foreign.'

'Who gives a shite if they'm in foreign?'

'You dunno what they'm sayin', does yer?'

'Who gives a…? Look, the point is, if you can see what's going on you don't need to know woss bein' said by em. Know what I mean?'

'I know but you can't see wh—'

'Ah, but you can.'

'No, Gerry Furlong says.' I were getting a bit fed up with him now. It's like I were saying about folks in the dole office. 'And Stan the barman says so as well.'

'Well, they ain't got what I got.'

'Fuckin' hell, John. Ain't you harkin'? They *have* got satellites. See?'

'Not like the one I got, they ain't.'

'Oh aye?'

'Aye.'

'Satellites is satellites.'

'I knows it, but mine's different. You know why? It's a fuckin' *professional* one. You can't get it in the shops. See, these is the ones used by the *secret services*, for spyin' an that. Only five of these uns in the world, there is. One in America, one in Russia, one in, er… Lapland, and one in Mangel.'

I looked at Johnny with newfound interest. 'Oh aye?' I says. 'And how'd you come to have it?'

'Erm…well, me sister's boyfriend, his uncle works for the secret services, see…and he gave it him. He gave it me brother's girlfriend, like. I mean me sister's boyfriend, aye. And, erm…he didn't want it, so he gave it to me. See?'

So I bought the satellite off Johnny Bengel for twenty quid, which I thought were a bargain. And he were right—there weren't no other one like mine in the whole of Mangel. I borrowed a bike and spend a couple of days riding around the different parts of town, looking up at the sides of the rooftops, and not one of em were even close to how mine were. It were like he'd said:

This one were a *professional* one.

Mind you, I couldn't get no secret things on it, for spying and that, once I hooked it up to me telly. One or two of the channels you could hear a bit of talking in the background and a lot of fuzz to look at, but you couldn't make the words out. And that were bollocks about the dirty channels as well. It were just like Gerry and Stan had telled it:

'You can get the channels but they'm all blurry, Blakey.'

I weren't happy about that. No man in his right swede would be. It's like sharing a pit with a nice bird…but you're blind. And paralyzed. And she's foreign. I made a mental note to break Johnny Bengel's jaw when I next saw him, then had a look at the other channels.

There were a marvellous one all about tractors racing each other. Truly, I never even knowed they went so fast, tractors. But it were in foreign, so…And there was another few channels where some folks was showing you things you could buy. Some great items there, I fucking swear. You wouldn't think it at first, looking at em. To look at em, you'd think em pieces of shite that you don't need. But once you started harking the people holding em, and hearing about all the amazing sides to em that you'd never know about just by looking, you realised that you couldn't hardly do without em. I couldn't buy em though cos I'd had me phone cut off donkeys back. Shame.

All the while I were doing this, flicking left and right and up and down through the channels, I were having little looks at the news ones, which went on all day and night and never shut up. I only had little peeks at first, just to see how well that channel showed up compared to the blurry skin channels, and having a little moan to meself about that. But the peeks got longer and longer, and soon I found meself watching news and not much else besides. And I'll tell you summat:

It were an eye-opener.

I'd never really thought about what were going on in the world, see, because I'd never paid no heed to news items on the telly and in the papers, and other current affairs wossnames. I'd been living a life of carefree ignorance, you might say. I used to be a like a daddy-long-legs, flapping around and knocking into things and people, not having no clue nor giving a shite about what were going on around him. And it's all right for the daddy-long-legs, see. He dunno nothing so he don't have to fret. But once you opens yer eyes (and you ain't a daddy-long-legs no more) all you does is fret. You can't help but fret, seeing how the world out there is turning to shite all around us. And soon it gets so you wish you could go back again, shut up yer peepers, and start flapping around and knocking into things again. But you can't.

You can't stop watching the telly news.

Mind you, I did like to watch things that weren't news as well. Especially copper programs. After watching all the shite going on in the world, it gave us a warm and cosy feeling in me guts to see a rozzer lay out a criminal, thereby making the world a better place. I found *Sledge Hammer!* to be the best of these types of programs. Have you seen it? I do recommend it to you if you ain't. Mind you, you ain't got a professional satellite like I had, which means you can't even get it.

So tough shite there.

Anyhow, none of the other shows seemed to take things serious enough. And it's the role of the copper I'm on about here, and how far he will go to do what he's got to. Sledge Hammer, who is the hero of *Sledge Hammer!*, he fucking knows it. He knows what it's all about. He don't fuck about with being nice and giving wedge to informers and that. He knows who's a crook and who ain't and he treats em according. 'Trust me,' he keeps on saying, 'I knows what I'm doing.'

And I'll tell you what—he fucking do as well.

Them's the sorts of coppers you wants out there. Brave, brainy, and rock hard. If I were a copper, that's what I'd be like. You mark my fucking words, pal.

Saying that, I did find Sledge to have his problems. And it's the togs I'm on about here. He didn't have the first fucking clue about how to dress and how to look the part. All you had to do were look at his shite jacket and you knew it. See, when yer a copper, yer a pillar of the community. Folks looks at you as an example of the finer things in life. A copper's got to wear smart gear and drive a beautiful motor, not the snot-green banger drove by Mr Hammer.

The doorbell went.

I ignored it, preferring to continue my telly-watching and scran-eating. I didn't get too many visitors them days, and you could almost say for certain that it were someone flogging windows or summat. When it went again, I started getting annoyed. They just don't leave it, them cunts. You do need good windows though. You got shite windows, you'll get robbed easy. My windows was a bit shite, truth be telled, but I were in the house nearly all the time so no robber would dare fucking try it.

Mind you, they might.

They says on the news about how they breaks in nice and quiet at night, kills everyone in the house, and don't even take nothing. Killing for kicks. That's the kind of folks who was out there in the world. That's why I hardly ever went out.

But I did need decent windows, I now saw.

The bell went again.

I put me empty plates on the couch beside us and went up, thinking how I might be able to get some windows out of him without actually paying. You can do anything if you sets your swede to it. Especially if you're big and the other feller's little.

Looking through the peepy-hole in the front door, I couldn't see no one. Either he were a short cunt or he'd fucked off up the street. I opened the door, hoping for a short cunt, but no one were there. When I shut it again I found a little handwrit note on the floor.

Blake

I have been trying to find you just to say hello really. The man in the corner shop told me you live here so I hope it is correct. I will call again some time.

Lot of love

M

Xxxxxxxxx

I found that odd. I found that exceptionally odd, actually. Odd in a nice way, though. I already telled you how I weren't doing too well with the ladies just then, on account of me not coming across many of em. Well, just look at it now:

Not only were there a posh bird asking about us in Doug's earlier on, but here were another one, also asking about us. And I knowed this were a different one cos Doug had telled us how he hadn't gave me address out to the first bird, but with this one he had.

Two fucking birds in one day. Both of em *quality* as well. You just knew this one were quality from the way she'd folded the paper in half perfect. And she seemed to fancy us as well, looking at all them kisses at the end.

I tried picturing her, using her handwriting as a sign of what she might look like. I'd seen a program on how they can tell all about you from your handwriting, see, so I knew how to do it. Blonde, I reckoned she were. You could tell that from the slightly slopey letters. And all them curvy lines—that means she's got big tits and nice round arse. The handwriting were quite neat and tidy, which meant she had an all right face. Aye, I were well certain of them conclusions.

I closed me eyes and imagined shagging her. After that, and with spunk all over me paw, I went upstairs for a shite.

4

I'd been sitting on the bog for about half an hour, thinking about them two birds, the posh one and the blonde one with big tits. I were thinking about em different now, in a non-sexual way. Wondering how come they was both after us, for example. Course, all you got to do is come within ten yard of us and you knows why that is.

I got sex appeal.

Not for you, you fucking chocolate speedway racer. For the *birds only*. Mind you, it's hard to tell in this light if you're a feller or a bird. You could be one of them lesbians, for example, which means birds who is too ugly to cop off with fellers so they got to try and shag each other, using cucumbers and the like. (I'd seen a program on em—honest to fucking god I had. They never actually showed you the courgettes but I'm pretty fucking sure one of em said it. And it weren't even in foreign.)

Anyhow, I ain't got time to tell you all about that, you mucky bastard. I were on about proper birds, and how I hadn't been getting much of em lately, despite what I got to offer em. In terms of having stuff to offer birds, I'm at the top of the tree in the Mangel area. Look south from the face and you'll find everything a woman wants, and in plentiful supply. It's like the fucking Garden of Eden down there. But with two apples. (Just the one snake, though. And he's a python.) So no, I knew why birds wanted us, even if they'd been deprived for a while. What I wanted to know were why was they suddenly coming after it?

And why two of em?

It's like the buses: you waits half an hour and fuck all. Then one comes, and you get on it and…and it goes to the wrong place, or summat. Actually I can't remember. But it is like the buses.

Mind you, summat occurred to us after a while of thinking about it. And it's the two birds I'm on about here, and the idea that they might actually be just the one bird. It *could* be, you see. And when you knows summat ain't impossible you gets to thinking how it might be possible.

Anyhow, after a while I lost me thought train and started looking around the place. There weren't much to see in my bathroom, besides a couple of towels and a bath, and some bits and bobs on the floor, and some stuff growing in the corner over there. Actually that stuff were quite interesting and I looked at it for a while. Sort of like a bunch of little brown trees, it were, the leaves like rubber and all stuck together. After a while that weren't interesting no more and my eyes lit upon some pages from the *Mangel Informer*, which were lying not two foot from me feet. It weren't the whole paper, course. I'd been using it to wipe my arse on and there were only bit left and I were looking at it and wondering if I had enough. Not that I had an especially shitty arse, but you just never knows how much you'll need cos it takes you by surprise at times. Anyhow, I were looking at the paper and I spotted an advert for FILTHY STAN'S EROTIC MOTOR EMPORIAM, and it had us scratching me swede and wondering what that were all about. Then I noticed the advert under it, which were entitled:

DO YOU HAVE WHAT IT TAKES?

I squinted and read on:

Most do not, but some do. And it's those ones that we want. We want the bravest men in the Mangel area. The most dynamic men. Intelligent men. Men of action. Men of honour. Is this you? If so, ring Mangel Police Force Recruitment Office on...

What a load of crap. Everyone knows they only hire runts for the Mangel Constabulary. Good and proper men, like what they're describing there in that advert—them sort ain't welcome. And that's cos they set off on the wrong foot many a year ago, when they started having coppers in Mangel and everywhere else.

I'd seen a documentary on it, see. It's called inst...instit... erm...it don't fucking matter what they calls it, cos it's the thought that counts, eh.

What it is, right, is that back in olden times the first police chief were a bad example of a man. He were a plain and pure wanker. And if the boss is a wanker, he's gonna want everyone below him being wankers as well, else he stands out and folks ain't happy and you have riots and that. So you ends up with an entire copper force of pure wankers. And when the first boss finally pisses off, everyone else there being a wanker, they makes sure the next feller fits the same shoes. And so it goes on down the years until the present day, which is where we finds ourselves here.

So you got turds all the way up and down the police force, and I found it laughable that they was putting out ads like this one here, making folks think they was taking on only the bestest. I found it so laughable that I dropped a big one into the pan, and it splashed cold water all over my arse cheeks and gave us a shock.

Then the doorbell went again, and I knew straight off that it were one of them birds after us.

I wiped my arse with the *Informer* and went down. Halfway along the hall I recalled how I hadn't washed me paws, and how first impressions is important ones and that. But it were too late. The bell went again and I could see the top of her head in the frosted glass in the front door. It were dark now, and the yellow streetlight framed her silhouette in a very pretty way, making her look like a top model, actually. She were a tall lass all right. Near as tall as meself, unless she were stood on stilts. Or high heels. Aye, that's it. I likes high heels in a woman. Especially when they're with fishnet stockings. And big tits.

I adjusted my hair and opened the door.

'Ah. Royston Blake, is it?'

'Oh,' I says. 'All right, er…Big Bob, er…'

'It's "sir" to the likes of you. And what were all that about, all that scraping and metal noises? How many bolts and locks you got on here? Eh?' He stepped inside and started looking at my front door.

It weren't one of the lasses who'd been after us. It were Big Bob Cadwallader, the police chief. Me and him had a bit of history and I knew he didn't care for us. Mind you, that were in the old days, when I couldn't seem to veer away from trouble no matter how hard I yanked the wheel. But things was different now. I kept meself to meself. And I didn't see no reason why the fucking police chief himself ought to be standing here in my hall, looking at my household security measures.

'Eh?' he says again. 'How many locks you got here? You got more locks on here than they got in the bank. But that ain't what I'm here about. I wants to know about that there big dish you got round the back of this house, on the roof.'

'What about it?'

Big Bob walked through the hall and into the kitchen. He stood there looking out the back window into the yard. I noticed there was some lights out there, beyond the back wall. Lights that was moving.

'I mean,' I says, 'it's just a satellite, ennit. For telly. It's the same as all the others you see, except a bit different in some ways. I buyed it secondhand. From down the market, like.'

I fucking knowed it. First I can't get no skin channels, now I got the coppers round after us. Next time I bumped into that Johnny Bengel, he were fucking dead. Thinking about it, I had a better idea.

'Actually, I buyed it off of Johnny Bengel. Know him? He lives down by the hairy factory. He told us that—'

'I don't give tuppence about who you got it off. It's too big, that's my gripe,' says the chief. 'And the wrong colour. You can't have a bright pink dish on yer roof. Not that big anyhow. It's a distraction for aircraft flyin' overhead. We've had complaints.'

'What? From airplanes flyin' overhead?'

'Never mind that. Why's you got a pink dish anyhow? You a poof, are you?'

'Fuck off.'

The police chief stopped looking out the back window and gave us his glare.

'I mean, I didn't mean *fuck off*, not literal, like,' I says, standing me ground. 'I just meant—'

'I can't think why else a feller might have a pink dish on his roof. You know what I wonders, Royston Blake? I wonders if you ain't a poof, and you don't even knows it. I wonders if that pink dish up there is like a proclamation to the world.'

'Get off it, Big Bob. You knows I ain't a poof.'

'I dunno nuthin'. I only sees what I sees.'

'Well, right now you sees a ladies' man. Women fuckin' *love* me, and I loves them. I can't even get enough of em, mate. I can have any bird I wants, just by lookin' at her. You knows that.'

'And then what you do with em?'

'Eh? What kind of a question's that?'

'I'm just askin', Royston Blake.'

'I loves em, don't I? Loves em and leaves em.'

'So you gets what you wants from their bodies and then you dumps em. That about right?'

'Spot on, Big Bob. See, feller like me, I got *needs*. I got needs and I can't ignore em, you know? I ain't got no choice in the matter. And it's birds I'm on about here. Their bodies, you know... when I needs it, I gets it. Know what I mean?'

REAPER STRIKES AGAIN

Earlier today the headless body of a young woman was found in South Mangel. Evidence suggests that this is the fifth victim of the Reaper, who has terrorised the streets of Mangel for several months. The corpse was found in a lock-up near Myrtle Crescent. As with the other victims of the Reaper, no head was found. Eyewitnesses report seeing a suspicious man in the area with long, curly blonde hair, "like a Viking". One such witness is said to have disturbed a man of this description in the act of committing the murder, although she is under sedation right now and unable to offer written testimony.

'I'm not saying anything,' said Police Chief Bob Cadwallader. 'If I says anything, you'll twist and turn it and make summat out of it that it ain't.'

Asked if he would now admit that this is a serial killer, Cadwal-lader was typically dismissive: 'It could be a succession of copycat killers. Actual serial killers are from films and books. You don't get them in the real world. Not in Mangel, anyhow.'

On the subject of the Mangel Constabulary's failure to appre-hend the murderer(s), he said: 'We've only got the best in this force, men who know what they're doing and devote their lives to doing it. And, er...women as well, I suppose. We're always on the lookout for new ones as well. This force always has room for new faces, as long as they are of the very highest calibre. And as for this murderer, believe you me, we will catch him.'

Challenged about his use of the word 'murderer' and the implicit admission of a single serial killer, he had this to say: 'So? So what if it is only the one murderer? Still don't mean he's a serial killer, does it? He might be a...a...But I'm not saying it is only one murderer, mind you. It still could be two murderers, or three. You just never know for sure, you see. Look, I'm out of time. Print what you like.'

5

I'd been in the cells at Mangel Police Station before, on many an occasion. There was twenty of em in total, I think, and I'm sure I've seen the inside of each one over the years. I were in one now, studying the work on the walls. It were fucking fascinating, I tells yer. Once you adjusted your eyes into ignoring the newer stuff on the top, you could see all the old writing, and it brung back so many memories. They was all there: Finney, Legsy, Big Pete, Ron, John, Don, Lon, Burt, Tommo. Even cunts like Nobby and Cosh. Course, I were there and all. BLAKEY, it said quite clear in big letters. There were another name below it, and I spent a good few minutes squinting and peering and working out what it were and I couldn't do it for the life of us. Looked like ISABELLE, but it couldn't have been cos that is a bird's name, and the birds is kept separate.

'Oi,' comes a voice from thither. And by thither I mean the other side of that selfsame wall. 'You're fuckin' dead.'

'Who's you sayin' that to?' I says.

'You, you cunt.'

'And who's me?'

You'll be impressed at my self-control here. Any other bygone era in my life and I'd already be through that wall and spilling the feller's teeth and sap on the concrete. But it's like I already told you: I'd been laying off the aggro of late. There's too much of it in the world, I'd now come to realise.

'Who are you?' he says. 'You askin' who you are? I'll fuckin' tell who you are: a cunt. Like I just said.'

'Oh aye? You got some proof of that, have yer?'

'Yeah, I fuckin' have. Roll yer sleeve up and read it. Can't get clearer than a label.'

He started coughing there, and while he sorted his lungs out I had a quick look under the sleeve in question. It weren't necessary though. I knew what were tattooed on me arm. And it weren't the word he had in mind, I'm glad to report to you.

'Well, I'm lookin' at me arm,' I says, smiling, 'and all it says here is AUNT MYRA.'

'AUNT MYRA?'

'Yeah, AUNT MYRA.'

The rude feller went quiet, and I knew I had him. Best thing I ever done, getting Tearful Terry the Tat Man to clean me arm up a couple of years back. I did sometimes think that the "A" at the start looked a bit odd, mind you. But Terry reassured us that it were a special letter from the French alphabet, or summat, so I weren't overly bothered. I thought it were quite artistic actually. Mind you, fuck knows who Myra is. I didn't have no aunts so I let Terry choose that name.

'Oh, I gets it,' the rude feller says. 'AUNT MYRA—very fucking clever. Very fucking stupid, more like. You've turned the *c* into an *a* somehow, probably using some fancy foreign lettering that don't look nothing like proper letters, and parked MYRA on the end. As I say, very fucking stupid. You think anyone's gonna be fooled by that? You can't hide a cunt behind a pair of old knickers, you know.'

I jumped up off me bunk and started booting the wall, shouting: 'Hoy, you fuckin' say that again, you cunt. I'll *murder* you, I will, fuckin' *murder* yer.'

The wall weren't budging so I tried getting me paw through the bars on the door and reaching round, but me forearm were too meaty.

'When I gets out,' I says, trying to squeeze the meat through, 'when I—'

Summat grabbed us by the wrist and held firm. I thought it were the bastard next door so I sent me other paw out there to sort matters out, but that wrist found himself grabbed and held firm and all. Next I felt cold metal and a couple of clicks, and me wrists was let go of. I couldn't get em back in though cos they now had cuffs on em.

'Funny you should mention murder,' says a voice much closer, a different voice. 'Cos that's what we was gonna ask you about, Blake.'

His face loomed across the bars from us and I'd know it anywhere. There's only one copper as ugly as him.

'All right, Jonah,' I says. 'Do us a favour and uncuff us, eh.'

'I'll uncuff you when you calms down.'

'I am calm. It's him next door, he's—'

'Listen, Blake—you're in serious fuckin' trouble,' he says. He'd put on a fair bit of lard since I'd last seen him, and the bit under his chin went on wobbling whenever he stopped talking for a sec. 'In a minute I'm takin' you out of this here cell and leadin' you to an interview room, where some people have got some very serious fuckin' questions for you. Ain't no skin off my nose either way, but if I were you I'd want meself straight in the head for it.'

'Fuck off, Jone. Just uncuff us and let us go. You wanna ask questions, fuckin' ask em. I ain't got nuthin' to hide. Big Bob knows I never distracted that airplane on purpose. He's just fuckin' us about cos he don't like us, cos he knows I'm more of a man than him. I got things to do, mate. Come on.'

'You knows I can't do that. And woss you sayin' about airplanes and—?'

'You mean you gotta ask Daddy before you can do summat? Come on and let us out.'

'It ain't like that. There's procedures, and—'

'Fuck off, you little prick. Let us out.'

'Just shut yer face and stand back from the door. *Now*.'

'How the fuck can I do that when I'm cuffed to it, fuck sake?'

'Don't get smart with us, you...you...Look, I'm uncuffin' you just now, all right? And I don't want no monkey palaver. Right?'

'I dunno nuthin' about no monkeys, Jonah.'

'That's *Sergeant Jones* to you.'

'Sergeant? How'd you manage that? You suck someone's cock?'

'Listen you, you little...Let me ask you summat, eh? Who's in there and who's out here? Who's livin' in a shite-hole with fungus growin' in his bathroom and who's got a nice semi-detached house with central heatin'? Who's married and got two young-uns? Who's on his todd? Who's got the stripes on his arm? Who's got the word CUNT tattooed on his arm?'

'Is that what it is, then?'

'What?'

'That stuff in me bathroom. Fungus, is it?'

The feller next door started laughing. I didn't care for that. I thought about doing summat about it, hauling backwards and yanking the door off his hinges. Then I recalled how far that had got us last time, and I just laughed along with him instead, thereby pissing off Jonah and turning him purple. He stomped off down the corridor, leaving us cuffed to the bars.

After a while I found I couldn't laugh no more. Especially since there were fuck all to be amused about, really. 'Come on, who's you?' I says to the wall.

'Never you mind. I knows who you are, and in time you'll know who I am. You will feel my wrath, and all will be well once again.'

I thought about his voice and racked me swede in vain for close matches. There were summat odd about it, a slight accent perhaps. You hear someone with an accent in Mangel and you remembers it. I just didn't know this fucker.

While I were thinking about that I looked at the writing on the wall, and the bit where it said BLAKEY, and I finally worked out that the name someone had wrote below it weren't ISABELLE, but ISA BASTARD. Unusual name, I remember thinking. But not unheard of. There were a teacher at school called Roger Bastard, for example.

'Come on,' I says. 'I ain't lairy no more. Just tell us who you is.'

'You'll have to sit tight and wait for me to present meself.'

'You ain't from round here, is yer?'

'Maybe no. Maybe so.'

'How'd you know us, though? I mean, about me tat and that?'

He went quiet for a sec, and I truly did believe he were gonna spill the baked ones. But a door opened up yonder and the moment were lost. Jonah had a mate with him this time. The mate were staring at us and I thought he looked a bit scaredy, to be honest. He uncuffed us, opened the door, and cuffed us again, Jonah standing behind him the whole while with his truncheon out, slapping it in the palm of his paw like he knew how to use it.

If I wanted to I could have it off him and up his arse in five seconds flat. But I didn't want to. He'd enjoy it a bit too much, like as not.

As they led us away I asked em who that feller were in the next cell.

'Him? He's just a *D & D* they picked up in town. But that's the least of yer worries,' says Jonah. 'The shite about to land atop of you, you won't even recall being in that cell.'

'Bollocks to that,' I says, trudging on. 'It ain't proper trouble.'

6

'Cigarette?'

The copper who'd just come in never even looked at us. Tossed the pack down on the table, then a file, then himself in the placcy chair across the table from us. I hadn't ever seen this one before. He were in his thirties, suntanned in an orange sort of way and wearing jeans and a shiny shirt, like he were just off out on the razz. Smelling like a tart's window box as well, although I did quite admire the pine-fresh fragrance of his aftershave. Big city all over him, mind you. He didn't look like the normal kind of twat you get for a copper. Ain't saying he weren't another kind of twat, mind.

'No, ta,' I says.

'I'm DI Borstal. You can call me Dave if you want but I'd be sure about that before you do. So, you don't want one of my fags? Your file says you smoke.'

'Well, I don't. Change it in the file, Dave.'

'I will.' Looking at us now. He had grey eyes that would have made him look a bit hard if they weren't so watery. I think I got to him there, calling him Dave so quick off the mark. Bet he weren't used to that. I knew he weren't used to the like of me. 'But you used to smoke, yeah?'

'Perhaps.'

'When did you stop?'

'About a minute ago.'

'Oh, I see. You don't want one of *my* fags. That right?'

'Yer gettin' it, pal.'

'Right, and let me guess: you don't want one of *my* fags because *my* fags are *copper's* fags. And you wouldn't be seen dead with a *copper's* fag between your lips. But hey, you've got your reasons. Of course, you're not blindly prejudiced against all coppers. Lemme see...persecution. Since boyhood the coppers have persecuted you. And not just you—your family and everyone you know. Again and again, they've locked you up for crimes you were innocent of. And on the flimsiest of evidence...things like fingerprints, witness testimony, and being collared on the scene. So the coppers must be cunts, right? Because you and your family and friends, you lot *aren't* cunts. You're good people, right? You never do *anything* wrong. In fact, you keep the peace. You're a stabilising influence on the town. Meanwhile, we coppers here are just out to make everyone's life a misery. And that's why you won't smoke a copper's fag. Isn't that right?'

'No,' I says, 'I just don't like Camels.'

He tried to use them grey eyes. I think he knew they didn't work cos he soon gave up. Maybe they'd worked for him once, before they went watery. 'I like you,' he said, lighting a smoke instead. 'You're good value.'

'Good value?'

'Yeah.'

He liked me but I didn't like him. I'm a good judge of character and I had him down as a pure cunt so far. And a twat. I fixed him with a *proper* hard look and says: 'I ain't a fuckin' frozen chicken, you know.'

He were taking his first drag just then and started coughing and spluttering and eye-watering even more. I looked around and wondered what to do, in case he passed out. I could change into his togs and slip out, perhaps. Bit short on the inside leg, mind you. While I were still thinking on that he sipped some coffee and got himself together again, saying: 'You're a funny man, Royston Blake. I've not laughed like that in a cop station in…well, I dunno.'

'Laugh? You was laughin' at us?'

'*With* you, Royston. I appreciate a man of spirit and humour, no matter what side of the law he's on. Know what I mean? We're all in the same game, cops and robbers, and it's good to get along.'

'I ain't no robber. I ain't robbed no one in donkeys.'

'And I'm not saying you are, it's just a turn of—'

'And I never distracted no airplane. Not on purpose nohow. I got that satellite off Johnny Bengel, so you can ask him about it being pink. Cos I ain't bent neither, right? You wanna know about bent people, ask Johnny. I told Big Bob that but he just wants to fuck us about and keep us here. Come on, mate, do us a favour and let us go.'

'No one gives a fuck about your satellite dish, Royston. Weren't you told what you were being arrested for?'

I shrugged.

'They should have told you. You're in here on suspicion of murder.'

'Oh for fuck sake…'

'You don't seem too bothered.'

'I am fuckin' bothered, I'm just used to it, is all. They'm always gettin' us in here on suss of murder and they never got no evidence. I ain't done nuthin'. Who's I meant to of carked, anyhow? You ain't on about them airplanes, is you? Don't tell us one crashed cos of my fuckin' satellite.'

'No plane crashed, so far as I know. And there is enough evidence to justify bringing you in. A red bomber jacket was found in the alley behind your house, and we think it belonged to the girl. Plus the chief says you made some highly suspicious remarks to him.'

'I never said fuck all suspicious to him. And what girl you on about? You sayin' a girl got topped behind my house?'

'A young woman, to be accurate. She was pulled out of the river earlier today, but we think the murder took place at a location about four hundred yards from your street. It was just the jacket that we found behind your house. What are you shaking your head for?'

'Nah, I'm just amazed, really. At the coincidence of it all. See, I were sayin' to some bird just earlier today that she ought to watch out, on account of bad folks roamin' around and murderers and that. They'm all over the fuckin' shop these days, murderers. You sees it on the telly.'

'I might be talking to one now.'

'Bollocks. Everyone knows I never kill birds. It's just Big Bob, fuckin' us around again.'

'*I* don't know it, Royston. And I'm the one who matters, not Chief Cadwallader. But don't worry, I'll find out the truth. You know what's going on out there? They've got about ten boxes of suspicious material found in your house. They're searching through it, looking for evidence.'

'You can't take my gear. It's my fuckin' gear, that is. And I ain't done nuthin'. Woss you took, anyhow?'

'Ah, all sorts…books, tools, and utensils that could be used for violent purposes, soiled garments, footwear, other odds and ends.'

'Soiled garments?'

'Yeah—you know, jeans, underwear…other clothes that might show up DNA or other incriminating material. I know it's an invasion of privacy but we can't take any risks in a case of this magnitude. Do you realise that this is the *fifth* vict—'

'You've swiped me dirty trolleys? How many pairs?'

'What? Oh…I really dunno. Look, it's not—'

'Cos I only got four pair. Woss I gonna wear for trolleys?'

'If they find anything incriminating, you won't need to worry about that.'

'They'd fuckin' better not. I ain't done fuck all wrong, like I says.'

'Well, if that's true then we'll soon know it. That's what a copper does, Royston. We're not all cunts. Although…' He checked that the door were shut, then leaned in. 'I can see how the ones around here might give you that impression.'

I couldn't help but smile, despite the trolley problem. He were all right, this copper. Hard to believe it but here were a copper, and he were all right.

'Why's you here, though?' I says. 'If you knows they'm all cunts, why's you workin' here? I mean, you ain't from Mangel, is you?'

'I transferred here from the city. I chose to come here, Royston. The city, it's not all they say it is. You can get bored of it like anywhere else. I wanted pastures new. And when I heard about Mangel, I knew it was for me. It's an all-action kind of town, you know? Bloke like you knows all about that, right?'

I were nodding slow. 'I seen a bit.'

He winked. 'I've seen yer record, mate. You've seen *a lot*.'

'Aye, well…it ain't all like it seems.'

'Nothing is as it seems, Royston. Like the birds in this town. They're rough but they're *quality*, you know? When you get em in the sack, I mean. I knew it before I came here, but I've had it confirmed since, if you know. Girls in the city, I've got no patience for them. The *demands*…Jesus.'

I looked at him, rubbing me chin and going: 'Hmmm.'

'You look pensive, Royston.'

'Eh? Nah, I'm just thinkin'.'

He seemed confused about summat so I went on:

'Thinkin' about you being a copper, see. I mean, you just don't expect coppers to pull birds.'

'Why not?'

'Cos no birds'd touch em, for starters. The ones round here anyhow.'

'It's like I was saying, Royston, there's all kinds of coppers these days. It's all about fitting in, not setting yerself apart. You wanna catch the crook, you've gotta live alongside him. Be like him. *Blend*, mate.'

'Hmmm…' I says again.

I had a couple of further questions for him, but the door opened just then and a uniformed copper walks in carrying a box marked R BLAKES SUSPISCOUS MATIERALS. On the top you could see a couple of books sticking out (one of em being *UFOs—Fact or Myth?* which were one of my favourites), a round metal thing that looked like my garlic crusher (I were getting quite into cooking just then), and some strands of the blonde wig I'd put on earlier in that lock-up. I'd forgot about it until I walked past a mirror at home.

'Don't you people ever knock?' says DI Dave.

'Soz, guv, but we—'

'Who are you?'

'PC Mard, guv. We got a—'

'Did you lot find any evidence or what, Mard?'

'Aye, we did. Most of them vids is Rocky ones, and Clint Eastwood cowboy ones and that, but six of em is just plain filthy. So, aye, we think we got him.'

'You can't lock a man up for having skin flicks.'

'Nah, but it says all about his psychological state, see. He projectifies women, see, and—'

'Objectifies.'

'—and he…What's that?'

'Just shut up, Mard. The man's sat right here. Show some respect.'

The copper looked a bit narked but turned it into a sneer. 'It's only Royston Blake, guv. When you knows him like we knows him, you won't worry about respect.'

'You cheeky fuckin' cunt,' I says, standing up. 'Didn't you hear DI Dave? He told you to shut yer mouthy fuckin' gob. And that's a fuckin' *order.*'

'All right, Royston, just sit down. Mard, are you just gonna stand there talking shit, or have you got something useful to tell me?'

PC Mard didn't look happy. He were clutching the box a bit too hard and the bottom fell through, but he were quick and got a paw under it. He had to lurch forward a bit though, and a couple of things fell off the top, namely the garlic crusher and the wig.

'Watch me fuckin' garlic crusher, you,' I says.

'Garlic crusher?' He looked at DI Dave, shaking his head firm and saying: 'It ain't, guv. Sergeant Jones says it's a secret device for tocherin' fingers, not an onion crusher.'

'*Garlic,*' I says. 'It's for garlics, you twat.'

'It ain't, guv. Jonah showed us. You puts the finger in there and squeezes it, like so, and it puts lots of little holes in the…*ow…*'

'Take your finger out, Mard,' says DI Dave. 'And get out.'

Mard stuffed the crusher and the wig back in the box, saying: 'They got the results back on that blood in the lock-up. It does match the corpse we pulled out the river. So we're lookin' at a feller in his mid to late thirties, with blonde, curly, shoulder-length hair and a look of the Viking about him, accordin' to that old dear's testimonial.' With that, he stepped back out and slammed the door. In the corridor you could hear him dropping the box again.

'What the fuck's that all about, guv?' I says. 'I mean, Dave?'

'It means you can go.'

'What? Serious?'

'Are you or are you not an innocent man?'

'Aye, course.'

'Clear off then. One of the grunts'll bring your gear round tomorrow. If they don't crush their fingers first.'

MANGEL TODAY—PUBS (PART TWO)

Russell Pank

A walk along Monk Lane and into Cutler Street brought me to The Shamrock—Mangel's only Irish-theme pub. The atmosphere inside was warm and lively, with no music but lots of friendly background chatter. I ordered a glass of stout and sat at the bar. The barman was a young man with dark hair and green eyes—a Celt through and through. I asked him if there were many of his kind in Mangel.

'No, we're pretty underground,' he said in a low voice. 'Most people sort of know about this place but they don't pay it too much attention.'

Surely advertising would help to get a few more punters in? Or at least removing the obscured glass from the front, so everyone could see what a lively pub it is?

'No, we don't want to attract attention. People around here, they just don't understand, you know? And anyway, if you're not "my kind", as you put it, what are you doing here?'

I told him that I was just curious.

'Oh, I see. One of those. Well, just take your time. No one's rushing you. It's your life.'

He went off to serve another customer. I took his advice and sipped my beverage slowly, looking around and noticing that there were no women in the pub. Most of the customers sported shaved or close-cropped hair. Many wore tight white T-shirts, some with leather trousers. One man seemed to be dressed entirely in black rubber, and another wore only leather chaps and a thong. I smiled warmly at these Irishmen who wore their national dress with such pride. It was great to see the old traditions kept up in exile.

A man with a large moustache approached me and asked if I was waiting for someone. I told him no, I was actually working. He laughed enigmatically and then looked me up and down, admiring my new trench coat. 'How much?'

I smiled and told him that it had cost a hundred pounds.

'Hundred quid? Blimey, it better be good for hundred quid. Er, where?'

I couldn't remember the name of the shop, so I described the location.

'Down by the bus station, eh? Mate, for hundred quid I'd expect a big bed, mirrored walls, and scented candles, not a quick fumble up a dirty alley. Although, saying that...'

I didn't catch the rest of the sentence because he walked away, rejoining his friends and sharing a joke with them. Thereafter I detected a certain froideur between myself and the other customers.

'Listen, pal,' said the barman a few minutes later. 'I think you better go.' Asked what the problem was, he said, 'Look, you just don't belong here, right? So you can take your hundred-quid cherry and get lost. OK?'

I finished my drink and got off the stool. I wasn't impressed with The Shamrock. As a theme pub I thought it didn't work, and frankly painted a poor picture of the Irish diaspora in Mangel.

7

DI Dave let us out the back door of the station, saying it'd be better that way. I thought that a bit odd but I didn't question him on it. I were happy to go along with whatever this copper wanted, cos he were the first one of em I'd ever met who seemed like a quality feller. A bit like me in that respect.

And it had gave us ideas.

Walking home, I had a think. About my life and the way it had gone as yet. When you really thought about it, you could see that I'd always had it hard. It showed on my face and I knew it. People wasn't so backwards in coming forwards about talking to us them days, due to my toning down of certain violent tendencies, and they spoke their mind. They'd telled us about the lines under me eyes, and the sparseness of the hair up top (only in places, mind). I'd heard all about how I didn't walk the same no more. Gone were the swagger, in were the measured gait of one who is a man of thoughts and not instincts no more. I'd learned that the hard way. I'd learned everything the hard way.

And it showed on my face.

Don't get us wrong here. I ain't saying it ain't my fault. I knew I'd made it hard on meself and I weren't in the job of blaming others, but any cunt could see how the coppers had took a dislike to us from the start, and had gone out of their way to give us special attention. It's all about making that first mistake that colours your life from thereonafter. You fucks up as a youngun, they keeps an eye on you forever, breathing down your neck and hauling you in on the slightest thing, even when they ain't got no evidence.

I'd hoped all that might have changed, what with me keeping meself to meself and living the quiet life. I'd thought, long as I stuck to me own patch and didn't mix with bad folks in town, that they'd leave us be. And then this, about the dead lass and the satellite. I wouldn't never be free from the long and greasy pole of the law. Not unless I done summat about it.

And I'd had an idea as to what.

I were thinking about it, and how I'd pull it off, as I let meself in the house. And that's how come it took us aback to find the state they'd left me place in. And it's the coppers I'm on about here. There's a way to search a man's house for evidence, and there's a way to trash his house. The coppers had chose the second way.

I walked around, picking up this and righting that, thinking about how wrong the coppers had got it, using up all their energy on tormenting a few innocents when they ought to be out there catching villains, like this feller who'd carked the lass. But when you thought about it and scratched your head a bit, you could see how it ain't so much their fault. And it's like I says before, about them employing nothing but cunts because cuntish is all they knows. They needed to be showed the way.

If someone showed em the way of the Sledge Hammer, for example, they'd be ticking along perfect with no worries, catching villains left right and middle, being nice to yer innocent man on the street, and generally making the world a more better place.

The cellar were the worstest, in terms of havoc wreaked. Down there were where I'd been spending most days for the past year or so. I had me telly set up there and me vids and books and everything. I just felt snug down there, and there were plenty of room to swing a cat if I'd had one. But it didn't feel snug no more. The fucking cunts had ripped the lining out of the sofa and swiped most of me vids and other gear. The telly were kicked over and didn't come on when I righted it and pushed the button. I looked round back and saw that some cunt had holed it and pulled all the innards out, wires and electrical bastards hanging down like entrails from a popped hedgehog.

I stood there for a bit, taking it all in. This cellar were my fucking headquarters, mate, and look what the cunts had done to it. It done me swede in just to look at it, and I felt me guts going jelly and me pins wobbling. I knew that this were a special moment in me life. A turning point, if you likes. I had a choice here. I were at a junction and I could go either way.

The one road led us to a barmy place. You could see it were red up there and there were a lot of aggro going off. I could see meself raging at coppers for what they'd done to me house and getting meself locked up again, doctors looking at me swede and cutting it open again.

The other road led a to a blue place. It were quiet that way, but for the sound of someone sobbing. And it were me, I soon worked out. I were sitting on me arse, feeling the weight of the world coming down around me lugholes, and I couldn't fucking cope with it. There were a big hole in the ground just next to us and I were looking down it, watching the tears fall and plop into the cold water down below. I were thinking about letting meself drop down there as well.

And it were then that I came aware of the third road, which is the road I took. This road led up the stair and into another room of my house, one where you had windows in the walls instead of just bare brick and darkness, and where it smelled a little bit of old chip fat instead of rising damp and the grave.

Half an hour later and I were sorted. It were better in here anyhow, in the living room. I ought to have been using it all along really, but the cellar had just felt like the best and safest place to set up camp, so that's where I'd been for the past fuck knew how long. And do you know what? I reckon it were down to this local murder, me hauling operations up the stair. It's strange but fucking true, I tells yer. You'd think I'd want a safe place to hide more than ever now, but you'd be thinking wrong. It's like it were all brung out into the open now, all the bad shite going on in the world, and there were no point in steering clear no more.

Do you know how I felt? I felt like I were the one to do summat about it.

The chosen one, you might say.

I'd always felt like a chosen one. As a babby I could have sweared someone had whispered it in my ear over and over. *You is the chosen one. You is the...*And it's me mam whispering there, her who carked it before I got to show her what a fine example I were turning out to be, feller-wise. And it ain't just the whispering mam what notified us to me being chosen. It's more stuff as well, like when I went to school and started hanging about with other lads. It don't take a fucking scientist to see how I'm a different breed from others. And it ain't just the swede department I'm on about there. It's the whole fucking package, my friend. Me, I could look at a situation and know all about it, straight off. Other lads'd have a clock at it, shrug, and get on with summat else.

Like all young lads, it weren't long before I were hauled up in front of the coppers and magistrates. And this is another thing what told us about me being a chosen one. See, I never seemed to get done for nothing. Every cunt knowed what I got up to, robbing houses and motors, shoplifting, a bit of mugging and the odd armed robbery. But there were always someone to pull us out of it at the right time. And it's doctors I'm on about here, and certain other notables in and around the Mangel area.

So what you had in Royston Blake, chosen-one-wise, were a feller who had a brain made for working matters out, and a unique ability to get others pulling for him. In short, I were a bit like a perfect copper.

And it weren't no coincidence that I'd come to that knowledge just now, when Mangel were walking through a shite patch.

The telly in the living room weren't such a big one, but I managed to wire him up to the satellite and get an all right picture. Besides that you had just an armchair and a sofa in that room, which were all I needed just then. Mind you, some curtains would improve matters. I'd have to put some up on the morrer. Until then I could keep the light off and watch telly in the dark.

I made meself a cup of tea.

Time were, I'd be sucking on the whisky bottle last thing at night. But I didn't have the urge so much of late. It's cos of staying away from town, that is. Places I used to frequent, you can't help but drink a lot of sauce. But if you stays in all the time and just watches telly and improves yer mind, you don't want it so much.

You should try it. Them bust veins on your nose, you could do with laying off the sherbet yerself. Eh? You knows I'm talking sense.

And I hadn't smoked a fag in months, neither. I can't say I didn't have the urge for that no more, but it had gone away a fair bit of late. I'd packed em in on doc's orders, after I'd coughed half me lungs up one morning, spraying the sheet red. He says I'd need a transplant if I coughed any more of em up, and that they costs a lot of wedge and you got to wait fucking yonks, carking it like as not in the meantime. I told him Butcher Fred in town does pigs lungs for a fair price and I'd sooner have one of them than cark it, but the doc weren't keen, saying they don't fit right or summat.

One Dead Hen

I took me mug of tea and trotted into the living room, slopping a bit over the edge but not fretting too much cos the carpet were tea-coloured anyhow. I sat meself down in the darkness and didn't feel too bad about being in there, though it were a bit odd without the bare brick walls of the cellar around us. I watched the news for a bit. Then I did some flicking, hoping to find *Sledge Hammer!* I didn't need no news no more. Not after finding out about that poor lass out there, getting butchered in me own backyard near as not. It's like all the telly watching had been gearing us up for summat, showing us how the world were getting so I could get off me arse and do summat about it.

And it's catching villains I'm on about here.

I couldn't find *Sledge Hammer!* but I did find *Miami Vice*. That program is quite good as well. The copper in it—Sonny Wossname—he ain't got what Hammer's got, in terms of knowing how to get results and not fucking about. But he do have what Hammer ain't got.

I'm referring to the togs.

And the motor.

If you want to know the way forward, tog-wise, *Miami Vice* is there for you. The gear on display in that program is an example to coppers everywhere. Impeccable tailoring, that's how I'd put it. And as for that motor he drives in it, you just cannot say enough about it. That's what a proper policeman needs, see: a pure *class* motor, to show robbers and hooligans how he's a cut above. He needs a Ferrari. Or a Ford Capri.

I thought about that as I fell akip.

MANGEL TODAY—PROSTITUTION

Russell Pank

Of course, Mangel is about more than just pubs. A dispassionate look at our town today will take in the bad things as well as the good. One such bad thing, arguably, is prostitution.

Step into any telephone booth in the town centre and behold the array of cards stuck to the wall, each one of them advertising the services of a prostitute and a number to call. As quick as the town council takes them down, up they go again. No one ever sees who puts them up, and no one admits to dialling the numbers. I decided to dial some of those numbers myself. And get some answers.

The first card I picked showed a young woman in black underwear, face obscured by the legend NEW IN TOWN. A bubbly female voice answered, 'Hello?'

'Hello. Is that "NEW IN TOWN"?'

'Oh, yeah. I'm new in town. Will you show me around?'

I told her that I was a local reporter and that I was doing a feature on prostitution. After a short pause, she hung up.

The next card was a young woman with Mediterranean looks, according to the picture. This time it was her chest that was obscured by the word EXOTIC.

'Hello. Is that "EXOTIC"?'

'I'm exotic, baby. What you want? I got it all. All for you, baby. Come on, what you want? You want come here, or me you?'

Again, the line went dead when I told her that I was a reporter. None of them wanted to talk, unless it was business. I could see that I might have to arrange a 'date' with one of them, and pay her for her time.

'Hello. Is that "HIGH CLASS"?'

'You want high class, do you?'

'I'm just wondering if that's what you are.'

'Well, I am.'

I went along with this banter for a while, trying to play the role of a punter out to pay for sex. It was surprisingly easy to slip into, and I can only attribute that to the prostitute's sales technique. But behind the patter I could detect something else, a certain self-awareness that I hadn't noticed in the others. I knew that this was the best chance I had, and that if I could get her to relax and open up I could really plumb her depths and come up with something earth-moving. And she would get something out of it, too.

'Tomorrow?' she said. 'You want to see me tomorrow? Well, it's your call. Tomorrow at three, then.'

CONTINUED...

8

I were having a nice dream. One of the best dreams I'd had in a long while, actually. Most dreams of late had been nightmares, but this one here, I'd rank it up there with the finest. I were in the arcade, see, slotting shrapnel in a fruitie and winning jackie upon jackie. There were a bucket beside us half full up of lids, cos I just kept winning and the lids kept on pumping out. Plus Fat Sandra—the bird who run the arcade—were being nice to us for a change. Here, hark this bit:

'You all right there, Mr Blake?' she says, her in her little kiosk.

'Aye. Ta, San.'

'You need another bucket yet?'

'Not yet. Do us a cup o' tea, though, eh?'

'Certainly, Mr Blake.'

'Nice one. And it's DI Blake. Right?'

'Of course, DI Blake. And would DI Blake like me to take my top off?'

'Nah, yer all right, San. Do us a favour and keep it on.'

'Are you sure, because—'

'Go on then.'

So you can see that it were going all right, this dream. But you'd be wrong if you thought that, cos it were about to turn shite-wise like no other. And it's guns I'm on about here, and bastards firing bullets at you. One of em came pinging past me lughole and into the fucking machine, making her blow up. I jumped back just in time and rolled under a pinball table. I think it were the *Rocky III*.

I could see Fat San's fat legs come wobbling over the floor. 'Here y'are, Bla—' She got as far as that before the bullet hit her. She went down hard, making all the machines jump an inch or so in the air. The mug of tea landed atop her swede and the handle broke off. I watched it roll towards us, wishing she hadn't spilt it cos I could have done with some tea just then. The mug stopped about a foot shy of where I were lying. I righted it and had a look inside and found it to be full up of whisky, which were odd. And it weren't actually a mug, but a whisky bottle.

There were a lull in the gunfire outside and I put the bottle down. I got me weapon out and stood up, edging doorward. I knowed it were only a dream but you got to look after yerself, even in dreams. I were keeping back-wise to the wall, gun up high just like you're meant to. Only trouble were the wall kept shifting away from us, no matter how fast I ran after it. Soon enough the wall went away and I were by the arcade door, hid behind a marble pillar. If I looked in the glass front of the fruitie across the way I could see the reflection of someone moving around outside.

'Hello,' says the feller, sounding like DI Dave. 'Come on out and see us, eh.'

'Fuck off,' I yells at him. And I seemed to be speaking in the voice of Sledge Hammer. 'I mean, throw down yer weapons. Trust me—I knows what I'm fuckin' doin'. I'm a fuckin' copper, see.'

'We ain't got no weapons here, son. Me, I'm your friend. You can't stay on your todd in there forever. Sooner or later you've got to—'

'I says you best fuck off. This is *my* fuckin' dream. Piss off and leave us be.'

'I can do what I like. I'm stood on the pavement here and I've a right to be here. This is a public byway. What was that about dreams?'

I woke up then and cottoned onto the reality of it all…me kipping in the armchair in me living room, the fat-face feller over there in the window, me not being a copper at all and Fat Sandra being liable to treat us like a cunt same as always, like as not. I were happy to know that I weren't being shot at for real, but otherwise quite grumpy, I do admit.

'Oh, welcome back from the land of nod,' says the fat face in the window. 'You do realise it's nearly ten in the mornin'? There's reporters here been waitin' politely on you for over an hour. They calls it politeness and I calls it summat else, but either way, enough's enough. Come on out now and answer yer questions. Tell you what—we'll give you two minutes to brush up and make yerself presentable, eh. Oh, and get yerself some flamin' curtains. People don't want to walk past and look at you lyin' there with yer belly out.'

I think I drifted off back into the land of nod there for a bit. When I woke again I got on me feet, recalling summat about a bloke at the window just now. I couldn't quite recall the details, and I had more important matters to fret over anyhow, such as getting me house in order. I did some more walking around, picking shite up and wiping dust off. While I done that I could hear that voice again outside, a bit further away this time:

'…useless, you are. All you got to do is knock on his door and ask him some questions, and you can't even do that.'

'But—'

'But nuthin'. You seen me wake him up, didn't yer? Do you see me quakin' in me boots? No. I employs you to get in there and get the story, then get out again and chase the next story. I don't pay you to stand around smokin' all day, takin' down the odd quote from neighbours. It ain't the neighbours I wants quotes from—it's him in there.'

'I don't smoke, boss.'

'Don't you give me lip. You ain't so big as I can't bend you over me knee.'

'Sorry, boss. It's just that, well, I see myself as more of a features writer, and I really feel like I'm onto something with these—'

'—"Mangel Today" things. Aye, I wanted a word about that.'

'And "Mangel Yesterday".'

'*Don't* you interrupt me, Pank. I'll not abide interruptions.'

'Sorry, boss. But—'

'Now, I'm off back to the office. If you ain't got this story filed in one hour, yer fired. And I wants a bloody good story, right? All questions asked and answered. Got it? Or else.'

'But—'

'I don't care about your wife and two younguns. You does this job right or you goes down the labour exchange. And you can forget them "features" of yours. Folks ain't interested in pubs and prostitutes.'

'Hoy,' I yells, pushing the window up and sticking me swede out, 'woss you doin', hangin' around the front of my house?'

'Like I says…er…' says a middle-aged feller in a grey suit. Sounded very much like the one who'd been talking just now, actually. 'I…I gotta get back to the office, and…' I couldn't hear no more cos he were off down the road.

'Go on,' I shouts at the remaining five or six. 'Fuck off.'

'Well, Mr Blake, I…er, we…'

'You deaf or summat? I says fuck off. That means you. *Now*.'

'But…'

He still weren't budging. A feller behind him took a photo, blinding me eyes with his flash. A bird stepped in front of them two, dragging a feller who were holding a microphone and a big lump of machinery with knobs on. 'Mr Blake,' she says, yanking the microphone off him, 'Barbara Knox from *Mangel FM*. If you could just answer a couple of—'

'*Mangel FM*?'

'That's right, the radio channel.'

'I knows what fuckin' *Mangel FM* is.'

'What did they say to you, Mr Blake?'

'Who?'

'The police. When they took you in.'

'Oh...they was all right actually. It ain't no big deal. I'm always in and out of that place. I helps em sometimes, see. Ain't been for a while but they still brings us in now and then, when summat happens. But they ain't all cunts, the coppers. I were havin' a long chat with one of em—DI Dave—and he were tellin' us all about copperin' and that. He reckons I'd make a good one, and I'm thinkin' about it. I think I'd be a perfect one, see. I'm almost like a copper already, when you looks at it. See, when I says about them bringin' us in now and then and askin' us questions, I mean on account of me being a sort of like an expert. On crime, like. In this area. I knows how it all works, see. And I'm a man of the people, and—'

'Mr Blake, *did* you kill that woman?'

'What woman?'

'The murdered woman, of course.'

'Oh, her. Nah. Mind you, I could get you the man who did do it, no fuckin' problem.'

'You could?'

'Oh aye.'

'You know who the Reaper is?'

'Reaper?'

'Are you the Reaper, Mr Blake?'

'Eh?'

'You're evading my questions, Mr Blake. The public has a right to hear answers. Are you or are you not—?'

'Royston...Dominic Sheft here from the *Mangel and Area Free Press*. Is it true that you killed your own father? And what about your wife? Who killed her?'

'What? Eh?'

'You have a history of mental illness, Royston, and you still seem to be suffering. Can you tell us about that? Are you still on medi—?'

I'd had enough. They weren't listening to us and I didn't know how to shut em up. It's cos I hadn't had a cup of tea yet, I knew it. Catch us early enough and you can confuse us, if yer lucky. But it's the only time you can. Fucking *believe* it.

Actually I did know a way to shut these cunts up, but I didn't want to go down that path. I didn't see why I had to, now that I'd broadened me swede to matters and enlightened meself. But I didn't know how else to do it, so I didn't have no choice.

I slammed the window shut and went to the front door. When I got there I didn't know where the keys was, which fucked us off no end. But I found that I hadn't turned the locks anyhow last night, so it seemed, and the door opened with a simple turn of the handle. I balled me fists as I stepped onto the pavement. I felt meself slipping into an old gear, one that I knew well and that could get things done for us. And that's where me swede kicked in and I put the brakes on.

Cos I didn't want that old gear.

Like I telled you, I'd made some changes in my life. I weren't into aggro no more.

I had to use me swede now.

I stood there, huffing and puffing, clenching and unclenching me paws. One or two of em hared off down the street, thinking I'd knack em, but seven or so was still in place, a couple of steps back but not budging like I wanted em to.

I had to use me swede here. I had to…

…to get em to move along…by means of…of…

'Mr Blake, I'm not your enemy.' It's the radio bird again, smiling now. She handed the microphone back to her mate and stepped right up to us. She were all right, actually. The fragrance of her perfume mingled with the masculine smell of my unwashed armpits, and it proved to be a heady brew. 'Tell me your story,' she says. 'I can help you. We can clear it all up for you. We can set the record straight with a live interview, then people will leave you alone. People will *respect* you.'

'Respect…' I were still trying to get me thoughts moving, but for some reason they was stuck. It were like I'd left em behind us in the house. 'People…respect…'

I felt her smooth and soft paw on mine. It were a bit cold, mind. And the fingernails was chewed ragged.

'Go on,' she says, squeezing me arm now, 'we could do it now. I've got a car back there. We could go back to the studio, where it's nice and private and cosy, and…You've got such muscular arms, you know.'

'Get the *fuck* away from him!'

I couldn't tell straight off who had shouted that. It were a bit of a confusing time. All I really knew were that there were two birds hollering at each other—one of em being the nice perfume lady just now—and there were a bit of aggro and then possibly one or two fists thrown. But not mine, oh no. Afterwards I checked me knuckles and they sported not scrape nor scratch. I just had a feeling of recent aggro in the air, later on, sitting down for a cup of tea with the other bird—the one who won the fight and got them bastards to fuck off.

'Milk and two, right?' she says. 'Unless you've changed yer ways.'

'No, nah…I ain't changed me…I mean, actually I have ch—'

'Ah…it's so good to see you again, Blake. I just can't believe I'm sitting here with you. It feels so…Blake? Have I changed so much? Do you really not recognise me?'

Well, no, as it happens I didn't know who the hell this bird in me living room were. But I felt a bit rude telling her straight, so I says: 'Course I fuckin' does. I'd recognise you anywhere, girl. Eh, were it you left us the letter last night?'

'That's right. Could you tell it was me, just from the letter?'

'Oh aye, course.'

I looked her up and down, wondering if I'd shagged her. You can usually tell. Once you touches a bird you leaves yer imprint on her for life, see. Mind you, it ain't always easy to spot it, later on. Birds around Mangel, most of em's got a lot of imprints.

But this bird weren't the normal Mangel sort. She had long dark hair in the straight and shiny manner, a fair bit of slap here and there on her face but not too much, blue jeans, and one o' them rolly-neck jumpers the colour of a sheep. All in all she looked like a bit of class in casual mode, and about twenty-five year old or thereabouts (although I ain't so good with guessing ages). Aye, a definite bit of class. And I hadn't shagged her. I'd remember it for fucking surely.

A funny smile came on her face—which were getting prettier each time I clocked it—and she says: 'Go on then. Who am I?'

It happens like this every fucking time. You tries to protect a bird's feelings and they ain't happy with it. They pokes and picks at it until the whole thing unravels and they ends up getting hurt all the more.

'I knew it,' she says, face falling and then coming up again, a bit grimmer. 'You don't really remember me. Why didn't you just say? No one talks to me straight anymore. Everyone lies and hides behind hidden agendas. No one cares about the truth, and—'

'I fuckin' does,' I says. 'I'm fuckin'…I mean, I fuckin' *loves* the truth, me. The truth? The truth is my middle name, girl. They calls me Royston Roger The Truth…No, I mean Royston "The Truth" Roger Blake. Er, I mean, Roger is me real middle name, actually, and I ain't sure how yer meant to…'

I stopped there cos I lost me thought train. I couldn't help but lose it, the way she were looking grim at us. But then her face softened up like a cup of lard on a warm day and settled into a nice smile. She went back out and came in again with two mugs of tea, parking one afore us on the wooden box that doubled up as a handy piece of furniture. I sipped it for a while and tried to relax, shooting her a little smile now and then and winking at her. She seemed to like that, and I knew I'd be getting in her knickers soon.

'Honestly, though,' I says after a while. Cos you ain't gonna get nowhere by sipping tea in silence, least of all a bird's knickers. 'I ain't got a fuckin' clue who you is.'

She started crying. I couldn't fucking believe it. Here in me own living room, her on the sofa and me in the armchair, I had a sobbing bird. It were good really cos it meant I still had the knack, like, but it didn't do much for my squirming arse. Time were, I knew what to do here. But not now. In terms of the ladies, I felt like a rusty old bike hauled out of the canal after twenty year.

'Ah…look…' I says, starting to get up.

She threw her face up and yells: 'Gotcher!'

'You what?'

She were smiling now and laughing a bit. 'I knew you wouldn't know who I was, and that you were fibbing. I was just foolin' you.'

'I ain't no fuckin' fool, right?'

'Right, OK. I'm just—'

'So who the fuck is yer, eh? You gonna tell us or is you gonna fuck us around some more?'

'I wasn't fuck—'

'Come on—*spill.*'

She flashed some genuine nark at us. I don't mind admitting to you that it shook us very briefly to the core, and if I were an apple I'd be hearing me pips jangling around just now. There's a certain way women has when they wants to, and a man finds it hard to fight his corner in the face of it. But this weren't that. This were summat entirely more of a core-shaking nature. It were like a demon had got inside of her, and you could see the little pointy-tailed cunt baring his ivories at us. But, you see, I knew who this demon were. He were dead now, so far as I knew, but he hadn't half caused us all manner of strife and turmoil, back when his heart were still ticking and mine were thumping. To be more precise, it were the face of the demon known as:

Lee Munton.

(If you dunno who he is, I ain't telling you. It's another story and I already told it. So go ask someone else.)

It were like he'd tarted himself up as a bird, lost a few stone and about a foot in height, made his voice go all high, growed his hair long, and turned pretty. I didn't believe that but it were like it. The more I sat there thinking about it the more I wondered if it might actually be the case, what with modern science and that. But then two things convinced against it:

1. Last time I'd seen Lee Munton, he were cut up into five or six portions and I were shovelling dirt atop him, out in Hurk Wood.

2. The bird here, of a sudden like, pulled her jumper over her head and tossed it. Her long hair fell over her face and tits. She swept it back and gave us a certain knowing look, which meant that she knew what were about to happen, and I knew as well, and she knew I knew, and I knew she knew I knew, and that's all the prompting a man needs. She came forwards and I watched her tits, realising that modern science cannot work them kinds of miracles.

3. She put a leg either side of us, jeans still on but button unpopped and zipper down, letting a bit of bush peep out. At that moment I looked up into her black eyes. And they told us who she were.

'Well, fuck me,' I says, 'if it ain't little Mandy Munton.'

'I ain't so little no more, as you can see…and feel,' she says. 'But I am still gonna fuck you.'

MANGEL YESTERDAY—PUBS

Russell Pank

Our 'Mangel Today' series of features takes a look at where we are today, and what people think of life in our fair town. But is it possible to know where we are now without knowing where we came from? The answer is no. Only by looking at the past can we see what has changed, for better or worse.

Much as they are today, Mangel's public houses have always been the lifeblood of the town. As far back as records go, we can see that they were the hubs of the community, places where important decisions were made, deals struck, alliances forged. More so than the Church, they performed a role as social glue, keeping people together and fostering shared thought and belief. It is difficult to say whether that glue still works today, but the history books paint a lurid and convincing picture of how it once did.

In 882AD, the area we now call Mangel fell into the grip of a localised civil war. It was a region at odds with itself, opposing factions dividing the settlement up into patrolled sections, each with a pub at its heart. In the West, The Bee Hive held sway over Norbert Green. Operations in the eastern district of Muckfield were carried out from The Hole Plugger (now known as Cheryl's). Divisions to the North and South are unclear, but the faction in control of the central territory (then known as Mangel) used as their HQ The Paul Pry.

The war came to a head in 1003, after 121 years of brutal inter-tribal bloodshed. A fierce battle took place in the South, in a clearing between Hurk Wood and East Bloater Road. Many lives were lost, and it is said that the bodies of more than a thousand soldiers were interred in Hurk Wood. The battle—and the war—was won by the Mangel faction led by Natenwulf, who then assumed control of all territories.

It is said that The Paul Pry (if not the entire town) has remained under the stewardship of Natenwulf's descendents ever since. I approached the current owner for confirmation of this, but he declined to comment.

9

'…just wasn't enjoying myself no more. D'you know what I mean? It was just work, and I was spending nearly every waking hour doing it. Jackie—my boss there—she was always off on holidays and health spas and the like.'

I found it fascinating, what she were saying, but I were just gasping to drop a big one, in terms of breaking wind. There was all kinds of complaints going on inside and I felt that if I didn't get shot of it soon I'd be looking at permanent damage to the gut area. I knew a feller once—George Farcourt, his name were—one morning he got on one and stayed on it all day. And it's drinking I'm on about there. High noon to high moon, necking pop like the world were filling up with it and he were the only one could save us all from drowning. But he shouldered too much for himself, and about an hour shy of closing time his bladder bursts. And by that I mean like a balloon going pop. But the balloon were full up of piss instead of air. And the pop were a bit muffled cos of it being inside his belly. But everyone knowed that's what happened cos his strides went wet and red of a sudden.

Now, in my case here I knows it weren't me bladder I were putting the strain on. Any twat knows that farts don't come from your bladder, but the principle remains the same. And the last thing I wanted were me lungs bursting for want of blowing off, lying here in the pit with Mandy Munton.

But, like I says, I didn't wanna drop the big one neither. I knew it'd be a serious one, and I knew it'd put little Mand off us for good. I truly were enjoying a spot of female company at long last, and I didn't want it changing just yet.

'Do you know what?' she says. 'I found out not so long back (and this was the thing that finished it for me)…they was *dryin' out clinics* she was going to, not health spas. The old bitch was rat-arsed all the time, leaving me to run the shop and…Oh, I'd just had enough, Blake. And it wasn't just the job. It was the city. It ain't all they says it is, Blake, believe me. Blake? *Blake*?'

'What?'

'Are you listenin'?'

'Aye.'

'What was I…? Oh, don't matter.'

'Nah, I were listenin'. I'm just…Here, I just gotta get up for a sec, all right? Half a minute tops.'

'Get up? You mean get *it* up?' she says, reaching down. 'I wouldn't mind that at all…'

'Nah, I just gotta…erm…'

'Just gotta what?'

'Well, I just gotta check summat, er…'

I couldn't hold on no more. I pegged it down the stair. Anyone else would pop over the landing into the bathroom, but I could feel how toxic me guts was and I knew the smell would waft through to Mand, having the undesired effect. I thinks of everything, me. Even in tight spots like this un. See, I could picture a future for me and little Mandy, and I didn't want her put off by my bad guts. Everything had seemed a lot rosier since she'd walked back into my life just now, and that's without me even knowing who she were at first. I knew I were meant to be with her—or at least shag her on a regular basis—and I weren't gonna put a foot wrong in making that happen.

I went into the living room and started farting.

It weren't pleasurable, like guffing can be at times, but it were better out than in for fucking surely. And I felt better after it, if a bit shivery. There were a clicking sound outside the window and I turned around, recalling how I were stark bollock starkers. No one there, but I really would have to put some curtains up.

I went back up the stair.

Mandy were sitting up in bed now with my blanket wrapped around the intimate parts of her chest, looking around the place.

'Here,' I says to her, 'you got a place to stay yet?'

'*Live*, Blake, not stay. I'm here for good. I ain't going back to the city.'

'Nice one. So where's yer place? Ain't in yer old brothers' house, is yer?'

'No, I'm never going back there, Blake. Too many bad memories. I've moved on from all that. Only good things now.' She gave us a little smile, and I smiled back at her. For a moment she seemed like the little girl she used to be. Then I recalled how she'd never really been a little girl, despite her being so little. 'Besides, I think there's someone else there now. Another family.'

'Oh,' I says. 'That's interestin', actually. I mean, you do wonder what happened to the house, after…you know…'

'After me and you killed my brothers?'

'Ah, Mand, it weren't like that.'

'Really? Who killed em, then?'

'Don't say that. You had to do it. I mean, *we* had—'

She cut us dead with a look. Not a nasty look but a look that says eh, do us a fucking favour. 'Only good things now,' she says again.

But summat in her eyes said different.

I laid meself down next to her and pulled her to us. The blanket fell off her chest and exposed her nipples. They looked quite hard, which I took as a good omen. I stared at em and realised that fate had tossed me and Mand together for a reason. We had a bright future together, I could now see, and she were another part in the jigsaw of getting my life back on track.

'Well,' I says, 'there's fuckin' loads of room in here, as you can see. I dunno how many dresses and that you got, but I got that big wardrobe there and another one in the other bedroom, which is full of, erm…papers just now. Aye, business papers. But our Sal used to get all her togs in that one there no problem, and Beth before her. So you'll have no worries, Mand. Mind you, the place needs a bit of a clean, and I don't really know how to—'

Her back went stiff of a sudden. She craned her face up and squinted at us. 'What's you on about? I ain't moving in here.'

'Oh, I thought…'

'You thought wrong,' she says, pulling the sheet up over them good omens and bringing darkness unto the world. But it didn't last long, her back relaxing after a few short seconds and the sheet dropping once again, spreading light all around once again and banishing the darkness forever, so it seemed. 'Blake…' she says, reaching up and touching me face. 'What happened to you?'

'Eh?' I says. But I knew just what she meant. The Royston Blake she knew were a community pillar, respected by all, fancied by most, envied by many and enjoying the kind of glamorous lifestyle you normally only sees on telly. The one she found here were summat else.

'Well, me hoover's bust, see,' I says. 'That's why I ain't cleaned up the place in a while. And also me razor is bust, which is why you sees the beard here. I'm cuttin' it off soon. But aye, I do realise that this place has seen better days.'

'Oh, I see,' she says, looking like she didn't see it at all. 'What about your job? Are you still a bouncer? I mean, please don't take this the wrong way, Blake, but you don't seem like a working man.'

'Well, I'm impressed with yer powers of…of…with yer…I'm impressed that you knows that, about me not workin'. Cos I ain't, just now. The Royston Blake you sees here,' I says, warming to it, 'is a man between careers. He's conquered the world of door security, and now he's about to embark on a new and excitin' mountain which he hopes and intends to scale. A mountain, he must say, that will put him right back atop the pillar, community-wise, as well as put some regular wedge in his pocket.'

'Oh,' she says. She seemed confused about summat. 'I didn't… I mean…'

'But just now,' I says, 'just lately I been havin' a well-earned bit of time off. And I ain't been sittin' on me arse, neither. I been learnin', see, expandin' me swede and enlightenin' me load, so to speak. Actually there has been a fair bit of sittin' on my arse,' I says, thinking about the telly, 'but it ain't like that. I mean, you just can't do it stood up.'

'Oh, I see. So you're sort of like takin' a sabbatical?'

'Aye, aye. What?'

'A sabbatical. It's like when you takes a break from your normal job in order to do summat else, but not go on holiday. My boss used to say she was on sabbatical all the fuckin' time. And by the time I got around to lookin' the word up, I already kind of knew she was a lyin', cheatin' old cunt.'

As a rule I don't approve of birds using such language, but I made an exception for little Mand, knowing what she'd been through. Plus she had no kit on, and I found it quite arousing.

'So,' she says, 'what is this new career you got? Cos I can't picture you in any other way than standin' on a door in yer dickie bow, watchin' punters file past. Or kicking someone into the gutter.'

'Actually it ain't much of a career change, when you puts it like that. Cos what I'm gonna do next, right, is be a copper.'

I found her reaction a bit strange. I mean, first of all she never believed us, which I didn't find so odd if I'm being frank. Everyone knows where I've always stood copper-wise, and it ain't a very favourable place. So the thought of me dressed in blue with a tit on me swede could well be a bit hard to credit, I do freely admit.

But then I told her all about how I were gonna be in plain clothes, and more of a detective than the normal kind of twat you sees plodding the beat. I explained to her how the boss pigs these days wants men of action like meself, rather than the usual breed of spindly cunt. I pointed out to her that coppering these days is all about fitting in and not setting yerself apart. If you wanna catch the crook, I told her, you gotta live alongside him. You gotta be like him. You gotta *blend*, mate. I told her all that whilst tracing a circle around her left nipple and poking me cock into her hip.

And finally she started looking like a believer.

Not yer usual sort of believer, mind you. In my book, believers is quite happy about things. I mean, they finally comes around to a way of thinking whereby they stops fighting the truth and accepts it into their souls, the truth here being that I were destined to be a copper. It's meant to make em happy, is what I'm saying.

But little Mand weren't happy.

She jumped up, grabbing her togs and saying summat about just remembering how she's meant to be elsewhere. I tried making grabs for her bare arse, all playful like, but she weren't having none of that no more and the milky white cheeks in question was soon wrapped in blue denim.

'Mand,' I says as she pulled the sheep jumper back on, 'I ask you summat?'

'OK, but you better make it quick.'

'Do you not think it'd be a good thing, me having a respectable job like that?'

'I think it's a great thing for you, Blake, I just…Oh, Blake, why be a copper? Couldn't you do summat else? There's loads of jobs.'

I hadn't really thought about that, but I opened me gob and answered her anyhow, and the words spilled out like they'd always been the truth and it couldn't be no other way: 'Mand,' I says, 'there is only one job for me, and a copper is it. I can make a proper difference, see, and…'

'Why are you takin' the piss out of me?' she screams.

'I ain't. You knows I wouldn't ever t—'

'You are. This is all bullshit. You're tryin' to be clever, right? This is all a big joke for you, yeah?'

'No, I'm deadly fuckin' ser…'

But I were wasting me puff, her being down the stair and out the door and slamming it behind her, shaking the whole house. I went after her and made a move to open the door, but I weren't really fit for running after her, being stark bollock starkers.

On the way back up the stair, as I were scratching me bollocks, I noticed summat moving near me bedroom doorway. I knew I had varmints in the house, but I hadn't reckoned em to have got up this high. I stopped dead, then crept closer, slow enough so me tackle weren't swinging and thereby startling the rat. As I got to the door the bugger hared off along the skirting board and behind the wardrobe. I went to shift the wardrobe but gave up after a second or so and sat down on the bed.

I just knew summat were up with Mandy there, her leaving so sharpish and acting all odd. She must have clocked the varmint.

Everyone knows where birds stands in terms of varmints, and she'd got a fright out of it. Plus she like as not thought me a scummer, harbouring rats in the house.

It gave us a bad feeling, knowing that's how she saw us. Put her off us for good, like as not, and I'd never get to touch her soft white tits ever again. I threw some togs on, frowning about that and getting a bit hard at the same time. Mind you, it ain't healthy to get down about birds. I had a wank and then went down the stair, where I made a cup of tea and thought nice thoughts.

10

'Hello?'

'Who's that?'

'Who is this?'

'Never mind that, when you picks the phone up yer meant to say who you is, so I knows if I rung the right number or not.'

'Not necessarily. By ringing this number, you are the one who has come to me. Therefore you should announce yourself. Otherwise I will simply hang up.'

'If you hangs up, I'll...'

'Yes?'

'I'll just ring you again.'

'And say what?'

'And remind you that actually it's you who came to me.'

'How's that?'

I got the bit of paper ready and squinted at it. 'It says here... "We want the bravest men in the Mangel area. The most dynamic men. Intelligent men. Men—"'

'Yes, all right, sir.'

'"—of action. Men of honour. Is this you? If so ring Mangel Police Force Recruitment Office on—"'

'I said *all right*, sir.'

'"All right" meanin' what?'

'All right meaning you've passed this interview.'

'Interview?'

'Yes. That's what you rang for, wasn't it?'

'Yeah, but I thought...'

'Congratulations.'

'Fuckin' hell…So I got the job then?'

'Of course not, this was just the telephone interview. Now you have to come in for the main interview. Name?'

'Oh.'

'O?'

'What?'

'Your name is O. Watt?'

'Eh?'

'Look, can I have your name?'

'Yeah, it's Royston fuckin' Blake. Why didn't you just ask?'

'I did, you stu…Hang on, Royston Blake, you say?'

'Yeah. Why, you heard of me?'

'Hmm…I'm not sure. Mr Blake, could you just hold the line for a second?'

'No, I will *not* hold the…Hoy, where's you gone, you fuckin'…'

I knew this would happen. This is the trouble with being a local celebrity: your reputation goes in front of you and folks starts assuming this and that about you, and then going off and conferring with their mates and deciding you ain't copper material, on account of your criminal past, even though none of it were actually your fucking fault, and a lot of it were for the good of society in general anyhow, being as I were by and large getting rid of bad eggs and nasty—

'Sir?'

'What?'

'Sir, you were shouting something? Something about eggs?'

'No, I were…Look, you don't wanna go listenin' to what they says about—'

'Are you free this afternoon? One o'clock?'

'Free? Why?'

'For the main interview, of course. We're moving fast on this recruitment drive. Is it OK?'

'OK? Yeah, OK. I mean yeah, it's OK. Fuckin' OK.'

'Great, see you at one. Come to the main desk and ask for PC Worrall. And mention your name, OK?'

'No fuckin' worries, my friend.'

Well, fuck me. It cheered us up no end to see that our pig force still knew how to recognise quality in a man when they seed it. I were surprised about it, for the reasons and prejudices I set out for you just now, about bad eggs and that, but I knew it were the right thing. I knew that this were my destiny, and it felt all snug and cheerful to hear the jigsaw pieces of fate slotting home in the required pattern.

There was a few little cards in the phone box and they caught me eye just then. I'd thought em plumbers' and sparkies' trade cards at first and paid em not much heed, but I noticed that they actually had pictures of pleasant birds on em, saying things like BUXOM BLONDE and FILTHY BRUNETTE. One of em said I LIKE MY JOB, with photo of a bird's arse on it. I quite liked that one and I took it down and pocketed it. There were another one I liked as well, showing a bird from the back but not her arse. She had long dark silky hair and pale skin. She didn't need to show her arse because you could just tell she were quality. And the words at the top drove the point home: HIGH CLASS.

I pocketed that one, too.

I lit a smoke and stepped away from the phone box, thinking about things. I were actually thinking about all the different matters I had to think about, rather than actually thinking about em, if you knows what I mean. I were writing a list in me swede, in order to grease the cogs of fate and make sure there weren't no fuck-ups. So far I had:

1. Togs. I had to wear just the right ones. Not too scruffy but not too smart neither. I wanted em to take one look at us and see that I could pull off the plainclothes wossname and bypass the boys in blue stage altogether.

2. Facial hair. I do admit that I hadn't been keeping me chin cleared of late. I'd seen summat on telly about some feller from the olden days who kept growing his hair, and then losing all his strength and carking it after getting it trimmed off for his bird, whose name were Delia or summat, and I were just trying it out for a while. But just on me face, like. Long hair atop the swede is for birds alone. I weren't proper beardy yet but not far off, and I don't think coppers is allowed to have beards. So I needed a shave.

3. Swede. Going in for an important interview like this, where you had at stake not only my future career but also the good of mankind in general, it were of the utmost wossname to make sure me swede were in the right place. You wouldn't know what I'm on about here cos you ain't a deep thinker like meself, but it's about getting all the bad thoughts out of yer head and making yerself feel like a lion. I'd found that I does all that by harking the opening few bits of 'Eye of the Tiger', by Survivor.

4. Scran. I were fucking starving. I'd had fuck all to eat all morning and I didn't want me guts whining like a tortured cat while…

The phone started ringing behind us. I'd only got about ten yard away but already someone were making for it from the other direction, 10p in hand. I made a dart for it (I'm sharpish over ten yard) and got there in about half a second, but somehow the cunt had got there first and picked up the handset, going: 'Hello? I'll have you know this is a public—'

I grabbed it off em and pushed em back. 'Hey,' I says into the blower. 'It's me, Royston Blake. Soz about that, some rude fucker pushed—'

'I just wanted to say that there's a free interview slot right now, if you fancy coming down. Erm, a candidate dropped out, so we're all geared up and ready. Fancy it?'

I've said it before and I'll say it now, to you: you got to strike the iron before it hatches. I mean, while the cakes is still hot, like, or summat. This were fate at work, pure and simple. Once she gets going, you cannot fucking stop her, my friend. And you can't stop Royston Blake neither. Royston Blake is like a raging bull, and—

'Er…' he says, 'that's all very interesting about hot cakes and raging bulls, but could you just confirm that you'll come?'

'Aye, mate. Aye. I mean yeah, I'll fuckin' be there all right.'

'All right. Ten minutes?'

'Oh yeah, you can fuckin' bank on it, pal. If I ain't there in ten minutes, I'll—'

I stopped there cos the line had gone dead. He must have hung up by mistake or summat. I stepped away and tripped over a thing behind us, which turned out to be the cunt who'd tried to steal me phone call just now.

'The fuck's you doin' down there?' I says to her.

She were mumbling summat or other but I couldn't hear it cos she were holding her face.

'I can't hear you,' I says. 'You'll have to move yer paw. Ooh, you got a nosebleed or summat, love? Here…'

I fished an old bit of tissue out me pocket and tossed it at her. Bit crusty but all right for blood mopping. However, instead of taking it with gratitude she aimed a swing at us with her walking stick, clipping me shin and making us hurt summat chronic.

I pulled me boot back to teach her a gentle lesson, but I thought better of it and turned me back on her. It's like I says: I didn't need violence no more. Sometimes you got to show em the other cheek. Personally I went one step further and showed her both cheeks, and the bit in the middle as well (making sure I weren't in walking stick range).

'Woss you doin', Blake?'

I pulled me strides up. It were Burt. Not the one from the caff—the other one. I says: 'Oh, all right, Burt.'

'All right, Blake. Woss you doin' there?'

'Where?'

'There.' He were trying to point behind us at my arse, but I kept moving and he couldn't. Fucker shouldn't have been spying on us, the fucking poof. 'And woss she doin'?'

'Who?'

'You blind or summat? Her,' he says, giving up on my arse and pointing past us at the phone box. 'That old granny there.'

'Oh?' I says, sounding surprised. 'Oh aye, I sees her now.'

'Woss she doin' there?'

'I dunno, Burt. Perhaps she were on the blower and she fell akip, eh.'

'She ain't kipping. You can see her tryin' to get up, look.'

'Oh aye.'

'But she can't.'

'No,' I says, scratching me swede. 'Look, Burt…I'm a bit rushed, mate.'

'Oh aye?'

'Aye.'

'Where's you off?'

'I got an interview, actually.'

'Oh aye?'

'Aye.'

'Where?'

'The police station.'

I knew just what he'd make of that, and couldn't help putting out a smug grin while I awaited the inevitable. He reckoned I were in for questioning, see, for some misdemeanour they had us up for. He were making assumptions about us, and I just couldn't wait to set him straight.

'What for?' he says, taking the bait.

'What for? Cos they asked us, is why.'

'No, I mean why'd they ask you? I mean, woss the interview about?'

I still weren't sure if he'd took the bait or not. He were a fucking annoying little cunt, Burt, at times.

'You mean woss they got us for?'

'Oh, they got you for summat, have they?'

'I never said that. S'what you was thinkin', though, ennit?'

'No.'

'Yeah you was. You was makin' assumptions about us, and… and…'

'You tellin' us what I'm thinkin' now, is it?'

'No, but…I mean aye, but…'

'Listen, Blakey, every cunt who ain't in jail has been down for that copper job they put in the paper. None of em gets it but they all has a go.'

'Oh aye?'

'Aye. I been along meself, but I can't say as I got very far. Everyone gets past the phone call, but they falls at the main interview stage, see.'

'Hmm.'

'It's the questions they asks, Blake. They'm just too fuckin' hard.'

'Hard, is they?'

'*Too* hard, Blakey. Some of em is actually *impossible* to answer, so they says.'

'Who says?'

'Me. And the lads down the pub.'

'Oh.'

'And in the bookies. You know what Clinton Barstow says?'

'Old Clinton, eh? I ain't seen him in—'

'He says it's like the legend of Arthur. Do you know the legend of Arthur, Blake?'

'Aye, course.'

'Go on then.'

'Go on what?'

'What is the legend of Arthur?'

'What, you mean about how he lost one of his knackers climbin' over them railings, and then he picked it up and put it in a crisp wrapper and took it home, and one of his dogs—'

'That's Arthur *Mold*, you twat. I'm on about *King* Arthur, and his nights round the table and that.'

'Oh aye? Woss that about, then?'

'Well, Clinton says there were this sword, called Ex...Exc...'

'X-ray?'

'Nah, more like...erm...'

'X-wing, like from *Star Wars*?'

'Nah, it's more like Excrement, or summat.'

'Woss that mean?'

'It's just a name. The name of this sword, like. And Clinton says the sword is stuck in this rock, and you can't pull it out, see.'

'How?'

'How what?'

'How'd it get stuck in the rock?'

'I dunno, Clinton never said that.'

'Hmm. Cos it's funny how a sword should be—'

'Anyhow, so the sword's in the rock, like, and this wizard feller called Marlon tells Arthur that the man who can pull the sword out is the…is…well, he's the king, or summat.'

'But I thought you says this Arthur were already the king.'

'Yeah, but…Fuckin' hell, Blake, it ain't the point. The point is that this here interview, for the copper job, is like the rock with the sword in it.'

'Excrement.'

'Aye. No one can pull Excrement out of the rock, and no one can answer the questions at the interview. Do you see?'

'Aye, I do see, Burt. But how's they gonna take on any coppers if no one passes the interview?'

'Ah, well it's like the sword again. No one can pull him out, says Marlon, except for one very special man. And only a special man can get through this interview. Do you see, now?'

'Hmmmm…'

'Blakey? You awake?'

'Aye, I were just thinkin'.'

'Right, well, all I knows is that the special feller ain't meself, and it ain't no one else what I knows of. And shall I tell you summat else, Blakey?'

'Aye.'

'It fuckin' ain't *you* neither.'

'Who says it ain't?'

'Ain't you been harkin'? I says they'm *hard* questions.'

'And who says I can't answer no hard questions?'

'Fuck off, Blake.'

'No, come on—who says I can't do it? Who says I ain't that special king feller?'

'You ain't got a fuckin' clue, have yer, Blake? You reckon cos you been hidin' away at home there, with that big fuckin' arse bandit satellite on yer roof, you—'

'It ain't an arse bandit satellite.'

'No? Well why's it pink, then?'

'Cos it's a fuckin' *government* satellite, you twat.'

'Don't talk shite. That what Johhny Bengel told yer? You thick fuckin' bastard.'

'You callin' us thick, then?'

'Aye.'

'Nah, come on—you callin' us thick or what? Cos I—'

'I says *aye*, you deaf twat. *You. Is. Thick*. And deaf and all. Woss you got to say to th—?'

I brung me right up from very low, near the hip, and landed a sweet and solid uppercut square under his jaw, slamming his gob shut like a trap door with a dead cow landing atop it. His heels left the ground and knees went jelly, and he curled up and went for a kip right there on the pavement. I were a bit put out cos I'd wanted to express meself a bit more, but I soon saw sense and got shifting.

As I walked along the road, rubbing me knuckles, I realised how that were the first time I'd twocked a bloke in anger since… well, since I promised meself that I wouldn't. But I weren't gonna fret too much over it. It were only Burt, after all.

And not even the one from the caff.

MODERN TECHNIQUES USED IN HUNT FOR KILLER

At a press conference yesterday, Police Chief Bob Cadwallader and PC Tim Worrall described the groundbreaking methods being employed by their colleagues as they hunt down the Reaper.

'Not only have we got the best men on the Mangel Constabulary working on this case, but we have also shipped in a top psychological profiler from East Bloater. This has enabled us to get a good picture of the man we are looking for, thereby narrowing down our search for him. We know what he likes to eat, what he does for relaxation, the sort of job he has got, and other notable details that I am not at liberty to disclose. Not with you anyhow.'

Asked to elaborate, Chief Cadwallader said: 'Well, we know that it is a local man. And a big man. A strong, physical man who is used to moving people around when he wants to. In terms of eating, he is a man of simple tastes. Full English for breakfast, steak and chips for tea when he can get them. Also beer. He likes to drink beer, and probably a drop of whisky as well, but a recent medical problem may possibly have turned him teetotal for the time being. And anyhow, this man is almost certainly without a job at the moment, and has been for some time, so his eating and drinking habits may not have been indulged to their natural extent. He has been in trouble a few times in his life, though it is highly doubtful that he has been incarcerated for any of it. However, it is likely that he has been treated for mental problems at some point. Most important of all is what the profiler has told us about this man's attitude to women. He just don't like them, so it seems. It is a deep-rooted resentment, possibly coming from a, erm...(What does that say, Tim? Oh, aye.) ...coming from a perception that women have put him out of a job, and might well be holding most of the cards in the future. We would also say that this man might well be important, and that his subsequent feelings of sexual inadequacy... Erm, excuse me.'

At this point Chief Cadwallader and PC Worrall broke off for a brief and heated discussion, suggesting that there might be a level of unrest within the constabulary. After a minute Chief Cadwallader tore up his prepared notes and threw them at PC Worrall.

'PC Worrall here seems to be telling me that it's not important. Well, I disagree. In front of all these reporters and wossnames here I do declare that I'm treating this case as the most important thing in the world, at this time. Until we catch him, no one on my force will rest. Except maybe PC Worrall here.

'Another thing I can tell about our murderer is that he is a coward. The worst kind of coward there is: a man who raises his hand to a woman. Not only his hand, in this case, but also a sharp, heavy cutting instrument such as an axe. And that's me telling you that, not Mr Psychological Profiler from East Bloater. Nor Mr "Not Important" here, who I'll be having words with.'

11

'There'll be someone along to fetch you in a minute. OK, love?'

'Nice one, darl,' I says, giving her a wink.

'That's all right, love.'

'Fancy a chip?'

'No thanks, love.'

'Suit yerself.'

I sat on one of them placcy chairs they got in there and stared at the wall, finishing me chips and trying to get meself into the ideal swede space. I wanted to be determined and yet mellow with it, a reasonable man who other fellers can work with and have a laugh with, yet one who will not be knocked off his path and will not allow his arse to get beat by no fucker.

The perfect copper, in short.

To achieve this aim I played the start of 'Eye of the Tiger' in my head, like I said I would, but also chucking in some snatches of 'Follow That Dream' by Elvis Presley, which is a light and cheerful tune whilst still exploring themes of not giving up. Elvis seemed to know what I were up to cos he came in with 'US Male' as well, which is about being hard. It were a good little medley and I listened to it for a while; then me eyes focused on the posters opposite and all them faces of folks who had gone missing and asking folks have they seen em. I did recognise one or two, as it happens. Arcade monkeys growed a bit older and more frazzled, or a youngun I'd turned away on the door at Hoppers, back in the good old days. And I knew that no one'd ever see em again. None of em. Not unless they went out to Hurk Wood and started digging.

I were thinking this, and trying to get the thought of all them rotting deadfolk out of me swede, when me peepers chanced upon a faded old poster up in the top corner, half covered by them around it. There was three faces on it but you could only see the middle one, and there were no mistaking the fleshy mug of Lee Munton. He looked quite sad in the photo, like he knew what were ahead of him, getting carked by his own sister and the rest of it. It is true that a man's fate is writ in stone before he's even popped out from between his mam's legs, I think, so perhaps a part of him did know it. I got up and peeled back the posters either side of him, revealing his two cuntish brothers, Baz and Jess. They didn't look sad, they just looked like cunts.

I stood looking at the three of em, rubbing the stubble on me chin.

'You Royston?'

'Eh? Oh, aye.'

It were a uniformed copper minus tit and jacket. He seemed a good five years younger than meself, and he looked a bit like a polecat, in a strange way. He stood in the corridor next to the desk, holding a clipboard and avoiding eye contact with us. 'I'm Sergeant Percival. This way,' he says, heading back to the corridor he'd just popped out of. Before going into it he stopped and says: 'You can't bring them back here.'

'What?'

'Them chips.'

'Oh. There's only a few left, though.'

'Well, you can't bring em. You'll have to get rid.'

'Fancy one?'

'No, I don't.' He turned and went down the corridor.

I screwed up the chip paper and dropped it, making sure the secretary didn't clock us. Then I followed the sarge, watching his back and thinking how there were a time when I knew nearly all the coppers on the local force. We went past five or six of em on that corridor and I didn't even know one of em. Which were good, in a way, cos it showed how I'd been staying out of trouble for the past couple of years. They seemed to know who I were, though, going by the way some of em was looking at us. And the one going past and saying: 'You just watch it, Blake.'

I turned to him but he'd gone past, and started blowing his nose and making noises like a trombone. Best to just leave it anyhow. I had to be calm in here. No cunt were gonna put us off me stride now. Someone grabbed me shoulder.

'Hoy,' he says. And it were the first copper again, Sergeant Polecat. 'Woss the matter with you?'

'Oh,' I says.

'Oh?'

'Yeah, I mean…I'm all right, ta.'

'Very glad to hear it,' he says, looking like he weren't. 'Come on, then. They're all waitin' on you.'

'All waitin'? Who's all waitin'?'

'The, er…the interviewers. Why, you expectin' someone else to be waitin' on yer?'

'Nah, I just…'

I stopped there cos he'd opened a door and gone through it, beckoning us after him. Through the door were a long room with a mirror running the length of one side. At the far end were a little desk and three chairs, two of em being sat upon just now by coppers.

'…but he just wasn't listening,' one of em was saying to the other in conversational tones. 'I was just trying to explain to him that the word was actually "impotent", and not…'

He clocked us and stopped, nudging his mate in the arm.

'Hold up,' I says to Polecat. 'I knows this place. I been here before a few times…although I can't seem to recall…'

But Polecat weren't there no more and the door had shut behind us. I tried the handle but it were locked, the fucker. I had an urge to kick it, but then I recalled about King Arthur and the Sword of Excrement, and how he went and pulled it out against all the odds. And here were meself, getting all flighty over a locked door.

'Come and sit down here, Mr Blake.' The other of the two coppers were talking now. I think he were the one from last night, the garlic crusher one. 'We won't bite. We're pussycats, ain't we, Tim?'

The other one kept quiet and just stared at us.

'Why's we in the identity parade place?' I says.

'It's the only spare room, Mr Blake,' says Garlic Crusher. 'You been in the ID Suite before then, have yer?'

'Once or twice.'

'I see. Well, that's good. You knows all about police stations and the things in em—that's a good start to yer interview, Mr Blake.'

I quite liked this copper here. He hadn't come across too bright yesterday, with the garlic and that, but it had been late at that time and him tired, like as not.

'My name is PC Worrall,' says the silent one. Although he weren't being silent just now. 'And this here is PC Mard. I understand you want to be a policeman. Tell me why you want to be a policeman.'

This one were starting to get on my rag, with his staring and long silences and hard questions. And I knew he were trying to trip us up, getting us riled so I'd say summat thick and he could mark us down. But I weren't gonna do it for him. This is where Burt and all them others had failed. I could see it now.

'Well, I've always wanted to be a copper,' I says. 'Ever since I were a youngun. I likes helpin' people, see. But only good people. Know what I mean? And I likes catchin' bad people. You catch the bad people and haul em off the streets and the world will be a better place. I truly believes that.' I looked at em both and gave em a nice smile. I thought I'd answered that one very well, but they seemed to want more from us. 'Erm...well, my background is in doormanship, see, which is very much like being a copper, but just in the one pub. Or club. And, well, I just feel that...erm...'

'What would you do, Mr Blake?' says the garlic feller, interrupting us. I found that a bit rude but I let him off. Being rude is part of the job at times, for a copper. 'What would you do if you was chasing a robber down the High Street and he knocked a pram over, spilling the infant to the ground, and then continued to run on?'

'Well, that is indeed a tough one, my friend. But I believe that I'd act swift and decisive. With my background in dooring, see, where you gotta think in yer boots and judge scenarios—'

'What would you do, Mr Blake?'

'All right, erm, what weapons I got?'

'Weapons?'

'Yeah. Tools. Woss I got to use on him?'

'Just your standard issue truncheon, I suppose.'

'All right, I'd stop by the babby and lob the truncheon at the robber. At his head, like. Hard. While he goes down, I'll put the babby back in the pram, makin' sure he's all right, like.'

'But what if the truncheon misses, Mr Blake? What if it hits an innocent bystander?'

'It won't.'

'You can't know that.'

'I can. And there's no such thing as an innocent bystander, nohow. Everyone is guilty of summat or other, you looks hard enough. And it's serious crimes I'm on about here, ones that is askin' for a truncheon lobbed at em. But I don't miss, like I says. Royston Blake do not fuck up, pal. He's got too much experience for that. See, he's been workin' on the doors for—'

'How do you feel about women on the police force, Mr Blake?' says the quiet feller.

'Women coppers? I likes em.'

'In what way?'

'In every way.'

'You mean you're attracted to them?'

'Only if they'm fit. Know what I mean?'

'But what about women in general? Do you get on with them?'

'Well, I fancies em and I loves shaggin' em and that, but they can be a fuckin' pain at times. I do admit that I've had me troubles with em, like any man has. They can't half get arsey. Don't you reckon?'

'And what do you think should be done with them, when they get "arsey"?'

He had us there. I just didn't know the answer to that one. But I gave him a wink and little nod, pretending like I did know but weren't letting on, it being a trade secret.

I thought I were doing marvellous here, in this here interview. I'd got all the questions right so far and I were really warming to it.

'Mr Blake,' says Garlic, 'do you have any past convictions?'

'Not really.'

'Yes or no.'

'Well, only a couple of little uns. From when I were a youngster, you see. Only the sorts that everyone gets, mind. But, right, the way I sees it, you gotta have a bit of form if you wants to be a copper. Not big jobs though, just little uns, like armed robbery and GBH and that. It's all about understanding the criminal mind, ennit. Seein' it from their angle.'

I gave him a little smile. I'd hit another big six, and we both knew it.

'You're a big man, Blake,' says the quiet one. 'You look like you could move bodies around with no difficulty. Especially women. Can you? Have you tried moving bodies around? Women, I mean?'

'Oh yeah. I can haul a woman no trouble. Two or three of em, I reckon. Even pissed ones, when they'm lairy and trying to claw yer eyes out. Being on the door at Hoppers, there were many a—'

'Do you find they're easier to pick up when they're unconscious?'

'Unconscious? Oh aye, no fuckin' question, pal. At Hoppers—'

'Or dead? A dead one must be easy to lift.'

'Well, you'd think so, but they ain't.'

'No?'

'No. They'm actually really heavy, dead. A lot heavier than alive, I can tell yer.'

I knew they was impressed cos they both just sat for a few seconds, gazing at us in wonder. They knew I were the one for the job, plain and simple. And I knew that it were my wealth of experience that were seeing us through. Especially with me on the door at Hoppers. That were the thing what separated us from all other cunts, like Burt and wossname.

I closed me eyes and pictured the Sword of Excrement coming out of that big boulder, like a spreading knife from a block of warm lard. Some clunking and scratching behind us had us opening em again, and before I knows it DI Dave comes storming in the far door, face all red and lairy.

'Summat I can help you with, Borstal?' says Quiet One. I sensed aggro brewing there. Personally I were on Quiet One's side if summat kicked off. Up to that point I'd been having the interview of me life, and I didn't want no cunt spoiling it for us. Not even DI Dave, who seemed like an all right one.

He weren't replying, but I could hear his shoes clacking closer behind us. I were watching Quiet One, and the pure lairiness brewing on his mug.

'This is a private interview, Borstal,' he says, 'and you can't just…erm…'

'Private, is it?' says DI Dave. 'That why all your mates are watchin' behind that glass there?'

'Who do you think you are?' says the quiet copper, all slow and drawn out. 'You think you're better than us, just cos you come from the city? No one gives a toss about that here. The fuckin' bets are off when you enters Mangel. You reckon you know this town? You *will* know it, Borstal. There's a lot of coppers here queuing up to teach you.'

There were more, but DI Dave had us by the arm and frog-marching us backwards before I could hear it. To be honest I weren't heeding much anyhow, what with things happening so fast. But when he got us out in the corridor and round a couple of bends and into a dark little room, scantly furnished with a table and three chairs, and turned the light on, I says: 'Woss you playin' at? I were fuckin' *pissin'* that interview in there. *Pissin'* it.'

'Blake, there's summin you gotta understand. The people here, the coppers in Mangel, when they make up their minds about people they don't tend to budge from that point of view. And they've got this idea into their heads that—'

'But I had em by the *knackers*, Dave…I mean, I were fuckin' *rattlin'* off the answers like a Sten gun in the trenches. That one about the dead bird being heavier…it were pure fuckin' *poetry*, DI Dave, the way I—'

'Blake, *listen* to me. That in there, it's not what you think it is. He can't bring you in for anything so he's trying to get some sort of confession out of you via the back door. He was waiting for you to slip up, Blake. And if I hadn't come in when I did, I dunno what…Oh, and why d'you think they used the ID suite? Do you know who was on the other side of that mirror? About twenty-five coppers is who. All of them baying for your blood.'

'Oh.'

'They all think the Reaper is you.'

'The Reaper?'

'Yeah, nuthin' I can say will take the scales off their eyes.'

'Scales?'

'Look, Blake,' he says, perching on the table. 'Let me tell you summin.'

He nodded at one of the chairs and I sat on it. Straight away he got up and started pacing, just like coppers likes doing. It's meant to shit you up or summat, but it didn't do that here cos I felt that DI Dave were a mate of mine. I watched him pacing up and down again, admiring the cut and sheen of his grey suit. It truly were a nice one, unlike anything you normally sees for sale in Mangel. Not that I went round the shops much them days. I knew I'd be doing that soon, though. I already had plans brewing along them lines.

'Blake,' he says again, 'this whole idea of being a copper, maybe it's a mistake. There's only two types of men on this force: bad men and morons. You—'

'Nah, don't say that,' I says. 'You're a fuckin' top copper. A top one, Dave.'

'No, I meant—'

'Who's been tellin' you different, eh? Tell us who called you a moron and I'll—'

'Blake, would you just listen?'

'I'll always listen to you, Dave,' I says. His suit appeared to flash a sort of turquoise when the light caught it just so. Other times you got some purple, and also a colour not unlike Alvin's chilli sauce, from the days when he had a kebab house and chippy. 'I've always got time to hark the words of a professional such as yerself. It's how a person learns, see.'

'Good, well, you can hark this: you don't have a hope in hell.'

'That Italian, is it?'

'What?'

'The suit. And the shoes—they're nice an' all. *Eyetie*, is they?'

'Well, yeah, I suppose, but—'

'Cos I been thinkin' about that, see. The togs you wears, as a copper. It's all about style, ennit? I mean, here's meself in me army strides, and a jumper with holes in it and some curry sauce I spilt the other day. And look at these fuckin' boots I got here—caked in mud. *Caked*. Looks like I been wadin' through shite.'

'Well…all right. In a way you're right, Blake. The job is a lot to do with image. The clothes, the car, the hair, the way you walk, the fags you smoke, the words you use…those things do come into it. And a lot of other image-related things. But, in a way, that's what I'm trying to tell you. Once people have got a certain image of you, it's very hard to shift it.'

'Interestin',' I says. Cos it were. 'So yer saying I gotta get meself some new togs, is it?'

'Look, let's not forget that police work is about results. The image is all well and good, but if the man inside the image cannot do the job, he's fuck all. And, no disrespect here, but I think that's your problem. Them in there, they would never see you as a man who can do the job. Never.'

'Oh,' I says, cos it came as summat of a shock, to be frank. 'You honestly reckon that?'

'I do.'

'Never, you say?'

'Well, I don't like to say never. Highly unlikely that their view will change, shall we say. You'd have to make a big statement if you wanna win em round. A *big* fuckin' statement, mate.'

'Sort o' statement?'

'Oh, I dunno. Do summin impressive that they can appreciate. But it'd have to be very, *very* impressive. Solve this case, for example. Tell you what—you solve that and I'll give you *my* job, heh heh. But come on,' he says, leading the way back into the corridor. He turned right and left and soon we was going the same way as last night, when he'd let us out the back.

'Nah,' I says, walking behind him. 'I don't wanna take your job, Dave.' Cos I thought maybe him and meself could be partners. Like them two in *Miami Vice*. Sonny Wossname and his mate, Tubby. 'Nah, actually I'm hopin' us two can work together one day. Tell you what, with your togs and crafty swedework, and my, er...my things, well, we could fuckin' *run* this town. *Run* it, Dave.'

'Look, why don't we just leave it for now, all right? I gotta work. This case, it's really stretching me.'

'Oh aye, I were gonna ask you about that,' I says. 'What is this big case you keeps harpin' on about, Dave?'

'What case?' he says, unbolting the back door. 'You takin' the piss now?'

'Dave, you knows me. When it comes to copperin', Royston Blake do not take no piss.'

'You really can be a daft prick, can't yer? The Reaper, of course. I'm the one who's got to find him. Well, I'm heading up one of the investigation teams, anyway.'

I found that a bit needling, him calling us daft and a prick. But he were all right, Dave, so the needling turned sharpish into the warm and cosy sensation of a good mate having a laugh with you, taking the gentle piss.

'Oh aye,' I says. 'Who's that, then?'

'Well, there's four of us. Five, if you include Sheila, our admin girl. It's small team but a very important one.'

'No, I mean who's this Reaper feller? Don't think I knows him. He from local, is he?'

He looked at us like I were swearing in foreign at him. 'Are you serious? You don't know what I mean by the Reaper? Jesus fucking Christ, Blake...'

Me fists was lightly bunched, but I were in control of em. It's good to know I were armed, but I had no plans to knack Dave. Mind you, I did feel that summat needed saying. 'Is you tryin' to needle us, Dave?' is what I said. 'I fuckin' hopes you ain't, cos I had you down as an all right one.'

His eyes went all odd, like he'd just died. Then he came to and smiled. He could be a strange one. 'No offence, Blake, eh? Let's just blame it on the case. Call it the pressure getting to us.'

And then he told us all about the Reaper.

12

'What I can't believe is how you been keepin' it a secret all this time. Feller goes on a fuckin' rampage of killing in a town, folks normally knows about it. They's got to know about it so's they can look out for emselves, keep an eye on their loved ones and that. And you're sayin' there's a feller with five under his belt already, and more to come, like as not?'

'You what, pal?'

'Eh? Who's you?'

'Who's you, more like? It were you talkin' to me, not me you.'

'No I weren't.'

'You fuckin' was, goin' on about rampages, and normal folks and the like.'

'I fuckin' weren't sayin' fuck all, right? And you say I were and I'll *lamp* yer. Right?'

'Er…yeah. Right. No worries, pal.'

I let go his jacket and moved off, stuffing the rest of the Cornish pastie in me gob. Cheeky cunt. Feller can't even think out loud no more without nosy bastard strangers sticking their big hooters in it. Not even when yer stood in a quiet spot round the side of the pastie shop.

Soon enough I forgot all about that, and I were back to me original train of thinking (but keeping it in me head this time). And the further I travelled on that train, the more I understood the wise words that Dave had doled out back there. What he were saying, in an arse-wise way, were that I gotta *prove* meself a copper before I can *be* a copper.

And not only that.

I'd set meself so much on the back pedal, getting involved in dodgy matters in the past, that it weren't even enough to just be a normal copper. If I wanted em to sit up and hark us, I had to be a better copper than all them others. Dave included.

I had to show em, on me todd and without the help of a badge and all them other things a copper uses, that I were the best fucking copper of all time, including famous ones like Sledge Hammer and Sonny Wossname, and them two in *The Sweeney*—Ronald Reagan and Jimmy Carter.

I were still thinking about famous coppers of yore as I neared the front doors of the Porter Centre for the first time in a long time. Like I already telled you, I'd been steering clear of the town centre on matters of principle and personal discipline, or summat, but I were on a particular mission here and a bit of shopping could not be avoided.

Bob Gretchum Jr were on the door. I weren't surprised to see him there cos they always was quite large lads, the Gretchum brood, and you could see em ending up in the door industry or thereabouts. Anyhow, I gave him a nod and a smile, cos he were doing the job I used to do and I wanted him to know that I weren't bitter about it. And I truly weren't. Quite the opposite. He could stick his fucking security guard job up his arse. Even if he were wearing full door regalia including dickie bow and DJ, while I used to have to wear a fucking woolly jumper when I were doing that selfsame job. But no, I were headed for special places, me, and soon every fucker would know about it. And be jealous of us. Especially when I started arresting the cunts.

I don't think Bob noticed us, though, cos he seemed to cast a bastard of a look in my direction and then turn his head the other way. I shrugged and moved on. I didn't have time for menial cunts like him.

I went up the moving stairs and onto the first floor, where I walked into Top Lad and started looking at suits. I knew I couldn't find spot on what I were after, this being Mangel, but I needed summat close. And I weren't resting until I had it.

'Can I help you, sir?'

She'd crept up behind us, like they always does, folks who works in big shops. You wants a little private mooch around and they has to come along and start badgering you. Why they don't leave us alone, I truly do not know. They don't fuck you around like this in supermarkets so I can't see the need in gear shops. Mind you, I turned and had a look at her, and she weren't so bad looking. A bit gormless perhaps but she didn't half have some shape to her, and you could see right down between it. On one side of it were an oblong badge saying:

BETHANY
I AM HERE TO HELP

'Aye,' I says, 'I were wonderin'...nah, you couldn't do that.'

'What's that, sir?' she says, all keen and sparky like a brand-new stainless steel cog fresh out of the mould, and with big tits on it.

'Well, it's a bit...nah, honestly, I—'

'It's all right, sir. I'm here to help.'

'No shite?'

'No, sir.'

'All right, well, it's me legs.'

'What about them, sir?'

'I can't bend em proper. Just at the moment, like. I had an injury and just I can't get strides on. Not on me own, like.'

'Oh.'

'And I fancies these uns here, see, but I daren't try em on in case I falls over and breaks a mirror or summat. So when you came up there and says, "Can I help you, sir?" I started wonderin' if you might come along to the changin' room and help us, er… you know. Eh?'

I gave her a wink.

• • •

The changing room were small. More like a big wardrobe really but big enough for what I were up to. You had bright lights overhead and mirrors all around, and I quite liked that cos it meant I could see meself as I moved. And I tell yer—I looked good.

'Sir?'

'What?'

'Are you the one wanted the zimmer frame?'

'What?'

'Bethany says there was a special needs case.'

'What? Who the fuck's you?'

'I'm Martin Counter, the duty manager,' says the voice behind the curtain. 'I've brought you the disabled equipment. Shall I come in with it?'

'*No.* I mean no, I'm just…' Truth were I already had the kit on, and were turning to and fro and admiring meself in the mirrors. It were fucking marvellous cos you had em front and back, so you could clock yer mug with one eye and cast a critical wossname over yer arse area with the other. And I had to admit—I looked fucking pukka on all fronts. But I didn't want Martin Cuntface seeing us, after I'd told that lass that I couldn't manage it on me todd. Mind you, why should I fret over the like of him?

'What'd you call us?' I says through the curtain, thinking about what he'd said.

'I didn't call you anything, I—'

'You did, you called us disabled. I heared it.'

'Not at all, sir. I was informed of your—'

'My what?' I says, wrenching the curtain open. I might have wrenched it a bit hard cos the whole thing came away in me paw, pole and rings and everything. Actually the pole flew off at a bit of an angle, and the rings pinged off the wall behind the feller like bullets. 'You wants a proper rail up for this,' I says, tossing the curtain. 'Them poles is shite. Can't even hold up a cobweb.'

Cuntface weren't listening though. Which I didn't find very polite, actually. He were turned away from us and had his paws up to his face, like he were having trouble containing some laughs that wanted out. I couldn't fucking bear that, folks laughing at us. Especially stuck-up little arse bandidos like Cuntface here. 'Hoy,' I says, 'woss so funny, Cuntface?'

'I'm not…the pole caught me in the—'

I gave him a slap on the back of the head. For being cheeky. Only a gentle one, as a warning, like. Just to say I ain't putting up with having meself besmirched, and I got a civic right to walk around and…er…not get besmirched, and that. I had to protect civic rights, see, in me new role as a copper.

Anyhow, he went down.

I fucking hates that, when they goes down for no good reason. It's like when you're a youngun and there's always some fairy who can't handle the proper lads' games, and they goes off squealing to mam, saying that Royston done this and Royston held us down and put eary wigs in me ears and whatever else. Fucking lying little bastard, that cunt were. It were only the one eary wig, and I just wanted to know if they did actually go up folks' ears, like the name says. And they did, as it turned out. I fed him in and he stayed there for at least five minutes before the screaming little fucker whose ear it were wriggled himself loose and hared off homeward, like I says.

Mind you, this one here weren't haring no place. He were mug-down in the carpet with his cripple frame atop him, pretending like he were hurt. This were another thing the soft lads used to do, and I knew just the remedy for it.

I shoed him in the kidneys.

Slightly harder than I'd wanted, possibly. I dunno, maybe not. Either way, his body left the ground and he bounced off the wall.

At this point I noticed another feller up the way, standing at the entrance to the changing room area, holding an orange T-shirt and a few pairs of trolleys. He seemed a bit scaredy and shocked and looking on the point of turning arse and doing summat silly, so I says:

'It's all right, mate. I'm a police officer.'

'Yer a…' He swallowed hard a couple of times. Poor lad were doing his best. 'A police, erm, off…offi…'

'Aye. This cunt here is a known criminal, and I were just catchin' him and that.'

'Oh,' he says, recovering sharpish and not looking so scaredy now. 'Oh, I see. So, erm, what was his crime? I mean, if it's none of my…'

'Nah, yer all right, mate. He's a fuckin' kiddie fiddler, this one. We been after him donkeys. He's been fiddlin' younguns for years and years, and—'

'Why'd it take you so long to catch him?'

I were slightly took aback, I don't mind admitting. The feller seemed narked about summat, and I did not know what. 'You what?' I says.

'Why? Why does it take so long to…I mean, why the hell is this sort of thing allowed to continue, in this day and age? We know they're out there, these bloody perverted bullies who take advantage of the young, and we know the…the *damage* they do, but…but…'

He seemed upset about summat, so I gave him a second or two to gather himself. After that I says: 'Listen, mate…first off, you don't fuckin' talk to me like that. I'm an officer of the law, and I got a right to demand a little respect from common punt—'

'And I've got a right to…to…I mean, *children*—small, innocent children—don't they have rights? Don't they deserve protection from dirty, filthy, evil scum like him?'

I looked at the feller saying this and I looked at the feller on the deck, and I were scratching me swede. I always had this, folks going barmy on us just when I didn't need it. But I knew that I had a responsibility now, as a copper. I had to look out for punters and sort matters out on the spot. Being a copper is all about solving problems, see. It's about nailing the wrongdoers and giving the wrongdone some satisfaction, or summat.

'Here,' I says, pointing at Martin Cuntface and addressing the other feller. Cos I'd just had a fucking top idea. 'You don't approve of cunts like this one here, do yer?'

'Don't approve? I…I bloody…'

'Nah, don't go all shy on us. I heard the way you was goin' on there and I can tell when a feller's got a gripe.'

'People like him, they…they just…'

'Yeah yeah…Look, you wanna give him a little shoe?'

'A little shoe?'

'Aye, like this.'

I gave Cuntface a little shoe, in the kidneys again. He groaned, suggesting that he might be waking up a bit. I had to move fast here.

'Go on,' I says, 'you hates him, give him some shoe. It's only fair, right?'

'But…'

'Listen, I'm a fuckin' copper. I says it's all right, it's fuckin' all right. All right?'

'Well…'

'Go on, get stuck in. Fill yer boots, pal.'

I dragged him over, whispering in his lughole: 'Think of all them kiddies he's fiddled, sittin' em on his knee and givin' em lollypops and that. How's that make you feel, eh?'

I didn't have to do no more cos he were in there. He weren't a big feller and I couldn't see him doing much damage, mind, with them little girls' feet of his, but he were a fast worker and I must of watched him put fifty in before I next blinked.

I went back into the shop and found the lass tidying up the jeans. 'All right, love?'

'Oh…hello, sir. Did you get some help in the changing rooms?'

'Aye, aye. Listen, there's some sort of aggro goin' on back there, a feller givin' your boss some GBH. You wants to call the coppers.'

'Oh…' While she thought about that I popped outside and kept on walking. Halfway down Frotfield Way I stopped and looked meself up and down in one of them big mirror windows they got down there. It were a nice suit. And do you know what? I looked just like a copper. And not just any copper neither. I'm talking about a proper detective here. Mind you, there was another couple of things I needed.

MANGEL TODAY—PUBS (PART THREE)

Russell Pank

Step off the beaten track and you will find a different breed of drinking establishment, one which shuns the glitz and glamour of mainstream nightlife, thriving on discretion and a slower pace. These unassuming drinking holes may not appeal to the common herd, but they are a vital and longstanding artery in the bloodstream of the town.

One such establishment is The Paul Pry, which can be found halfway along an apparently nameless backstreet to the West side of the town centre, nestling almost imperceptibly between a garage and a junk shop. To the untrained eye, the ornate letters "PP" carved in the ancient oak door are simply an emblem from yesteryear…perhaps the initials of a former resident. There is no other external sign of the pub that lies within.

I turn the handle and go inside.

A waft of ancient beer welcomes the adventurous wayfarer as he enters the bar…a sensual reminder of drinkers from centuries gone by.

'No, that's just old Mr Fillery. He spilt his half a mild on himself about twenty minutes ago,' says a portly man behind the bar. 'And don't go using words like "sensual" in here, please, ladies being present.'

I look around, failing to spot any ladies, but the daylight is scant and the corners are obscure, and there is movement in the shadows. I cross the crepuscular floor—cold flagstones said to have been laid more than a thousand years go—and perch on an ornery barstool.

The barman takes note of my brief grimace and says, pointing his chin over my shoulder 'If you don't like the stools, there's hard pews over yonder.'

I remain on the stool and order a pint of whatever flows best in this backwater.

'The lager's special,' he says, pulling an ancient ceramic lever lined with fine cracks like the veins of a Stilton. 'Did you know that lager were invented here? Aye, it's true. They invented it in the cellars hereunder, going back…oh, a good several hundred year, now. Couple of centuries back, a man fled this town and went overseas, taking the magic formula with him and flogging it to a Kraut brewer in return for a year's supply of what he came up with.'

I asked the barman what became of that man, but he didn't seem to hear me. I asked him again and he picked up a tankard and started polishing it. At last he said, 'We don't talk about that.'

The lager was good and cold, with a full body and a slightly fruity flavour. I drank it and looked around. My eyes grew accustomed to the poor light, and before long I discerned two men sat at a table to one side, and another sitting alone to the other side. It was hard to tell, but I had the feeling that they were all watching me.

I remarked to the barman, in conversational tones, that there were not many women.

'Women?' he said, apparently offended. 'Women? I won't have women in here no more. Women? This is a working man's tavern, laddie. Shall I tell you about women? It's women who've got us to where we are today, regarding this town of ours. All the ills and shortfallings that beset our daily lives, such as they are, you can lay 'em at the door of women. Harlots, actually. Aye, harlots and harridans—if they're not the one, they'm the other. Either way, it's their flamin' fault. All of it is. Tell that to your readers, eh? Go on and tell em it, that's what I say.'

I drank my lager while he polished his tankard furiously. After a while he seemed calmer, putting the tankard down and setting both hands on the bartop before me. 'If you don't mind,' he said, 'drink your pint and be on your way, eh.'

13

'What's in the bag, though?'

'Never mind woss in the bag. Can you help us out or not?'

Filthy Stan rubbed his chin. His chin were covered in black stubble, but he made it even blacker by rubbing it, all the dirty motor oil on his paws. He were the filthiest bugger I knew, and I knew some fucking filthy buggers. There weren't an inch of Filthy Stan's body weren't covered in summat or other. Not that I'd ever seen him in the nod. You could just tell by looking at him. The filthy bastard.

'I'll help you out, no problem,' he says, 'long as you tells us woss in the bag.' He lurched Blakeward and made a grab for me carrier bag.

'Fuck off, Stan. I got me new suit on, ain't I? Don't want none of your muck on it.'

'Oh aye?' he says, stepping away and sparking up a fag. He'd only just got it out and there were hardly a white patch left on it. 'You sayin' I'm dirty?'

'No, I'm sayin' I'm clean. This suit is anyhow.'

'Aye, but why would you say that to me? You wouldn't say fuck off to a tasty bird who moved towards yer.'

'You ain't no tasty bird, Stan.'

'You sayin' I'm dirty, though? You sayin' I stinks?'

'Fuck sake, Stan, I'm just *sayin'*, like. Watch the gear is what I'm sayin'.'

'Hmmm.'

We was standing in the forecourt of his garage. It weren't really a forecourt but it's where he flogged his motors from, and there was about twenty parked there at this time. I hadn't had a good look yet but none of em seemed much cop. I still held out hope, though. Fellers in the motor trade, like Filthy Stan, they got a lot of contacts and that. All it takes is a call or two.

'Where's you been anyhow, Blakey? Ain't seen you in donkeys. You been' out o' town?'

'Out o' town? Don't be a twat. Nah, I just been keepin' me swede down, like. Livin' the quiet life. A *satannical*, they calls it.'

'Satannical? Woss that mean?'

'Means when you goes on holiday, but you ain't just gettin' pissed all the time. You're doin' a bit of graft as well, see. Only not on yer normal job. And you ain't actually workin' at all, see, cos yer on a satannical.'

'No shite?'

'That's right, Stan.'

'Hmmm.'

'You callin' us a liar, Stan?'

'Course not, Blakey. Just seems a mite odd. I ain't never heard that word before.'

'Well, you knows it now. Look, can you help us out or not? I told you what I wants. Can you get the fucker for us or not?'

'Ah well…depends, dunnit.'

'On what?'

'On if you shows us woss in the bag.'

'Fuckin' hell, Stan.'

I opened the bag and let him peep inside, hoping none of his grease would drip into it.

'The fuck's them? Slippers?'

'Course they fuckin' ain't slippers, you twat. Ain't you ever seen espadrilles before?'

'Esther who?'

'Drills.'

'They ain't drills.'

'No, it's just what they calls em. They'm shoes, ain't they? Special shoes made out of material, and with soles made out of… well, it's sort of like a string, or summat.'

'Hmm, most odd. Woss you got them for?'

'They ain't odd, Stan. You just ain't got no style. They'm very fashionable, actually. Like this suit I got on.'

'It is a nice suit, Blakey. You off to court, then?'

'No, I'm…look, I showed you in me fuckin' bag, now you gotta help us. How's I gonna get me motor back?'

'Hmm.' He were rubbing his chin again. The rub moved round and ended up behind the back of his head on his bald patch. He slapped enough motor oil on it, you wouldn't see it no more. 'Capri, you say?'

'Aye, 2.8i. You knows the one. Everyone knows the motor I once had. I were famous for it. Best Capri in Mangel, that one were. Come on, who'd you flog her to?'

'And yer sure it were me you flogged her to?'

'Aye, I'm sure. Well actually no, it weren't *me* flogged her to you. I'd never do such a twat thing as that. It were the bird, see.'

'Oh aye? You got a bird, Blakey?'

'No, me old bird. I'm goin' back a few years here.'

'Hmm…I do recall summat about you havin' a bird. Beth, were her name? I thought she carked it…got burned in that fire, down the old Hoppers?'

'No…well, aye, she did get burned but it ain't her I'm on about. It's Sal, the later one.'

'Oh aye? She carked it as well, ennit?'

'Aye. I mean no, she…erm…she went missin', like.'

'Oh, I heard she carked it.'

'No. She run off.'

'Too bad, Blakey. Happens to the best of em.'

'What do?'

'Birds. Runnin' off with another feller.'

'She never run off with no other feller, Stan, she just…run off. Or summat.'

'Ain't no shame in it, Blakey. All it takes is them coppin' off with a feller who's better lookin' or summat. Or better at protecting her. Or maybe he's got a much bigger wanger.'

'Shut it, Stan. That kind of shite don't happen to me. It happens to stumpy little shite-hawks like you.'

'Oh, I see.'

I looked at his pack of fags shoved down the top pocket of his overalls, and wished I had one. Even a filthy one, after he'd touched it.

'Look, Stan, I never meant to—'

'You know what I heard, Blakey? I heard all the birds who goes out with you carks it in the end. *Mysteriously*, like.'

'Woss that meant to mean?'

'Nuthin', Blakey. Just what I says, is all.'

'I know but woss you sayin'? You sayin' I knocks em off?'

'I ain't sayin' that. Bit mysterious though, ennit? I mean, if you looks at the facts. Anyone'd think you don't like birds. You know what anyone'd think, Blakey? That you *hates* birds. And if you hates birds, you probably likes—'

I got him by the overalls and lifted him skyward, holding him overhead for a moment or two, me roaring up at him, before dumping him back-wise on the bonnet of a nearby Morris Ital.

Then I hauled him off there—him whimpering like a babby now and not giving us no lip at all—and planted him face-down in the black, oil-drenched mud and gravel that passed for a forecourt. With a knee planted between his wing bones, I says:

'I wants me fuckin' Capri 2.8i. And do you know what? I fuckin' wants it *now*.'

'I dunno who got it, Blakey. Honest, I...aaarrggh, I can't fuckin'...'

'Who'd you flog her to?'

'I dunno, Blakey. It's fuckin' yonks ago and I don't...urrgh...I don't keep no records. Actually, I...'

'What?'

'I think she went for scrap, Blakey.'

'Scrap? Fuck off, she were *mint*.'

'No, the fuckin' chassis were knacked, and the engine were just...'

'I thought you says you couldn't recall her?'

'Aye, well, it's all comin' back now, ennit?'

'Hold up a min, Sal traded her in for a Viva Estate. How come you gave her a Viva Estate if the chassis were knacked?'

'I...er...'

'*How come?*' I eased up a bit on his back, giving him space to talk.

'All right, fuck...she were a persuasive lass, Blakey.'

'Eh? Woss you sayin'?'

'You knows what I'm sayin'. Come on, Blakey, let us...'

'You sayin' you shagged our Sal?'

'You knows what I'm sayin', Blakey. Ain't like she's your bird no more, so you can't—'

I picked him up again and took him inside. He were quite heavy for a short-arse, and I could feel his overalls coming apart at the seams. On the floor next to a stripped-down Cosworth were a nice-looking air compressor with a hose attached. I picked up the hose and stood weighing it all up, and while I were doing that Stan's overalls tore clean out of me grasp and he went deck-wise again, leaving us with a fistful of polyester. It were the seat area that had come loose, and as he got on his knees and made a very sluggish bid for escape, his horrible bare arse were exposed to the air for all to see, not that anyone wanted to see it and least of all meself.

But it did give us an idea.

I looked at the hosepipe and looked at the horrible arse. Then I turned the compressor on.

• • •

'Maestro, you says?'

'Aye.'

'MG Maestro?'

'Aye. Zero to sixty in seven, no problem.'

'Seven?'

'Aye. You fuckin' try her if you don't believe us. I been workin' on her and she's a dream, Blakey. You take her up the East Bloater Road and—'

'Woss wrong with her?'

'Fuck all. I ain't shittin' yer, Blakey. Honest I ain't. Come on, Blakey. Call it a present from me, to…to say I'm—'

'I wants the paperwork done and everything.'

'Aye, aye.'

'And I'm comin' back if you does it wrong. Whatever happens, first chance I gets I'm comin' back lookin' for you. And I'm bringin' me own air pump.'

'Don't fuckin' worry, Blakey. I said it and I means it. There's no fuckin' problems, all right?'

I still weren't sure. Didn't seem right, this. Didn't seem fair on our Sal, whose honour I were looking after here. And I'd never liked the look of them Maestros. No class, not even the MG ones. I went to turn the compressor back on.

'Blakey, don't...*please* fuckin' don't...Look, I says I'm fuckin' sorry. What more can I do?'

I frowned at him and reached for the switch.

'*No*. Look, I got a better idea. Any motor out there in the yard. All right? How's that? Any motor you wants out there, you fuckin' take her, no problem. As a gift from...Oh, except...er...'

'Any motor at all?'

'Well, er...aye, all right. Any one of em which is for sale, all right? Cos I got some punter's motors out there, see, waitin' on pickin' up. But any ones with a sale tag on em, you can have it. No problem.'

I thought about it, and then I said all right. Straight off he got up and went outside, not even stopping for summat to cover his hairy arse with. I knew he were up to summat so I followed him, and I'm sharp over twenty yard so I caught him easy. He stopped and pointed over the one side, saying: 'Most of em's over there. Aye, the best ones is there. You go on and have a gander, eh.'

I took a step that way but went no further. Stan went the other way, turning his hips and skipping like a fat and hairy ballerina between an old Moggy Minor and a bright green Princess with black vinyl roof. I went after him nice and quiet. I couldn't do the ballet bit but I stayed close. He went behind a brown Datsun up on bricks and ducked, disappearing from view. I took a gamble and went the other way around the Jap car, planting a paw on the bonnet and vaulting her like Starsky and Hutch. The bricks gave way though and I went arse-wise in the mud, coming up sharpish with a brick in me paw just in time to see him making a leap for summat in the far corner, roadside. I lobbed the brick. Actually it were two bricks. Stuck together with mortar, like.

I were just trying to slow him, you see, cos I could tell he were up to summat.

And it did slow him.

I went over, to make sure he were all right and safe and sound and that. That's when I clapped eyes on the thing he'd been trying to reach ahead of meself. I could see what he meant. She were a fucking beauty, and I'd not seen the like of her in Mangel in all me borned days. I looked all around her, and although I did find a minor blemish here and there, and signs of corrosion under the front driver-side wheel arch, I fell in love. Shocking colour, mind.

Truly fucking shocking colour.

But I couldn't stand about ogling her all day. Filthy Stan were lying on the pavement with his swede hanging over the gutter, dripping blood and snot onto a little heap of pale dog shite. One or two motors had gone past, but you gets a lot of winos around this part so they wouldn't have paid him no particular heed.

I bent down and gave him a slap, getting nothing back. I noticed his eyes was open. I ain't no expert but I took that as a bad sign. So I closed em and gave him another slap, much harder this time and with some knuckle. After that I held his nose and put a paw over his mouth, keeping it like so for a minute or thereabouts. I wanted to catch the sly fucker out, see. Cos he *were* a sly fucker, trying to get to that motor before meself and swipe the sale tag off the front. Which were not only sly but quite dishonest, I thought. So really, when you looked at it, he'd brung this upon himself. All I'd tried to do were prevent a wrongdoing. Which is what all decent coppers must do.

'Fuckin' hell,' I says, thumping him in the thigh. Cos it didn't matter how much I were in the right here and acting like a proper copper and all, I still had a fat, dishonest bastard on me hands who weren't breathing. This were all I fucking needed, at this important time in me life. I were all set to go respectable and fulfil my destiny and that, and *now* look.

I always had to have obstacles, me. Never the smooth passage for Royston Blake, oh no. Always some cunt getting in the way with his fat head.

I got Filthy Stan by the heels and dragged him inside.

FILTHY STAN'S
EROTIC MOTOR EMPORIAM

Mangels premier used
car dealer and repare shop

Family, excecutive, and sports models at a price
you can afford no problem. And now EXOTIC models as wel!

~ CAR OF THE WEEK ~

1982 FERARRI DAYTUNA SPIDER*
A genuine Italian throughbread at a price you can afford
no problem. Only 10k on the clock and vgc
inside and out. FSH. Tax & 10 month MOT. Pink.
£POA

~ OTHER GOOD CARS ~

1980 ESCORT
Blue. Good runner........£100.00

1979 DATSUN CHERRY
Lovely number. One careful old lady. Brown. No weels...£50.00

1985 SIERA
vgc……………..4£00.0

1983 SIERA COSSWORTH
Must sell due to some one dying…$1500.50

1986 MG MAESTRO
0-60 in 7 no problem. Full body kit. No brakes…..£41.000

*Plus many many more great vehicals at
a price you can afford no problem.*

*First registered as a Capri 1.3

14

'You made up yer mind yet?'

'No, I'm still thinkin.'

'You only got two to choose from.'

'But I just wants black. Ten tins of black.'

'You can have black.'

'Giz em, then.'

'I already explained it to you: I got two types of black here. Coal or jet. You got to choose.'

'Black is fuckin' black, fuck sake.'

'No swearin' in here please, Blake. And it ain't as simple as "black is black". In this shop, we got two types of black.'

'Woss the difference?'

'One is black like coal, and the other is black like snow. What d'you think the flamin' difference is? Flippin' heck. You make up yer mind, eh.'

I were trying to make up me mind, you see, and Lionel in the hardware shop weren't helping matters. I fucking hated pushy salesmen, like I think I already told you, and all he'd done so far is get on my back about making up me mind, when all I wanted were a minute or two.

'Just giz a fuckin' minute, right?' I says. 'Or two.'

'You wants a minute, you got yer minute. But no swearin' in here, please, Blake.'

I stood to one side and closed my eyes, trying to concentrate on the matter. The bell went behind us and someone came in, but I weren't about to let em distract us. I had special powers of concentration, see. That is another thing every top copper needs.

'All right, Ray.'

'All right, Li. I wants a short-arm, three-be-thirty-two allen key, please.'

'Short-arm, you say?'

'Aye.'

'Three-be-thirty-two?'

'That's the one.'

'I can get you that, Ray. Mind you, have you seen these nine-piece sets we got here? You gets em in a nice black case, and—'

'I just wants the one allen key.'

'We got a seven-piece set as well, if yer interested. They got a balldriver on one end, so—'

'I just wants the three-be-thirty-two, Li.'

'I can get you that.'

'Nice one. Hey, you hear about that fire?'

'What fire is that, Ray?'

'The one across town. Stan Fletcher's motor shop.'

'Oh aye? A blaze, you say?'

'Blaze? Blaze and half. The whole fuckin' place, explosions and every fuckin' thing.'

'No swearin' in here please, Ray. Mr Fletcher not there at the time, I hope?'

'Well, they do think he might of been. Can't find him elsewhere, you see. And until they gets the flames under control…'

'Oh, no. And him with a wife and four younguns.'

'Well, let's hope he's off down the bookies or summat.'

'Mind you, I ain't surprised.'

'Nah, nor me.'

'Some of the death traps passes through the gates of that place...'

'I knows it. Always got a fag in his mouth and all. Fire hazard, see.'

'Surely is, Ray. Anyhow, there's yer two-and-half mil.'

'Two-and-half mil? I asked for three-be-thirty-two.'

'Two-and-half mil is three-be-thirty-two in metric, Ray.'

'I ain't havin' no metric.'

'Ray, I keeps tellin' you—it's the same thing, only expressed in a different way.'

'No, I don't trust it, Li. You can't trust nuthin' they throws at you these days. Look at this Reaper feller—he walks amongst us here in this very town, so they says. How can you trust yer fellow man, knowin' that?'

'Er, Ray...'

'Mind you, they thinks it's that feller, don't they? The one in the paper there. That Roy bloke.'

'Ray, would you just keep it d—'

'What I don't understand is how come they ain't locked him up? First they brings him in, then they lets him go, then the paper names him for us, along with that dirty picture of him. I mean, why'd they name him if it ain't him? I ain't complainin', mind you. Forewarned is four-armed, as my nan used to say. I don't quite understand it, but—'

'*Ray*, would you just look over there. He *stood right there*, you flamin' fool.'

'Eh? Oh, I never noticed...Fuckin' hell, you reckon he harked us? Fuckin' hell. Should we call the coppers?'

Nah, it were no fucking good. I'd racked me swede up and down and hither and thither for a goodly old two minutes or so, and still I couldn't decide for the life of us if it were coal black-or jet-black.

'Here, Lionel,' I says.

'Yes, Blakey? What can I do for you?'

'You knows in *Miami Vice*, the motor he's drivin' there? Well, she's black, right. That weren't a problem before I came in here, but now it is. I dunno if she's coal black or jet black, see. I just can't picture her right.'

'Well, I must say, Royston, I ain't too clear on…er…'

Lionel were fucking useless, and I ought to have knowed better than to ask him. '*You* knows it though, eh?' I says to the other feller stood there. He looked a bit younger and like he might know about *Miami Vice*. 'You knows *Miami Vice*, right?'

'Me?'

'Who else am I pointin' at, eh?'

'Oh. *Miami Vice*, you say?'

'Aye, *Miami Vice*.'

'I dunno it.'

'Fuck off, course you fuckin' do. Come on, *think*.'

'Er…'

'Come on, it's about a copper with a jet-black Ferrari with spokes on the wheels. And all I wants to know is what colour of black is she? Cos I can't fuckin' recall it, no matter how hard I racks me swede.'

They clocked each other for a bit, and I must say I didn't have very high hopes. I'd forgot how thick folks in Mangel could be and generally was. All that time spent indoors and staying away, watching news and documentaries and that, it had blinded us to the true reality. Folks just weren't up to it, swede-wise. That's the fucking problem with the world as it were. No wonder they was crying out for a higher standard of copper to keep em all straight. Lucky they had me, is all I can say.

'Well, Royston,' says Lionel, surprising us, 'I truly thinks it's jet-black that yer after.'

'You sure? I thought you says you dunno it?'

'True, true, but I seem to have picked up that bit of knowledge somewhere. And I'm quite sure that it's probably correct, I think. Aye, spoked wheels, jet-black Ferrari. That help you, do it?'

I thought about it for a bit, chewing me lip. I chomped down on it a bit too hard and tasted blood, which I took to be a good omen. 'Aye, all right,' I says. Cos I couldn't hang about here forever. I had work to do. Serious fucking work. And I were doing it in the name of humanity and for the benefit of it and that. 'I'll have ten cans of jet-black spray paint, then.'

'Doin' a body job, is yer? You wants a compressor, that's what you wants.'

'I ain't got time for no compressors, Li. Just giz the fuckin' paint, eh. Oh, and, er…you got any spades?'

'No swearin' in here, please, Blake. Spades? Course I got spades. How many you want?'

'Just the one.'

'They're over yonder. You can choose one, can yer?'

I went over and chose one.

'Oh, and Lionel?' I says, coming back.

'Yes?'

'Can you put that on the slate, mate?'

'Slate?'

'Aye. Slate.'

'What slate?'

I looked at him, and then I looked at the other feller. Then I looked at Lionel again and held the spade in a certain way.

15

I didn't like walking about with a spade and a bag of spray paint, but I didn't want to go home just yet neither. I were enjoying meself, just being out and about in town. Like I says, I'd been steering clear. Watching the news all that time, I'd got the impression of how everywhere were overrun with thieves, murderers, and bad folk, and I didn't want no part of it. But it weren't so bad once you got used to it. There were bad folk about all right, like DI Dave had spelled out for us, but you looks at it different when you're wearing the shoes of a copper. And it's the espadrilles I'm on about here. They fitted us perfect, like a fucking dream. And Filthy Stan hadn't been too far wrong in likening em to a pair of slippers. They was well comfy. Mind you, you had to watch out for dog shite. I'd trod in some back there in Cutler Road and I couldn't get it off the top bit, which were made of white curtain material or summat. There were a big brown stain there now and it fucking stunk. I'd have to stick him under the tap later and hope for the best.

'Hay-eurgh!'

That's what it sounded like anyhow. Fuck knows what he meant by it but I'd know that cry anywhere, anytime. 'All right, mate,' I says I says to him. Cos I'd never actually known his name.

'A nasty business,' he says, handing us a *Mangel Informer*.

'What?' I says, walking away from his little newspaper stand and glancing at the front page. There were summat there that seemed to catch the eye, but the paper man got us by the arm and held firm. For an old man, he were a strong man.

'Three bob,' he says.

'Eh? Three bob?'

'Aye. Papers ain't free. Not this one anyhow. If it's a free paper you wants, try the *Mangel and Area Free Press*. This one here's three bob, though.'

It were a fair point. Might seem obvious to you that newspapers cost wedge, you being such a fucking know-all, but I weren't in the habit of buying em and I hadn't been in yonks, if ever at all. I put paw to pocket. 'I ain't got three bob.'

'You ain't havin' that paper, then,' he says, reaching for it. The other one got a bit tighter on me arm.

I looked around. There were plenty of folks about but none looking in our direction at that precise moment. Being a copper is all about making the most of yer opportunities, I've always thought. I went to scratch me nose, doling him a gentle uppercut on the way up. He were a strong bloke but an old one, and I didn't want to hurt him. He went down.

One or two folks was paying attention now and coming over, cooing over the fallen feller and crouching down by him, but I don't think they'd clocked us chinning him. 'He just keeled over,' I says, slipping the newspaper in me bag. 'Got a heart condition, has he?'

'Heart condition? Nora—you give him the kiss of life?'

'Me? Why me?'

'Cos you're a woman. A man can't kiss another man.'

'I ain't kissin' him. Look at that big wart on his chin.'

'Never stopped you kissing Pete Malcolm.'

'I never kissed Pete Malcolm!'

'Don't start denyin' it again. I saw you both at the office party, and...'

While they was arguing the toss I slipped away and sat down on the bench by the Igor Statue, where I got the paper out and had a gander.

And you would not fucking believe what I encountered there on the front cover.

I went into shock, and I didn't truly know what I were doing for a long old while. I took to wandering, and when I found meself again I were up in Vomage Park, crouching down in some bushes. The paper were still there in me paw, and fuck only knew how many folks I'd passed on me travels, pointing at us and laughing. It were too fucking much, and I didn't know as I'd ever live it down. Mind you, I still didn't know why I were squatting in them bushes. Me strides was done up and I didn't feel in need of a shite, so that weren't it. And there really were very little of interest to a feller like meself, down there in them bushes. I'd never really been into bushes, and I could now see that there weren't much else besides them to look at, other than an old Coke can and a used johnny. And I weren't into used johnnies neither.

I were starting to wonder if me true intentions was to hide here in them bushes from here on in and ever thereafter, such were the shame and true fucking embarrassment that had befell us with that front page photo there. I were wondering that, and weighing up the pros and cons, when I clapped eyes on the two birds. They was sitting not twenty foot away from us, on a bench which were not unlike the one I'd been sat upon by the Igor Statue a while back (although it seemed like hardly no time at all). The only real difference were that this bench had two birds atop it, like I says, and one of em had a paper.

They was both looking at it.

'Didn't you shag him once, though?' says the one.

'No I did not. And you dare go tellin' no one about it.'

'You did, though. Didn't yer?'

'Hmmm...well, I honestly can't remember, Shell.'

'You dirty slut. *Look* at him. Fancy shaggin' a perv like that.'

'You *dare* fuckin' tell, Shell.'

'Woss he doin', though?'

'Looks like he's stickin' his arse out.'

'But he's got no kit on. Why's he stickin' his arse out like that with no togs on, though?'

'Why's you askin' me? I dunno.'

'You shagged him. He do that when you was on the job with him, did he, though?'

'I told you, Shell, I don't recall it. I never can recall none of them kinds of stuff. Woss it say about him there, anyhow, in the writin' bit? Why's he in the paper? Just cos he got his arse out in his own living room?'

'No, it's all about him being took by the coppers and let go. They says he might be the Rea—'

I felt a bit sick, actually. How could I have let such a shite thing come to pass? I knew when it had happened, course—me popping downstairs for a guff when Mandy were in me pit, earlier on today. I should have fucking knowed it, sneaky fucking cunts with their cameras. And all because of that wossname they found behind my house, belonging to the dead bird.

And that got us to thinking about what I were doing here. Not here in these bushes, like, but the whole thing about getting nice togs and the motor and that. 'Make a big statement,' DI Dave had said, or summat like it. 'Like catching this Reaper feller. Catch him and you is guaranteed a job on this force. And I mean a fuckin' *top* job, Blakey.'

Where to start, though? I'd had it all straight in me swede not so long back—get the duds right and the rest will follow. But now, with the whole town having a laugh at my bare farting arse in the paper, I felt more lost than ever. I felt like a boxer on the ropes, knocked pillar to post and not knowing his gloves from his tonsils. One more punch and I'd be canvassed for good, I fucking tells yer.

'Mind you,' says one of them two birds. The pretty one, actually. 'He has got quite a nice arse though, ain't he?'

'Mmm…I do quite like a body like that. See his muscles? Mmmmm…Ain't he lost weight since he were bouncin' at Hoppers? Weren't he more of a fat one back then?'

'You'd know. You shagged him.'

'I know but I didn't shag him lookin' like this. This feller here shagged us, I'd remember it. Look at them powerful arse cheeks. You don't see many like that around here.'

Suddenly it all changed. And it's me being like a boxer I'm on about here. The moves came back to us. I ducked a right hook and slammed in a left of me own, breaking two of his ribs and sending him to the canvas. On his way down, before the ref could step in, I gave him a straight right and bust his jaw and near enough killed him. Mind you, I still didn't really know what I were meant to do next, and how to go about catching this murderer feller. At the back of me swede a little thought were hanging about, like a filthy little gyppo child in a sweet shop, waiting for his moment to rob a bellyful. The thought were that I weren't really up to this, on account of me not truly knowing the first thing about coppering, besides how to dress and what motor to drive. But it weren't a very big thought. All I had to do were smack it on the ear.

But the slippery fucker kept moving about, and I kept missing him.

'Look, Shell, I gotta go and get my Phil's tea on. Give you a buzz later though, all right?'

'Yeah, see yer.'

You could hear em giving each other a friendly kiss. I loved it when birds done that. Gave us a warm and cozy feeling inside, like a warm and cozy rolling pin in me pocket.

The fat one walked off, leaving the fit one behind. I were thinking about stepping out and making meself known, seeing if I couldn't interest her in a feel of me powerful buttocks and whatever else she might want to get hold of, in exchange for me shagging her. But she got up sharpish and headed off down the path, which were wise of her, considering how dark it were getting. I stood tall and squeezed the cramp out of me pins, grunting and stretching and farting and wishing I had a fag, then set off after her. Not that I were bothered about catching up with her. Nah, I felt like I were on duty now—as a copper, like—and I had to show that I could resist the urge. I'd just see her out of the park at a safe distance, making sure she were all right, doing me copper thing. Mind you, I had to get a move on cos I couldn't see her no more.

I got a move on.

I'd always had trouble in Vomage Park. Ever since I were a youngun, when we used to come up here and catch minnows in a bucket and tip em down lasses' knickers, I'd got confused with all them different paths that went through that woody bit on the town side. Some went down to the river and some off to Barkettle Road, and others ended up on Waterworks Lane, and all of em twisted over each other and done me swede in summat chronic every fucking time. I got to a bit of a crossroads (although it were about eight paths meeting and not four), and stood there, scratching meself. I heard a noise off to the right somewhere and stopped scratching, staying perfectly still and just harking. I were like one of them birds of prey—a pigeon, or summat—lying in wait until he spots his furry little dinner.

'Cunt.'

This weren't the sound I'd been lying in wait for, but I pricked me lugs up nonetheless. I pricked em up high and swivelled me neck round, like an owl now, cos it were a man's voice that had said that bad word just there and I weren't sure from which way it were coming.

'Yeah, you, cunt. Or "Aunt Myra", as you prefers it.'

'Aunt Myra?' I says. I still couldn't see the fucker. I thought it might be up in a tree but I couldn't spot him there. I knew who it were, though. Not cos I knew his voice but cos I just sensed the fucker, and the pure hatred coming off him in waves. Just like in the cells the other day. Last night, actually. Fucking hell, don't time fly?

I wheeled around and looked the way I'd come, and that's where I found him. Skinny little speccy feller, about so high. Holding a rounders bat.

'Oh, all right,' I says. 'Bit late for ball games, though, ennit? You'll have a nightmare findin' the ball.'

'I ain't got plans for ballgames,' he says, swinging his bat. 'Not unless your head's the ball.'

'Nah, my head's a swede, not a ball. You can't play rounders with a swede.'

'It ain't rounders, you twat. This is a fuckin' baseball bat. And if I wanna play with a swede, I will. You just try and stop us, cunt.'

'Aunt Myra.'

'All right then, *Aunt Myra*.'

'So you wanna play baseball with us?'

'Yeah, and you ain't—'

'Only I dunno the rules, see. And we ain't got no gloves. You needs a glove in baseball, I knows that much. In *The Great Escape*, Steve McQueen has got this big baseball glove, right, and in the other hand he's got a ball. A baseball, I suppose you might call it. Like this, see...'

I picked up a big stone off the side of the path and lobbed it paw to paw.

'And what he does, see...'

'Put that down.'

'...is he goes—'

I lobbed the stone hard, aiming for the head. I'd only meant to fuck the feller around and scare him off, but you gets carried away easy in these situations. (And don't say you don't cos you're no different from the rest of us, you po-faced bastard.) So anyhow, the ball (or stone) (actually more like a rock) is heading for the rude feller at a fucking stupendous rate of knots, and already I'm starting to curse my bastard luck and wish for a more gentle nature, thereby steering us well clear of this kind of shite, with dead bodies and that. And the feller seems to know it as well, cos you can see in a man's eyes when he's cacking himself. And if you can't see it in his eyes, you can smell it. And I could do both just then, the moonlight behind us and the feller stood upwind.

The rock hit his baseball bat, splitting it clean in two like I'd snapped it over me knee.

'You...' he says, finding it hard to speak cos he were short on puff. I noticed his cheeks and jaw was rough and pockmarked, like orange peel. His greasy hair glinted blue under the moonlight. 'You ruined my life, you know! My wife, she...she never forgave us. No matter what the coppers told her, about there being nothing I could do about it, she just wouldn't listen to em. She called us a coward. She said I weren't a real man, and it's all cos of *you!*'

I went for him. I don't mind a cunt having a go with a rounders bat but this were going too far, spouting shite at us and making out like I'm a villain. About five yard off he grew wise to the danger of Royston Blake, and turned and scarpered. I already proved to you how sharp I am over twenty yard or so, but there ain't no point in haring all over a park after skinny cunts like this one. Everyone knows them sort can run on forever.

I picked up half his bat and lobbed it after him, then fucked off.

• • •

On the way out, and with the moon waxing gibbous and yellow overhead, I went past the Mam Fountain and stopped for a clock of it. Used to be knowed as the Piss Fountain, but then one time I witnessed the statue in the middle come to life as my mam, and I'd hitherto called it the Mam Fountain in honour of her, with no referring to piss at all. The three little angel fellers still slashed into the water without no let-up, but I couldn't stop them. Mind you, as I stood there now, gasping for a smoke and feeling a bit down about life in general, I wondered if I couldn't do summat about that. It just didn't seem right and correct, three little stone bastards surrounding my mam and doing a piss.

I had a look around for summat or other, and then I came back.

The first one missed and went over the other side of the fountain, landing on the bench there. The second half-brick hit one of the little bleeders and knocked his right arm off, but he still kept on pissing. I knew I'd have to knock em clean off if I wanted to stop em doing what they was doing, and I knew I'd need proper bricks for that, and lob em hard. A minute or two and I had five of em lined up in front of us, and I were warming to the job. I picked up the first and took aim at the pisser in the middle.

I were smiling.

Playing about with that feller and his rounders bat had got us nice and limber, and I were swinging easy and able to call upon untold reserves of pure strength. I lobbed the brick hard, hitting Mam in the face and knocking her head off before flying off into the trees with nary a deflection. I got in the water and waded over to Mam, already fighting back the sobs. I couldn't believe what I'd done.

Her head were in the water behind her body. I picked her up and sat down on the side with her in me lap. I looked down at her and she looked up at us, and my tears splashed down upon her careworn face and pooled in her eye sockets. 'Ah, Mam...' I says, fighting to get the words out. 'You knows I never meant to—'

'Shut your whiny little face, you little fool,' she says, spraying little drops up in me face.

I wiped em off, wondering if they was the water from the fountain, my tears, or her actual flob. 'I...' I says, shaking me swede, 'I don't under...'

'No, you don't understand, does you? When will you wake up and get that brain of yours workin' proper? There's things in this town needs addressing, Royston, and you ain't addressing em. Instead of addressing em, all you're doing is going around tartin' yerself up and causin' trouble.'

'I ain't, Mam...I'm just...I mean...'

'Just shut up and listen to me. Women in this town are being killed, Royston. They are having their heads chopped off and used for unsavoury ends. And it's *men* doing it, Royston. They thinks it's all for the greater good, and that they're justified, but it ain't and they ain't. Shall I tell you what it is, Royston? It's a *shame*. Truly it is.'

'I know but—'

'But *you* don't have to be like that, Royston. Do you know why? Because when you was a babby I looked into your blue eyes and saw summat different. I knew that you'd be treading your own path, Royston, and that others would follow. Where men once treated women bad and struck them down and killed them, I saw that you would treat them nice and look after them, and respect them as equals in every way. I were a victim, Royston. Your mam were a victim of men and their ways. But you was always gonna make up for that. And other men would follow in your footsteps. They would, I honestly did think they would, but...'

'Mam, I just wanted to—'

'I only ever wanted the best for you, Royston. I used to close me eyes and picture you as a grown man, just like you are now. Except you was wearing a nice suit and tie, and you had a proper job. You had a car and a lovely young lady, and you gave her a beautiful ring and made her your wife...and then you had a nice house and everything, and I were a granny. Did you know that, Royston? I used to dream about being a granny.'

'You will be a granny, Mam. Actually, I think you might already...No...I mean, I ain't sure...but—'

'But it weren't being a granny that made us proud, as I sat there with you on me lap and dreamed about things to come. No, it were you, Royston. It were always about you, and the thought of what you might make of yourself. I always had such high hopes. You'd turn out a proper man, not like all them other fools. And you wouldn't stand by and watch womenfolk suffer.'

'No...no, I never does that. I am actually—'

'But then I sees you now, and it ain't there. The son I used to see when I closed me eyes, he ain't you. It's a disappointment, Royston, that's what it is. You sets your hopes so high and the real world can't reach em. It's just hard, Royston. It's hard to look at what is, and remember how I dreamed it might be…'

'But…'

'But it ain't too late, Royston. There's still time to make your mam proud and shine like that star in the sky. All you got to do is follow the path. Follow the path, though it be dark and full of nasty things, leading you to places you don't want to go.'

'But, Mam, I just wanted to—'

'The path, Royston. The path.'

'*Mam*…'

MAN ARRESTED FOR GBH

A man has been arrested for a violent attack on the manager of Top Lad in the Porter Centre. Owen Gladbeck, an accountant from the Danghill district of Mangel, is said to have knocked out Martin Counter in the changing room area of the popular menswear outlet, and then proceeded to kick him repeatedly until interrupted by concerned staff members. Mr Counter suffered broken ribs, cuts and bruises, and concussion.

'He came up with a cock and bull story,' said Sergeant Doug Percival of the Mangel Constabulary. 'He had the gall to suggest that a police officer told him to do this, saying the victim was a known paedophile who deserved some corporal punishment. I've never heard anything so stupid in my life. A police officer, I ask you. Here, let me read you some of his statement here. "I was a victim of abuse myself when I was a child. A larger boy held me down once and fed earwigs into my ears, and I've suffered nightmares and anxiety ever since. When I saw the policeman standing over

the prone body of that man, for some reason all these memories came flooding back and I just snapped. All of my pent-up feelings of frustration and anger seemed to come out at once, and I took it out on that poor man." The things they'll say to get out of trouble, honestly. I'd like to make it clear at this stage, so as to avoid any confusion, that no policeman was in Top Lad at the time. And never do members of the Mangel Constabulary resort to corporal punishment, or otherwise license members of the public to do so.'

Gladbeck will appear before magistrates on Monday morning.

16

I wanted a fag so bad me lungs was itching like bastards. And I were fucking starving. The bottoms of me strides was wet and cold from wading in the fountain. Plus I were knackered, what with all the events of the day.

But I weren't down about it. Not none of it. How could I be down, after getting a visit from Mam?

It is true that I hadn't ever knowed her proper, her carking it when I were so young, but I'd come to learn all about her and her ways since then. I knew how she worked, see, and what she got up to and for why. Things like her living in that statue in the park. It were cos of the trees, see, and the flowers and birds. There were plenty of that in the park and she felt drawn to it, even though the birds shat on her head quite a lot. Another thing I knowed were that she only ever came to us when the shite's flying, most of it aimed at meself. And that's what she'd done there, just now in the park. She'd wanted to give us a message.

And I'd heard it loud and clear.

Do not stray from the path of being a copper, were what she'd said, in her way. Make us a proud mam and get yerself a proper respectable job, where you can be a proper pillar and order cunts around. And she were going on about birds as well, I think. And it's womenfolk I'm on about here. I think she wanted us to be more polite to em, opening doors for em and that.

I were thinking about that and trying to ignore the werewolf pining in me guts, when I noticed a little light up yonder. I were on Shirt Street at the time, which is more like an alley, and a place frequented by few on account of it not really leading to no place, unless you was taking the long and quiet route home like I were. Didn't want folks seeing us, see. Tomorrow were the day to get out there and start coppering, and until then I wanted me profile kept low. Also I thought it were a nice opportunity for a bit of training in the art of coppering. It's important for a copper to glide invisible through the night, see, and since leaving Vomage Park back there I'd clocked at least thirty folk and not been clocked once meself, which I thought were well good.

But as I neared the little light up yonder, and read the words "Alvin's Kebab Shop & Chippy" on the sign outside, and let out a growl from me guts so loud that a stray cat over the way looked up from his piece of batter, I knew I'd have to spoil me perfect record.

'All right, Alv.'

'All right, Blakey. Chips, is it?'

'Er…how much is they?'

'Thirty-five pence for medium. Fifty-five large.'

'Thirty-five?'

'Aye.'

'That's a fuckin' rip-off, Alv.'

I knew I'd made him feel bad cos he looked down and got on with moving his fish around.

'Look, I never meant it that way,' I said. 'Thirty-five p is all right, for medium chips. Go on and do us some, eh. Actually, large. And a saveloy, all right?'

'Large chips and a saveloy. Right you is, Blakey.'

'Two saveloy.'

'Two? Yer sure?'

'No, three. Three saveloy and large chips.'

He went about his work. I felt like there were summat stood between us, me and Alvin, summat that stopped us from being the mates we once was. It were like a big block of ice, even though the Kebab Shop & Chippy were quite toasty just then, and I knew it were down to me to smash it.

'I just…' I says, 'I just thought you could of said summat else to us, just then. Other than "All right, Blakey." Know what I mean, Alv?'

'I did say summat else.'

'You what? You never.'

'I did. I says, "All right, Blakey? Chips, is it?"'

'Nah, I don't mean that. I mean, you know…'

'I dunno, Blakey.'

'I mean, you ain't seen us in fuck knows how long. You could of asked us how I is, and that.'

'I did. "All right, Blakey?" I says. That were a question.'

'No, I mean…'

'What?'

He put the scran in front of us.

'Don't matter,' I says, picking it up and opening it. I were fucking starving.

'That'll be two pound and sixty-five, Blakey.'

'Here, I thought you closed down the shop?'

'Aye, I did. But I opened up again.'

'In a different place, though.'

'Aye.'

'How come you closed down, and then opened up in a different place?'

'It's a long story, Blakey.'

'Go on.'

'Well, I got drove out of business by them burger bars and the like, and I had to turn me hand to some other things for a while, makin' ends meet and that. But after a while I realised that I weren't no good at them other things, and chips and kebabs is what I'm best at. It's what I'm meant to do, Blakey. I honestly feels that in me bones.'

'I could of telled you that meself, Alv,' I says, cramming some of his life's work into me gob. 'You does some fuckin' marvellous chips, no doubt about it. Kebabs as well.'

'Ta, Blakey. That'll be two pound and sixty-five, please.'

'But how come you was able to open up again? In a different place, like? I thought you was drove out of business?'

'I were, Blakey. But, you see, I been lucky. I got a benefactor.'

I frowned and shook me swede. 'Nah, I dunno him. Benny Factor, you say? He from local, is he?'

'Blakey, benefactor ain't the name of a person. It's more like a word. A very special word.'

'Special word, eh?'

'Aye, and—'

'You mean, like, a secret code?'

'I…I dunno about that. And perhaps I oughtn't to be…erm…'

He were backtracking, the little cunt. He'd opened up a little door to us and gave us a sniff of the good things beyond it, and now he'd gone and changed his mind. He wanted to keep old Blakey out of the good life.

Well, I weren't having it.

'Fuckin' *spill* em, Alv. And it's the beans I'm on about here.'

'Eh? There ain't nuthin' to—'

'*Beans.*'

'All right…bloody hell. Let go me apron, will yer? It ain't even such a big secret. Not with you knowin' him already. And if you'd of stayed in with him, instead of turnin' yer back on him and goin' yer own way, he might of been a benefactor for you as well. Nathan is a fair man, and a good man, and he—'

'Nathan?'

'Aye. And it ain't just me. He helped out Bob Gretchum with a new pickup he needed. And Old Mr Fillery—Nathan bunged him a bit for some new stock, after he fell over and smashed every singe ornamental figurine in his shop.'

'No shite?'

'It's gospel, Blakey. He slipped on a teabag and—'

'No, about Nathan. He's really been helpin' folks out, has he?'

'Course he has. And there's Filthy Stan, too. Ah, you heared about him today, Blakey? It's a bloody tragedy, burnin' to death in his own—'

'Never mind about that, I'm askin' about Nathan.'

'And I'm tellin' you. Nathan really helped Stan set himself up as a dealer. Especially with this new line in exotic motors he were plannin'. Did you know Nathan went and found him an actual Ferra…'

I weren't really harking him no more. Me swede were going turbo, bombing down one line of thought and sussing every angle before shooting off down the next. It's like I were saying just now about things coming to us without me even trying. This here were one of them things. I knowed how to catch the murderer now, thereby making my big statement, like DI Dave had said, and thereby becoming a proper copper.

'…a flamin' shame about Stan, it really is,' Alvin were still saying. 'Oh, I didn't mean…'

'What?'

'I didn't mean it like that. About the flamin' shame, see. I mean, I weren't thinkin.'

'Woss a flamin' shame? Stan gettin' burnt?'

'Aye, but I never meant to—'

'Oh, I gets it. "*Flamin'* shame"—ha ha…That's fuckin' hilarious, Alv. Anyhow, nice to see yer, mate. Hey, Benny Factor, you say?'

'What? Oh, Nathan? Er…aye.'

'Nice one, Alv. Say no more, eh?' I tapped me nose, letting him know I knew the score. Then I put me empty wrapper down and headed doorward.

'Hoy, Blakey, what about me two pound and—?'

17

I were fucking sorted now. All I had to do were ask Nathan the barman who the murderer were. He'd tell us, then I'd go and catch him, tie him up, and haul him in. Bob's yer fucking uncle and I'm the hero, all over the papers (with me arse covered) and set up for a top job on the force. No fucking problems.

Except the one.

If you were being harkful, you already knows it. Alvin mentioned it just a short while back. But I'll be honest with you and say that you don't strike us as a careful harker. I reckon you was too busy sniffing the fishcakes and thinking about your belly. So I'll spell him out again. Just for you, you fat fucking bastard:

Me and Nathan the barman, we wasn't on speaking terms.

It's a long old story, and I ain't even sure I knows it all meself, but I'll just say that Nathan the barman were one of the things I'd had to turn away from, back there when I cut meself off from Mangel life. Nathan were a part of it, you see. Every spot of bother I got meself into, he were right there in the middle of it, stirring the shite like no other. Seemed like he were helping us at times, but I wouldn't need no help if he hadn't got us in trouble to start off with. So no, I hadn't missed Nathan and his pub, the Paul Pry.

Mind you, sometimes you need to crack a few heads to make an omelette. Know what I mean? And I ain't saying I wanted to crack Nathan's swede. Far fucking from it, my friend. Cracking the swede of Nathan would be the doziest thing any man can do, as he'd soon find out. No, I'm just saying that…erm, I'm saying… I'm just fucking *saying*, like. I'm telling you how come I were walking into the Paul Pry on that evening, saveloy and chips in me belly and not a penny in me pocket.

'All right, Nathan,' I says.

It were quiet in the Paul Pry at that time. Too fucking quiet. So quiet I could hear the bubbles popping as they hit the surface of Bob Gretchum's pint of lager, Bob being sat bar-wise at the time.

'All right, Bob,' I says as well.

In response, I got fuck all.

This came as no surprise to us. The silence, the harsh looks in my direction from the four or so punters, the atmosphere that made you feel like you was walking blind into quicksand...all of that were spot-on as you'd expect, considering how I'd been staying away in recent times. To them I were a wrong un, and I could understand why. But I didn't let it knock us off me perch. I knew how they worked, see, Nathan and the Paul Pry contingent. I knowed how to get around em.

'Fair enough,' I says, addressing the Paul Pry as a whole. 'Fair fuckin' play to yers. Who the fuck am I, coming back after stayin' away for fuck knows how long, like a prostitute son? And well might you—'

'Prostitute?' says Fat Ron. 'He got prozzies with him, has he?'

'He means prodigal.' This were Gromer, the miserable cunt from the offy down Cutler Road. 'He's on about the prodigal son, returnin' after a long time of wasteful livin'.'

'Oh. He ain't got no prozzies, then?'

'Look,' I says, 'I'm just fuckin' sayin', right? I'm sayin' how I knows how it looks. But, you see, I've had me reasons. And fuckin' good reasons as well. Do you know what they was?'

I had me eye on Gromer when I says this. I knew he'd be the one to bite, and I knew a bit of peeper contact were like a rag to a red bull where he were concerned. And I weren't wrong.

Like I says, I knew these cunts.

'I don't like to ponder on what passes for "reasons" in your head, Royston Blake, and I don't want to hear em neither. But I can tell you the likeliest truth, from where I'm stood.'

He were blazing away like a wood stove with four good logs in it and a lot of kindling. Seemed his eyes was all set to pop out of his face, bulging like they was, and I wondered if they'd field some damage on the stone floor of the Pry if they did. Or they might bounce. Then I recalled how they got little cables on the back of em, eyeballs have, which is how they're plugged into your swede. And I never learned that from school neither. Nor telly.

'No,' he says. 'My estimate says you stayed away, Royston Blake, on account of your opinion of yerself. And your opinion of us, here at this here tavern. One of em, you ranks it significant higher than t'other. And it's you I'm on about here.'

I rolled me eyes. 'You got summat to say,' I says, 'fuckin' say him.' But I were smiling as well, being friendly and not arsey at all, despite Gromer talking a load of shite there, and trying to confuse us and make us look a twat in front of the assembled here today.

'What I'm sayin' is you ranks yerself far higher than the common herd. And by that I means us in here. That is what I'm flamin' sayin'. You been stayin' clear of this establishment cos it don't accommodate your swede, in short.'

'Fuck's he on about, Burt?' I says to Burt.

Burt ignored us and looked down at his pint of mild. He'd always been a bit off since I knocked him stone cold the one time.

'I can tell you woss wrong wi' you,' says Bob Gretchum, tapping his swede. 'You're flamin' wrong up here, thass you.'

'It's more than that,' says Fat Ron, pouring a pack of smoky bacon into his trap. When he started talking again, bits of crisp sprayed all about like muck out of a spreader. 'It's like Mr Gromer here says: he's got *airs*, that one. The like of us, he don't hold as high.'

'Hoy, you,' shouts Nathan. To Fat Ron, so it seemed. 'Don't you spray them crisps all over my floor, you mucky pup.' He ducked down and came up with a dustpan and brush, and put his evil eye on Fat Ron, who came and took em like a bad dog.

While Ron cleaned up his mess the rest of us fell to silence and stayed there. It were like we felt short-changed by Nathan the barman, who were now going about his barmanlike affairs and showing no hint of further utterance. The matter of me turning up after a long stay away hung heavy in the air, like a fart by someone with very bad guts. Mingling with the fart were the echo of Nathan's voice, ringing in your lugholes like when you gets a thump aside the swede. While the fart and the echo lingered, no one could pipe up. Nor move on to other matters neither.

I were stood bar-wise, leaning on it and letting me eyes wander. I couldn't keep eye contact with no one without em slithering away. After a bit everyone were looking at the floor, which were now free from bits of crisp. I looked over me shoulder at Nathan. I didn't really have to do that to know how he were, cos I could feel it. He were raging, turning pink and polishing his pint glass with a bit too much elbow for my liking.

'You'll smash that,' I says to him. Sometimes you can't stop words before they're said. Do you find that yerself? Mind you, you don't really say much, does you?

Nathan lobbed the glass at us. Hard. I ducked, me being sharp as a new pin in terms of reflexes, and the glass kissed the back of me swede without smashing and flew on.

'Ooh, Nathan…' says Gromer, putting a paw to his gob and looking at the floor. 'Ooh, that weren't a good outcome.'

Bob Gretchum got up and hared to the back of the room, kneeling down where I couldn't see him. Fat Ron went over as well, but not haring. Gromer stood over em, looking down and going: 'Ooh, Nathan…' Burt watched from afar, shaking his head.

There were someone else in the room, somewhere, and I couldn't recall who it were. I leaned back and peered around the table at the floor where they was fucking about, and clocked the sole of a very large boot, a bit of white shirt with some red on it, and what seemed to be a dickie bow.

'You've gone and smashed my lad,' yells Gretchum Senior, his irate face peeping over the table.

'Shut your flamin' hole, Bob Gretchum,' blares Nathan from behind us. 'That weren't me who done that. Any blinkin' fool can see that.'

'I never seed it that way, Nathan,' says Fat Ron, keeping his swede low, quite wisely. 'I seed you pitch a glass and it hittin' Bob Junior here.'

'Aye, I pitched it all right, but it bounced off this un here's head. Any old fool could see that.'

Gromer rubbed his chin and goes: 'Deflection, eh?'

'Aye. Blake here deflected it with the back of his head. He hadn't of done that, it'd of smashed his face instead of the boy. Or if he'd ducked proper, like a man with a grain of sense, it'd of hit the jukebox there.'

'Hold up…' I says.

'No, *you* hold up. As I were sayin', that were meant for Blake and Blake alone. By gettin' his swede in the way he upset the natural order of things and…well, right there's what happened.'

'Jukebox don't work, Nathan. You told us you'd fix her, but you—'

'Shut up about the flamin' juke box, Ron.'

'Woss we gonna do about my boy?'

'*All right*, Bob, I heared yer. Erm, how bad's his face?'

Nathan wandered over to the damage with a couple of bar towels and a little box of summat or other. While he done that, I reached over and pulled meself a couple of pints. I know I weren't a drinker no more, but I felt right on edge, in terms of nerves, and I needed summat. I pulled meself another couple before Nathan stood up.

'Aye, he'll be all right,' he says, packing his sewing kit back in the little box. 'When he wakes up, just tell him not to stretch his face too much.'

'Too much? How much is too much?'

'Just use yer common sense.'

Nathan came back to the bar alone, leaving them others helping Bob Junior onto his arse. I were glad of that. Not the helping onto his arse bit, but the Nathan being alone bit.

'Hey, Nathan,' I says low.

I wanted a word, see. You knows what the word is, but Nathan didn't. And, to be honest, I couldn't recall it meself at that time.

'What?'

'I wants a word.'

'Aye. Go on then.'

He weren't looking at us. The only time I think he'd clocked us were to take aim at us.

'I says go on then.'

'Aye, I will, I'm just...'

'You forgot what you come in for.'

'No, I ain't forgot, I just...I'm just tryin' to get the words right, before I—'

'Well, the answer is no.'

'Oh.' I wished I had some more lager. 'But you dunno what I'm askin'.'

'Don't give us that. You knows I knows what your question is, and you knows I knows the answer. And it's no.'

'Oh,' I says again. 'Well, yer wrong, actually. See, all I were gonna ask were can I have a pint of lager?'

'How d'you know I'm wrong? I ain't said what I think your question is, yet.'

'Yeah, but—'

'And the answer is no either way. You can't have another pint, and I ain't telling you who's decapitatin' these young women.'

'Come on, Nathan. Be a fuckin' mate, eh?'

'A mate? You wants us to be a mate?'

'Look, I just needs to know it. I got shite planned, see, and it's good shite. I got good intentions, Nathan. You'd be fuckin' proud of us.'

He didn't say nothing to that.

'Hey, Nathan,' I says, looking left and right and leaning in. 'Benny Factor. Eh? *Benny* fuckin' *Factor*.' I gave him a wink, just to drive it home.

Nathan didn't wink back at us, for some reason. He weren't even smiling. 'I see,' he says. 'You wants us to be your benefactor, eh?'

In response, I just winked again. I loved all this secret password business. Made us feel like a proper spy.

'You ought to know better than to come in here askin' for benefactors, Blakey. You ought to think about the things you done, recent things, and how they stands in my book. Cos I'm the lord and master around here, Blake.'

'I ain't done fuck all, Nathe, all I—'

'The name's Nathan. You ought to know that.'

'I does know it, Nathe…I mean Nathan, but…'

He put a finger to his lips, brushing the low-hanging moustache hairs slightly. It had got a fair bit bushier since I'd last seen it, Nathan's moustache, and I thought it were better that way. Then I noticed that he'd actually trained his nose hairs to come down low and spread amongst the tash hairs, padding it out. It took us right aback, realising that, and I actually did stagger backwards and almost keel over.

Still aiming his watery peepers at mine, he stepped backwards himself, towards that door that led behind the bar. 'Would you please come down here, Blakey?' he says, opening it. 'You just come down with us, and I'll set it all straight for you. I'll settle it once and for all, Royston.'

I were still going backwards. I heard someone shout, 'Hoy!' and felt meself going down, tripping over the arse-wise Gromer lad and knocking a table over. Then I were on me feet again, backing towards the door.

When I got to it, and opened it, I fucking pegged it.

REAPER STRIKES YET AGAIN

Earlier today the headless body of a young woman was found in North Mangel. Evidence suggests that this is the sixth victim of the Reaper, who has terrorised the streets of Mangel for several months. The corpse of Shelley Turnbridge, a housewife from Shatter Crescent, was found under a bench in Vomage Municipal Park. 'I just can't believe it,' said husband Phillip, a labourer.

As with the other victims of the Reaper, no head was found. Eyewitnesses report seeing a suspicious man in the area at the time, carrying a wooden-handled implement that could have been an axe. He is described as short and weedy-looking, with thick-rimmed glasses, lank brown hair, and a pockmarked complexion. This is at odds with the 'Viking' description given by witnesses to the previous murder. Elsewhere in the park, the fountain was vandalised.

'We will find him,' said Police Chief Bob Cadwallader. 'No one gets away with vandalism in this town. Especially when it's sites of public beauty, like the fountain at Vomage Park. Generations have grown up playing in that park, and it boils my blood to know that someone can bring such wanton destruction to it.'

Asked to comment on the murder, Cadwallader said: 'We really do think we are onto something now. We can discount the "Viking" description because that witness has since been undergoing psychiatric treatment and is therefore unreliable, so we are sure this weedy man with glasses is the one. I'd like to point out that appearances can be deceiving, and just because he looks weedy does not mean he is weedy. My brother-in-law looks like he's made of pipe cleaners, but he doesn't half pack a punch. Wiry is the word. So what I'm saying is beware of this man. Do not approach him if you see him, unless you're quite handy.'

Asked if he would now admit that this is a serial killer, Cadwallader's stance remained resolute: 'I've said what I'll say about that. I don't like the term "serial killer". I prefer the word "murderer". Murder is a crime in this town, as is vandalism, and anyone who does either will be apprehended and dealt with. I don't care how many times you do it, you will be caught. And it's you I'm addressing this to, weedy man with glasses. I know you killed those women, and I know you damaged that fountain. We'll get you, wherever you're hiding.'

18

Walking up the main road, I found myself whistling a tune. And it weren't a merry tune, which were odd for me. Normally I'm a cheerful chap, as you knows, and if I whistles it's to let the rest of the world share in my sunny nature. But no, this were more like a funeral march, and I didn't have no clue from where I'd picked it up and why it were piping out from between my puckered lips.

Thinking about it, I could see why. It were coming up from the depths, see, from the place where I knowed the truth about matters close to my heart and couldn't kid meself otherwise. And it's the coppering I'm on about here, the whole plan of me catching this Reaper feller and thereby becoming a proper policeman. See, in me heart of hearts—which is the name for that deep place I just told you about—I didn't have the first fucking clue how to go about catching him. I mean, you ain't gonna catch a rabbit if you dunno where the rabbits goes running. Do you know what I mean? I just didn't know where to start, and who to ask. Nathan had been my best hope and he'd fucked us off, which left us on square one without a paddle. So really, when you was honest about it, you could see how I weren't ever gonna be a copper that way. So it's just as well I had another plan.

And this is where the funeral march comes in.

See, if you casts yer swede back to DI Dave telling us how I ought to go about it, you'll recall his precise words. Actually you won't recall his precise words at all, will you? I bet you don't even remember what you had for tea last Monday, you dozy twat. What he said were that I got to *make a mark*. And then he said, as an example like, that catching the Reaper might be a way of doing that. But he never said it were the only way.

And that's where Plan B comes in.

It had first came to us in the copper station, when I were waiting on me interview, and the more I thought about it, the more I could see how it'd work. I'd even got meself a spade without thinking about it, a spade having a vital role to play in Plan B. The only part of it I didn't like, if I were being picky, were the bit about grassing on someone. Especially after Mam saying all that about being nice to birds. And the more I thought about it, the more I knew that I couldn't do it. Plan B were for a cunt, and that cunt weren't me.

Which left us with Plan C.

I went along a bit further, trying to think up a Plan C. After a bit I forgot about that and started whistling again, this time 'Love Me Tender' by Elvis Presley. It's how I felt right then, see, underneath it all. I felt somewhat knocked about, and I wanted a nice bird to love me tender. I were a working man again now, when you looked at it in a certain way, and at the end of a long shift I just wanted a nice bird to shag.

I were thinking about that, and still whistling the Elvis tune, when I spied a light up yonder. And it's the bedroom window of my house I'm talking about here. Someone were in there. But for some reason I weren't too bothered about it. It's like the light weren't on in a narky, burglarising way, but a soft way, suggesting a bird waiting there for us.

And it's Mandy Munton I'm on about here.

Soon as the thought went in me ear, I knew it had to be true. Do you recall how she'd fucked off this morning a bit sharpish, and frankly none too polite? Well, it stood to fucking reason that she'd come back and apologise about that, and perhaps suck me cock. That's what I liked about Mandy Munton—you just knew she'd suck yer cock whenever you wanted her to. It's the look in the eye they got. Do you know what I mean?

I were well hard by the time I got the door open. She'd know I were here now, and she'd like as not be adjusting her hair and making sure I could see some of her cleavage. I went to open the door, thinking about that. Or perhaps she didn't have no kit on at all, and were just lying there on the bed with her legs spread.

I rubbed me paws together and went up the stair.

She weren't there. Not in the bedroom anyhow, though there were a mug of tea over there on the shelf with steam coming out of it. I stood still and heard a noise off to the side, coming from the bathroom. I crept over there and harked, hoping she weren't doing a shite. There's one thing I don't like in a woman and it's shitting. I just don't think they're meant to do it. Or if they gotta do it, they ought to keep it hid, and pretend they don't. Mind you, when I put lug to door I heard a definite pissing sound, so that were all right. I don't mind pissing in a woman, long as she's quiet about it.

I went and laid meself down on the bed, stretching my arms along the pillows and making meself cosy. Some more noises in there now and I knew she'd be out in a sec, so I pulled me jacket and T-shirt off sharpish and tossed em across the room. Give her a nice surprise, me lying there with me bare hairy chest, and hopefully we wouldn't have to waste time talking and we could get straight down to shagging. Just to drive the point home, and as the bathroom door started opening, I undid me belt and strides and pushed them down a bit, taking me trolleys with em. Top of my hard dick were showing but it were too late to change that, and she'd only be wanting it out anyhow, so I thought fuck it and yanked the lot of it out sharpish. Then I put my arms behind me head and sat back with a sexy look on me face.

When she came out and stopped for a few moments in the doorway, looking at us, she didn't half look like Jonah. And it's the copper who preferred to be known as Sergeant Jones I'm on about here. The light weren't so good but the Jonah look about her were fucking uncanny, I swear. After a bit the sheer uncanniness of it got to us, and I could feel me cock inching south to safety. And when she opened her gob and said summat, and her voice were very much like that of Jonah, I didn't feel so well.

'Look,' she says, 'I…I ain't like that, all right? I'm gonna go back in here, where I forgot to wash my hands, and then come out and I'll *reconnoitre* with you in the kitchen, or thereabouts, and I'll address the official business I'm here on. Eh? Oh, and your bog don't work.'

'It do.'

'It don't. Flusher's bust. You ought to get it fixed.'

'Well, I never bust it. You must of bust it.'

'I never, honest.'

She went back in and shut the door, leaving us high and dry and limp and frankly quite cold. I pulled me trolleys and strides up and my top back on. I noticed I were breathing hard, and that I were riled about summat.

'Hoy, you,' I says, yanking the bathroom door open. I had to yank cos it weren't coming easy. 'Where's Mand? Woss you done with our Mand, you bent fuckin' arse bandit?'

'Mand? Who's Mand? And don't call us an arse bandit, you fuckin' arse bandit. Get away from us, you fuckin'…you fuckin' arse…erm…'

I got him by the throat. It were easy cos he had a fair bit of slack there, being somewhat of a fat bastard them days. You'd think a fat throat would give you trouble, what with all the blubber sliding around and that, but if you just thinks of it like a dog's scruff you'll do all right. He were trying get in some potshots at me face, and one of em even clipped me eyebrow and had us blinking, so I brung me knee up and gave it him full in the ribcage, possibly doing it some serious. I weren't thinking about that, though. I were thinking about turning him arse-about and sticking his swede down the shitter, which I went on to do.

'No cunt calls us an arse bandit,' I says, holding him down the pan. 'No fucker. Specially not true arse bandits like you.'

'All right…' he says. 'All right, you ain't a…an arse…'

He were right about the bog being bust. Must of been bust since the last time I'd used it, cos there were a lot of brown water down there. I held Jonah's face in it, trying to drown him. Mind you, he were like as not enjoying it, the dirty pervert. It were a bit of a surprise, learning that about him. He'd never before struck us as one who pots brown. I let go of him, wiping my paws on me trousers.

'Honestly, Jone,' I says, 'I never thought it of you. You really goes for a pair of hairy bollocks over a nice fanny?'

'Fuck off, you bastard,' he shouts, spraying brownish flob all over. 'It's *you* who's—'

I got him and dunked him again, this time putting more weight on it and getting him to the solids down there at the bottom. 'Say it,' I says, letting him up a bit. '*Say* it.'

'All right,' he yells, gurgling. 'All right, fuck sake…I am an arse bandit. Let us go, you…you…'

'What? Me what?'

'I don't fuckin' know…not an arse bandit, or summat.'

'Fuckin' right,' I says, letting him go. '*Not* a fuckin' arse bandit, me.'

He fell sideways off the pan and tried to get up, falling again. He had the shite soup all over his face and tried wiping it off with his sleeve. I left him to it and went down the stair, where I washed my hands and put the kettle on. Watching it for a while I noticed a smell, and I knew that Jonah were creeping up behind us.

'Watch it, you,' I says, turning to face him and pressing my arse against the cupboard in a defensive way. 'And what the fuck's you doin' in my house anyhow?'

'I only came in because you left yer front door open. I just popped upstairs for a tinkle when you came in.'

'I never left me front door open.'

'You did. It were hangin' wide open. Go and look in the hall—there's dead leaves and everything blown—'

'I never left it open, right? I never leaves me doors and windows open. I'm careful like that. Got that, Jonah?'

'All right, Blake. The door weren't open. All right.'

'Oh, I see,' I says. 'So you broke into me house?'

'No, I never...I mean...'

'That's fuckin' breakin' and enterin', that is. I been had up for that meself, many a time, in me wayward youth. Mind you, I don't do it no more. I left all that behind us and went responsible. Just goes to show, dunnit? It's the fuckin' coppers in this town that is the problem. They does what they wants and gets away with it. Well, that's about to change.'

I let him go, realising that I had him by the wobbly throat again. I didn't want to be so close to his face anyhow, knowing how it'd just been dunked in that muck in the bust bog. I could tell from his rosy cheeks that he'd had a quick wash but he still hummed like billy-o.

'You want summat, does you?' I says. 'You ain't gettin' us for fuck all, cos I ain't done nuthin'. I'm a model citizen these days. But I'll tell you summat—the more you hangs about, the more

I feel like gettin' up to aggro. And do you know what the strangest bit is? I don't even know why that is.'

'Well…' he says. He didn't look happy in himself. Face were like a hanged man, like he can't get no puff and his tongue's set to bust. 'You might want to know that I'm here on official business.'

'That's odd,' I says, 'cos I thought you was here on a social visit.'

'We both knows that ain't ever gonna happen.'

'Shame. Fuck off then.'

'Hear us out first, eh.'

'Go on then.'

I made meself a cup of tea. Jonah could fuck off, like I just telled him.

'We need your help. The coppers…as in…well, I am here to put a proposition to you. It's a small job, but a very important one. And it's a job that only you are in a position to do, Blakey.'

'Don't call us Blakey. Only mates calls us Blakey.'

'What shall I call you, then?'

'Royston.'

'Royston? But that's your…'

'Fuckin' *Royston*, right?'

'All right. Well, Royston, it's about the Reaper.'

'Oh aye?'

'Aye. See, we knows who it is.'

'Oh aye?'

'Aye.'

'Go on then.'

'I will. And I'll also tell you all about how you can help us— and it's the Mangel Area Constabulary I'm speakin' on behalf of here—about how you can help us to catch him.'

He told us all about it, the plans they had for catching the Reaper. It were more like meself catching him on me todd—single-pawed, like—but I could see how that were the only way to play it. About halfway through his telling of it to us, I made him a cup of tea. He had four sugars.

'Sweet tooth,' I says.

'Aye. And it's tomorrow, this plan I'm sketchin' out to you. It must be pulled off tomorrow night, OK?'

He told us the time and the place and made us repeat em back to him two or three times. I reckon he would have had us saying em over and over all night long, if I hadn't got fed up after a while and told him to fuck off.

'Just so long as you got the details straight, all right?'

'Aye. Fuckin' hell, Jonah.'

'Look, is there summat about this you don't understand? I mean, you don't look like you're takin' it in.'

'Nah, I am takin' it in.'

'Why's you frowning, then? You don't reckon it's a good idea?'

'Well, in truth, I don't reckon it's that good of an idea. I can see *how* you came up with it, and *why* you came up with it, but I can also see that it won't work. See, this Reaper feller, why's he gonna play along with it? He don't know us, see. I'm a fuckin' stranger to him, so he ain't gonna play.'

'Ah, but he do know you. The Reaper, turns out he's someone you knows quite well, in a strange way.'

'Who?'

'Can't say. You'll hear in good time. So long as you agrees to do this.'

'Go on and tell us.'

'I can't, because—'

'Just fuckin' *tell* us, you cunt.'

'Flamin' heck, Blake. Can't you learn some flamin' respect? I can't impart that information to someone who ain't on the team.'

'All right, I'll do it.'

'Ain't as simple as all that. You gotta sign a contract.'

'A fuckin' contract? What fuckin' contract?'

'This one here.' He got a contract out of the inside pocket of his jacket. He handed it to us and I had a look.

'This is a nice contract,' I says.

'You read it, then?'

'No, I mean it's on nice pukka paper. And I likes them coats of arms and that along the top. Nice.'

'Here, give it us and I'll read it for you…'

I gave him a look. 'You sayin' I can't fuckin' read?'

'No, I'm just speedin' along the pro—'

'You is sayin' that, ain't yer? You'm sayin' I can't read fast enough.'

'I'm not, Royston, honest. Go on and read the contract. I'll just sit here and drink me tea. Ooh, it's a bit hot.'

I did like he said. It were like this:

I, Royston Roger Blake of South Mangel, do hereby solemnly promise to go along with the plans for catching the so-called "Reaper", as drawn up by members of the Mangel Area Constabulary such as Sergeant Cecil Jones. I will carry out my part of the plans to the utmost of my abilities, which is to say that I will not be late or say the wrong things. In addition, I do solemnly promise not to breathe a word about this to anyone except Sergeant Jones and his immediate team. If I break this promise, I understand that I will go to Mangel Jail for a long time.

'I ain't signin' this. You can fuck off with it.'

'Wuh?' he says, wiping dribble off his chin. 'Where…? Oh, right. Blakey. I mean Royston. Must of dozed off there.'

'I says I ain't signin' this. I ain't even wiping my arse with it.'

'Wassat? Oh, the contract?' he says, picking up his mug. 'What part don't you like? Pleurgh…this tea's cold.'

'Says I'm goin' in Mangel Jail if I fucks it up. Bollocks to that—I ain't goin' in no Mangel Jail.'

'Ah, but we got to have that bit there to make sure you don't spill the beans, or try to wriggle out of it.'

'Well, stick it up yer arse,' I says, tossing it on the table. 'Get some other cunt.'

'I knows where yer coming from, Royston, and I can see how the jail bit is a big disadvantage to you. But you got to weigh it up against the advantages.'

'What advantages? There ain't no advantages here.'

'Aye there is. There at the bottom, there.'

I had a look, and sure enough there was the advantages, right after the Mangel Jail bit.

In return for my services, I understand that I will be recompensed to the tune of £250. The Mangel Area Constabulary agrees to this.

'Recompensed means paid.'

'Fuck off. I knows what recompensed means.'

'I were only—'

'Two-fifty is shite,' I says.

'Well, we can adjust it slightl—'

'I wants three ton.'

'Three hundred?'

'Aye. Cash.'

'Oh, well…we can stretch to that, I imagine.'

'Can you? Make it four ton, then.'

'Now hang on…'

'Stretch to three and you can stretch to four. Or I ain't signin'.'

He pursed his lips and stared at us. He truly were an ugly bastard. 'Well, all right,' he says. 'If you'll just—'

'There's summat else I wants.'

I put it to him.

Take or leave.

'And not just any old job,' I says, in addition. 'I ain't wearin' no uniform. It's plain togs for me, or you can tear up yer fuckin' contract.'

'You want us to give you a job as a detective?'

'Aye, like DI Dave.'

'Dave Borstal?'

'Aye, him.'

'Well, that is interesting. Hmm…tell you what, I reckon we can actually swing it for you.'

'Course you can. It's a piece of piss for you. I ain't just any old punter, you know.'

'I does know. With your knowledge of the policing system, and your background as a security guard, I reckon you'd be a shoo-in.'

'Good. Nice one. Shoo us in, then.'

I thought this were going a mite too well. Don't you? I mean, you'd expect a cunt like Jonah to fight us to the last, in terms of blocking my path into the force as a copper. And not only a copper, but his own boss, in a way. See, he'd be wearing uniform, and I'd be in me fashionable togs, which makes me more higher up than him on the old job ladder, or whatever they calls it. So aye,

I were well surprised by his agreeing to it. Plus I didn't like the look on his face. Actually I hadn't ever liked the look on his face, him being so ugly, but it were a worse one than normal just now. And he knowed it, cos he says:

'Oh, I'm only smilin' here cos I reckon it's a great idea. You on the force, it's just what this town needs. Truly and honestly, Royston. I knows we had our ups and downs, but I always admires a man who can turn himself around, like you has. Truly, you are an example to us all. And the town of Mangel will be all the more better for having you on her streets, as a copper.'

'But I ain't wearin' no uniform.'

'No uniform, no.'

'So it's a goer, then?'

'Aye. If you'll just sign—'

'You got us down as thick, have you? I ain't signin' shite unless it says I'm gettin' to be a copper. A fuckin' full-bore plain togs detective. Right?'

'Not a problem, Royston. Not a...' He stopped there while he wrote out the new bit at the bottom, then passed it to us:

In addition to the £250 £400, Mr Blake will be welcomed into the Mangel Constabulary as a plainclothes detective. If he goes along with the aforestated requirements, that is.

'And summat else,' I says. 'I wants to drive my choice of motor. As me work motor, like. And I wants the coppers to pay us for it, cos I actually already bought it. But only I can drive it, see. You know in *Miami Vice*, his Ferrari? It's like that. He needs his flash motor cos he's got to look flash himself, in the line of duty, so they pays for it and not him.

*In addition, the Constabulary will pay for Mr Blake to drive
any vehicle he so chooses. We will hold the ownership docu-
ments but only Mr Blake can drive the vehicle. Refer to* Miami
Vice *for an example of this arrangement.*

'And petrol. I ain't payin' me own petrol.'

And petrol. He is not paying his own petrol.

'And...er...'
'What? I'm running out of flamin' space here.'
'Turn it over then.'
'I have done already.'
'Write smaller, then. Fuck sake.'
'Just get on with it, eh. I got a home to get to.'
It stopped us in me tracks, him saying that. All the while, here's
me looking out for meself and not giving a butcher's flange about
no one else. And there's him, Sergeant Jonah, stood here, earning a
crust for his wife and younguns at home. It brung home to us how
life is all about priorities, and not just yer own personal wossnames.
It pointed out to us in a fair and unflinching way how a man counts
his success by them who he's got at home, meaning that he's fuck all
if he's on his todd. And I could picture it, me sat here in me kitchen,
supping a nice and sophisticated cocktail after a hard day's catching
villains. But it didn't look right, that picture. It were a picture without
colour, and one that just looked a bit shite overall. It needed summat.
It needed what Jonah had.
I told him what my last thing were.

*And a diamond ring. A nice big one made of gold and with a
big diamond in the middle.*

MANGEL YESTERDAY—THE MANGEL STONE

Russell Pank

Of course, Mangel is about more than just pubs, and always has been. Our town was built upon beliefs, conflicting though they may have been for a time, but ultimately uniting in an approach to everyday living that saw it through the dark ages and into modern times. Inevitably, pubs had a role to play here. Whenever a common belief is being forged, you can bet that it takes place in a pub.

It is hard to see it today, looking at its drab, unassuming exterior and even drabber interior, but for many long centuries the most influential pub in Mangel was The Paul Pry. Natenwulf, the all-conquering chieftan of the civil war, was to give seed to both a dynasty of potent rulers and, incredibly, an entire religion. Unlike other religions, the nameless one fostered within the bowels of The Paul Pry was centred around an object rather than a divine entity. But this object was worshipped with at least as much fervour and passion as any god. The object was the Mangel Stone.

Little is heard of this legendary artefact nowadays. Some say it is a myth, others that it is buried somewhere beneath the tarmac and concrete we see around us today. Most have never heard of it. But what cannot be denied, if the history books are to be believed, are the deeds done in its name.

For countless centuries, men believed that the well-being of Mangel depended upon the Mangel Stone, and that the only way to influence their own fate for the better was to make offerings to the stone. Indeed, a document exists which lays out precisely how and when such an offering should be made. "When the moon is gibbous, on the wax, a hen wrapped in bay leaves may be offered unto the stone. When four gibbous moons have waxed, and four hens been offered, you may offer two hens on the next gibbous moon. A seventh and final hen must then be offered unto the Stone when the moon is next full, and it will bring about great things. All ills will be lessened and all turmoil alleviated." This is my own rudimentary translation of a badly deteriorated manuscript, and I may have missed some of the meaning (the word suggesting "hen" could possibly mean something else) but the sense is clear.

What is also clear is how far we have progressed since those dark times.

19

'Aye, aye, you just get all that stuff together for us and I'm yer man. Tomorrow night, no worries. I'll be there. Don't forget the fuckin' ring, right? And I wants it all done up in a posh box, right? And don't go tryin' to fob us off with one o' them placcy ones from the market. I knows a diamond when I sees one. You fuckin' understand that? Good.'

Jonah started to say summat in response but I slammed the door in his face. He were an ugly bastard and it didn't do us no good at all to look at him, nor hear him neither. Mind you, if he could pull off all that, like I'd asked him, I'd give him a big kiss on the lips.

As I trudged upstairs to me pit, yawning and stretching, I could still hear the echo of some of them words I'd just said. They bounced around inside me swede, pinging off the sides and slowly coming to settle right in the middle, which is where most of the deepest thoughts goes on.

I knows a diamond when I sees one.

And it's Mandy Munton I'm on about there, not rings. Mind you, it's rings as well. Cos it's her who were set to have one off us. Mandy were the bird for me, and I could now see it loud and clear. We'd been through a lot together, me and her, and it's a certain time out in Hurk Wood I'm on about here, whereby she blasted her own kindred brothers and I put em in the ground for her.

(But I don't want you thinking bad of her by that. They was pure cunts, her brothers, all three of em. And if she hadn't carked em, I would have, like as not. In fact I think I did cark the one of em, although I can't recall it for sure. And if I did, you can bet it weren't my fault.)

Plus Mandy were just the sort of wife I needed. Me being such a smart and fashionable plain togs copper, I needs a bird at home who ain't gonna look ugly and boring stood next to us. Mandy were well fit and very sophisticated looking, with her smart jeans and her sheep jumper. Plus she had marvellous tits.

I knowed it would turn her around, giving her the diamond. And with the job as well, and the motor, she'd soon forget about them varmints. Mind you, I still had to get shet of em.

I were only joshing there, by the way, about kissing Jonah on the lips.

• • •

Next morning, while I were hauling on me army strides (I had some dirty work to do, so I weren't putting on me new suit just now), a couple of little cards fell out of the pocket. It were the two from the phone-box—the one with the bare bird's arse and the one saying HIGH CLASS.

I looked at em both, weighing up the goods and bads, and went for the posh one. I were going up in the world now, and if I were gonna get me bog fixed, I might as well use a posh plumber. Mind you, I were still a bit surprised to see so many of em being birds these days. Used to be a fellers' trade. I weren't complaining though.

• • •

'Hello?'
    'Hello?'
    'Yes?'

'Hello.'

'Who is this?'

'Is you…"HIGH CLASS"?'

'Oh, right. Yeah, I am high class. I'm too high class for this town, let me tell you. But I'm here and I'm in service. I don't come cheap, though.'

'Oh?'

'No, I don't. What is it you was after?'

'I just want me bog fixed.'

The line went dead. I fucking hated phones, and I were glad I didn't have one no more. I put another coin in and dialled.

'Hello?'

'Hello?'

'You again, eh? Look, are you takin' the piss?'

'No, I just want…Here, does I know you?'

'I dunno. You do sound a bit familiar. You sound a bit like… Oh my God…'

The line went dead again. I only had one coin left and it were a fifty. I dunno why, but I just couldn't leave it alone with this HIGH CLASS bird. Summat in her voice—and the long dark hair in her picture—wouldn't let us walk away. Plus I truly did want me bog fixed, because Jonah had been in it and I found that unhygienic, and a bit disgusting actually. I crossed the road and went into the paper shop.

'Got change for a 50p, Mike?' I says to the feller there.

'Oh, all right, Blakey.'

'All right, Mike. You got—'

'You'll have to buy summat.'

'I don't want nuthin'. I just wants change for me 50p. I got a call to make, and I ain't wastin' the whole fifty.'

'And I ain't a change machine. You buys summat, I'll give you change. See?'

I picked summat up and goes: 'How much is this?'

'It's 2p,' he says. 'You tight-fisted beggar.'

'You callin' us a beggar?'

'I called you tight—'

'Did you, though? Did you call us a beggar?'

'Well, aye…but it's because of, erm…Look, rules is rules. You got to buy summat if you wants change, and not take the mickey by pickin' up a tuppenny gobstopper.'

I'm a big feller. You knows that by now. And Mike ought to have knowed it as well. They all fucking knowed it, but it didn't stop em being cheeky. I'd learn em soon enough, though. Soon as I got me badge I'd fucking teach every one of em some respect, thereby making the world a better place. But I didn't have no badge yet. I just had Mike here in the paper shop, giving us lip like no other. And like I says, I'm a big feller. Plus I got moves, mate. I got angles and dummies and the lot of it. I got options. I could have been a boxer, you know. Only thing stopped us were the thing about using yer fists only and no other part of your person. I fucking hated rules, sometimes.

'I fuckin' hates rules,' I says to Mike. 'Sometimes.'

'That ain't my bother. If you don't intend on stickin' to the—'

'Open yer till.'

'You what?'

'Open the fuckin' till,' I says, glancing over me shoulder. The shop were empty. 'Go on an' do it. You don't, I'll waste yer fuckin' face. Know what I mean?'

Mike narrowed his eyes at us. Like it'd help him.

'Go on and call my bluff,' I says. 'Go on. I needs the exercise.'

'You can't—'

I reached over and grabbed his arm, then put his paw up to his face. He were a weak little runt and offered no fight whatsoever.

'Feel that,' I says. 'Feel that face. You makes us wait three seconds longer and that's the last time you'll be feelin' that face like it is. One…two…'

I admire the sound of a cash till opening. Actually, I loves it. But I admire it as well because it tells you all about order. And by that I mean a society that runs smooth, money flowing this way and that and everyone being happy, unless they didn't have none. I didn't have none.

'All of it,' I says. 'Just the notes, mind. In a placcy bag.'

He opened his gob.

'Don't talk,' I says. 'Just pack the fuckin' bag, eh? And I'll tell yers what—you grass to the coppers and they'll shut you down. Do you know how come? Cos I *am* the fuckin' coppers. Eh? How'd you feel about that?'

Crossing back over the road, I looked in the bag and got the notes out. The tight-arsed cunt had only put thirty-five lids in. I stopped and went to go back, but an oncoming bus blared at us.

I stood me ground.

The bus stopped about a foot shy of me toes, making my hooter about three foot from the driver's and level with it. I stared at him. He stared back and honked the horn again, but only a short one this time. I were filling up with darkness and rage inside, but I knew I couldn't do nothing here. Soon as I went to get in the door he'd drive off, and I'd look a twat. What I needed were a badge, a proper metal shield that I could hold up to him and make his heart sink. Then I'd haul him down the nick, put him in a cell all nice and cosy, and then beat the shite out of him. Stood there, and thinking this, I knew that I could waste no more time in becoming a copper and fulfilling my destiny. The world needed it. I could feel it in all them faces behind the bus driver. They wanted us to fucking have him. They wanted us to have every cunt in town and make the world a better place.

I pointed at the driver in a meaningful way, then moved off, feeling a bit calmer now. I knew his face and he could wait.

Mind you, I felt riled all over again when I got to the blower and put paw to pocket. I'd only gone and forgot to get change off Mike. But rules is rules, like the man said, and you cannot break em. I dialled the number. The phone on the other end rang and rang for a long time.

No one answered.

• • •

Couple of hours later, and in another part of town, I heard a voice and looked up.

'Woss you up to in there?'

'Nuthin,' I says.

'You was. You had this car in there, didn't you?'

'What car?'

'This car here. This plastic one.'

'Plastic? Fuck off, this is a genuine Ferr—'

'I don't give a monkey's what you thinks it is, you was in Don Creswell's lock-up just now. What the flamin' hell was you doin' in Don Creswell's lock-up with this car?'

'I told you, I weren't in there. Get out the fuckin' way or I'll run you down.'

'Get out the way? I'm callin' the flamin' police, that's what I'm doin'. This is Don Creswell's lock-up and you ain't got no business in there.'

'Go on then—call the coppers.'

You had to laugh (although I didn't). The poor cunt didn't realise that I were actually on police business here, sort of. Everyone knows that coppers can use other folks' property if they needs to. Well, I fucking needed to. Not no more though cos I'd finished. I opened the driver door and got in.

But the old feller weren't budging. I couldn't drive around him cos it were only a narrow little track here.

'I ain't fallin' for that,' he says. 'Moment I goes to phone em, you'll drive off. And woss that smell? You been sprayin' paint in Don Creswell's lock-up?'

'For fuck sake,' I says, getting out. 'I just needed a fuckin' lock-up for a few minutes, to do some work on me Ferrari. I ain't nicked no gear and I ain't done no damage. Now fuckin' *shift*.'

'Aye but you used the leccy, though. Eh? You used Don Creswell's leccy.'

'I only had the light on for a few minutes. Listen, you don't understand woss goin' on here. I'm on official business. Anyone stands in my way, I got a right to put em down. You hearin' us?'

'Official business?' he says, screwing his wrinkly face up. 'You from the council?'

'Look,' I says, sitting on the bonnet in front of him. 'Look…'

'You bloody fool. The paint's still wet on that and you've gone and sat on it. What'd you do that for? You bloody fool.'

I got up sharpish, cracking his face with me swede. He were only a short little fucker and I had to get down quite low to do it, although it were an accident, sort of. The old cunt shouldn't have been stood there anyhow. And he shouldn't have called us a bloody fool.

'You've…' he says, lying on the ground and holding his jaw. 'You and yer bloody…you've gone an'…an'…'

I couldn't have him holding us up no more, so I laid one on his left eye. I knows old folks has got bones like bamboo but that weren't my fault, and I had a job to do. He went flat on his back for a couple of seconds, face starting to look like a plate of old mutton now, then started getting up again. I couldn't fucking believe it.

'Hoy, you,' he says, pointing a wobbly finger at us, 'I were a boxin' champ in the army. Come on—put yer dukes up an' let's see who's who, eh? Eh?'

I stood there for a moment, scratching me swede.

20

I couldn't believe it.

I plain could not fucking credit it.

And I'm on about a good thing here, not a bad matter. Things truly did seem to be turning right for us at last, and I sat back and just enjoyed the moment. I'm on about one of the bestest, most beautiful and precious things you can have in this life of ours: the magic that is created when man and machine is cruising along in perfect harmony, up the East Bloater Road.

I'd drove her before, course. I'd drove her away from Filthy Stan's yesterday and stowed her under some old branches in a quiet spot down by the river. And then this morning, waking up all rosy-cheeked and full of hope, I'd got her out and went off in her, hunting down a suitable lock-up in which to carry out me plans. But it were different, now I'd carried out them plans. She hadn't seemed right in pink, you see, and under the slick coat of black I'd sprayed on she just came alive. It were like a beautiful and sexy woman slipping into a little black dress, trowelling a bit of slap on, necking half a bottle of voddy and going out on the town for the night. It's like that song by Derek Clapton, where he goes on about her brushing her long blonde hair and asking him if she looks all right.

'*And I says yes*,' sings Derek, '*you don't look too bad tonight.*' Summat like that anyhow.

I felt that way about my new motor, actually. It filled us with pride to be in her saddle, coaxing her along with the kind of expertise that cannot be learned. See, you got to understand that

I'd always been meant to have a Ferrari. All them years with the Capri, it were like preparing us for it. Do you know what I mean there? I mean, you cannot just jump in a Ferrari and expect to drive her. There's a lot of matters you got to be aware of in such a motor, and you'll end up pranging her if you ain't in the know.

The long bonnet, for example. Your Ferrari Daytona has the longest bonnet in the world, and you just dunno what to do with it when you first gets behind the wheel and has a peep to the fore. But that's where your Capri comes in, see. Your Ford Capri, obviously, has got the second longest bonnet in the world, so you can get some good experience of long bonnet driving with her. And that will come into play when Ferrari time comes.

I were thinking about that, and wishing I had a fag, when I spotted someone roadside, town end of East Bloater Road. Just past the shops.

I pulled in, honking me horn. I hadn't honked it before, and therefore I didn't realise that it played the same tune as the General Lee in *The Dukes of Hazzard*, right the way through, no matter how lightly you touches the button. I found that a bit odd, considering how this were a thoroughbred Italian stallion and not a Yank motor, but it were a pleasant surprise nonetheless. I got out.

'Fuck me,' I says. 'All right, Rache?'

I hadn't seen Rache in donkeys. And when I says donkeys, I means a whole field of em. Last time I'd seen her had been a fraught affair, with misunderstandings either side and ending up with Rache missing out on her big chance to go out with us. I truly had been keen on the girl, despite her leading us up and down the garden path regarding one or two matters, and causing us no end of grief. But no, I didn't hold that against her. Rache were a good one, and you knew that no bad could come from her.

She had her little lad with her, bending over him and saying summat to him just now. I weren't sure if she'd heard us, so I goes: 'Hoy, I says, "All right, Rache?" You fuckin' deaf or summat?'

I laughed a bit afterwards, to show that I were just joshing and not being arsey.

She went on saying summat to her lad for a little while longer, then looked up and gave us a death stare, saying in a well pissed-off and sarkey tone: 'Thank you very much, Blake. Thank you *very* much.'

It took us right aback, I can tell yers. All I'd done is pull up in me new Ferrari, wanting to impress her and her lad. Truth be telled, it were her lad I were after impressing as much as her. Last time I'd seen her she'd telled us this big story about how his dad were Don, a feller she'd been knocking about with for a while back there, but I knew it weren't true. The lad were mine, in plain gospel truth. And she weren't even the mam. Our Sal (God rest her rotting corpse) were the mam, and…Ah, I can't be arsed to spill it to yers. And to be frank with you, I hardly even knows it meself.

So anyhow, what the fuck were I saying? Oh aye—anyone could tell that the lad were mine just by clocking him. I could understand how she didn't want to admit it to us, mind. She just didn't want to put pressure on the poor lad, having him grow up knowing his old man is one of Mangel's top pillars. Women can be funny like that sometimes, and you just got to let em get on with it.

'What?' I says, in response to the death stare and harsh words of welcome. 'Woss I fuckin' done now?'

There were a bus stop just back from the pavement, and she led the boy over to it and sat him down, stroking his cheek and cooing to him. I could see him turning into a soft lad if she weren't careful, and I started wondering there and then if I shouldn't try and get him off her while he still had a chance in life. He could have the cellar all to himself. Aye, it'd give us a reason to do it up a bit, put a little bed down there for him. Him down there and me up above, we wouldn't get under each other's feet that way. I'd even let him have his own telly, if I could find one in a skip and get it working. Maybe a video as well. He could watch my Rocky vids on there and learn all about being a man, and rising up to the challenge of our rivals.

'Look, Rache,' I says. She were approaching now and I wanted a word with her about all this. 'I wants a word with you about—'

'Do you ever think of *anyone* but yerself?' she says.

'Eh?'

'You, pullin' up behind us and blastin' that big daft horn.'

I truly found meself stumped for words. She were taking us aback like no other, Rache were, with the nasty way she had about her. She used to be such a mild girl, and one with big tits and quite a nice face. Here she were, acting like an old harpy. And looking like one as well.

'Hold up a min, Rache, all I'm doing is stoppin' here and sayin' hello to an old friend, which is how I seed you just now, before you started havin' a go. Honest, I don't see what the fuckin' problem is.'

'You wouldn't, would you? You've been hidin' away for two years, looking after yerself and not caring about others.'

'Woss you on about? I only honked me fuckin' horn, fuck sake.'

'Yeah, and nearly frightened my little Roy out of his poor skin.'

'Eh? Honkin' me horn? I fuckin' swear, Rache, you're makin' that lad go soft. I've a good mind to...'

'What? Good mind to what?'

'Never you mind. You just stop wrappin' him up in…in bog paper, or whatever they—'

'Shall I tell you summat about my Roy, since you're suddenly so interested? He's *hard of hearing*.' She stopped and gave us the look, the one they all gives you when they reckon they got you. But I couldn't see how she had us. She were talking pure shite.

'Hard of earring? Woss you on about? Lad his age shouldn't even be wearin' an earring. No wonder his ear's gone hard. Fuck sake, Rache…'

'*Hearing*, Blake. Or *deaf*, as you'd probably call it.'

'Deaf?'

'Aye.'

'The lad's deaf?'

'Well, partially so, yes.'

I glanced over at him. His eyes were on summat in his hands, and he were clicking away at it with his thumbs.

'Don were a bit like that, weren't he?' I says. 'A bit deaf, I mean.'

'Don?'

'Aye. His old man. Don's his old man, ain't he?'

'Yeah, course he—'

'Course he fuckin' is. No question. I mean, they're like two peas off the old block, Don and that lad there. They got the same, erm…ears. Which are very different to, say, *my* ears. Don't you reckon? I mean, I had a son, he'd look more like Clint Eastwood. Don, he were more yer Sean Connery. Just like your lad there. A young Sean Connery, before he started doin' James Bond.'

We both looked at the lad. He had his hood up now. It weren't even raining.

'Well,' I says, 'maybe not so much just yet, but you can see how it'll come out in time. The Sean Connery, like. And Don used to be a bit deaf as well, didn't he? "Hoy, Don," you'd say, and he wouldn't even look up. So it ain't surprisin' that the lad here—'

'—that my Roy is deaf. No, it's not a surprise. Right. Thank you, Blake.'

'Nah, I really does feel sorry for him, like. Course I fuckin' does. Must be a bloody nightmare, not hearin' stuff. How can he watch telly? And…and…and it must be a bit hard for *you* as well. What if yer tellin' him off, like? Can't be easy if he don't hear you, and he goes on being naughty.'

She turned away from us and shook her head, so I know she agreed with us.

'Tell you what, though,' I says, putting a soothing arm around her. She did feel a bit bony. 'Any time you wants a shoulder to cry on, and maybe a bit more besides—if yer lucky, eh? So what I'm sayin' is, er…Hey, hold up a min…you says he were upset by me honkin' the horn just now. How's he gonna get upset by that if he can't—?'

'I said he's *partially* deaf, not stone deaf. Just like you're partially intelligent.'

I thought about that for a bit, then goes: 'Oh, cheers, Rache.' Cos it's nice that she should say that about us. I mean, she didn't have to. She were a nice girl, Rache. 'I always thought so meself, truth be telled. Only you don't like to say it. In front of people, like. I ain't big-headed.'

We looked at each other for a bit. Her from under her long curly eyelashes, me sideways-on. And I could tell she weren't so narky with us no more. I think it were cos she'd suddenly realised how partially intelligent I were, and how she couldn't really win an argument against someone like meself. Not that I'm saying Rache is thick. She ain't. It's just hard for other folks, pitting emselves against wits like I got. And anyhow, Rache had other things that made her special.

'Do you know what?' I says to her. I had to choose me words and tone careful here cos I didn't wanna sound like a ponce. And I didn't want her thinking I were just saying it to make her happy. 'I think you're partially quite pretty.' I gave her a wink.

I don't think I'd ever said such nice things to a woman before, and I found meself quite enjoying it. Rache liked it as well, blushing a bit and trying to hide her smile. I thought I'd lay on some more while the going were good, so I says: 'And yer hair looks nice today, partially. Aye, you could say I'm well fuckin' partial to it, all tied up at the back like that. And you ain't even got hardly no grey at all in it, even though you must be gettin' on for, what—?'

'What's that?'

'I said yer hair's not that grey, even if—'

'No, what's that noise?'

'Eh?'

'It's comin' from your car. That banging. You hear it?'

'Bangin'? Nah, there ain't no bangin'.'

'There is. It's comin' from—'

'Hey, Rache, come on and introduce us to your little Roy. I bet you told him all about us, eh?'

'Blake, there is a faint knocking sound coming from the boot of this car. What have you got in there?'

She went to open it, so I stepped in sharpish and flicked her paws away.

'Just leave it, Rache. There's some things a woman oughtn't to question, and—'

'If you think I'm gonna walk away from here and pretend I heard nuthin', you can think again. I want you to open this boot.'

I couldn't understand why Rache were being such a cow. First I'd stopped to say hello, then I'd said nice things about her, even offering to comfort her about her spazzy lad. And here she were, giving us grief.

'If you're gonna be like that,' I says, 'I'm off. I don't fuckin' deserve this kind of—'

'Open this boot or I call the police. Just do it, Blake, please. If you're in trouble, let me help you. I can get you help. I know what you've been through in your life and I understand how you get confused sometimes, and let things get—'

'Fuck sake, Rache, I ain't confused. It's just…it's just sortin' matters out, is all. I'm just goin' about me business, overcoming obstacles and that.'

'Open the boot, then.'

'Fuckin' hell…'

I popped the lid and stood by it, in case he jumped out. So far he'd proved himself a spry old one, and you never knew. As it happens, he did try getting up, so I put a paw on his face and leaned my weight on him, tucking him back in. He were a perfect fit, actually. Skinny and short and surprisingly limber. I shut the lid again.

'Blake, you…you…'

'Just don't get involved, Rache. You sees a poor old man locked up in me boot, it ain't like that. Ain't like that at all. I got a right to put him in there.'

'A right? There's no possible reason for you to have…He's got blood on his face, and—'

'You don't know me now, Rache. You dunno what I'm up to. I'm on official business these days, and this here old feller, he… well, I am gonna let him go, course. I were thinkin' on droppin' him out by Hurk Wood. That way, see, by the time he yomps all the way back home he'll like as not forget all about us, and how he got there. And if he don't make it back…well, he's old anyhow. Do you see what I mean?'

'Get him out of there right now. Let him out now or I…or I'll never talk to you again. I can't believe this, Blake, not even from you.'

I had a think, leaning against the boot. He weren't knocking no more and, truth be telled, I were getting a bit worried about him. You got to be careful with old people. They needs a lot of looking after. It's easy to ignore em and leave em to die. And sometimes it might be best to do just that, for their own sakes. But you can't forget that they're people, too, with stories to tell and shite like that. So I got off the boot and put a thumb on the button, ready to spring him.

'Tell you what, Rache,' I says, 'I'll let him out on one condition.'

'Don't come at me with conditions, you bastard. I never knew you was such a nasty piece of work, Blake, I really never knew. Let him out now, or I'll—'

'Come on, don't be like that. I'll let him out right now if you promise to do us one favour. All right? It ain't a hard one neither. Take you a couple of minutes tops and the old man gets out. You wants him out, right?'

'What favour?'

'Tell you after. You gotta promise to do it first, though.'

'All right, I promise.'

'On your lad's life.'

'Blake…'

'Else I won't let this poor old man out.'

'Yeah, all right, on my lad's life. Now let him out.'

'Honest? You'll do it?'

'Yeah. Let him out.'

I opened the lid and had a look at him. Didn't seem so lively now, but when I picked him up and parked him on his feet he seemed to get going again, opening and closing his toothless cakehole and lifting his boots up and down. 'Yer all right, eh?' I says to him, looking him in the eye. He couldn't seem to focus on us, and didn't answer. I were glad of that. 'He's all right,' I says to Rache, winking at her. I led the old feller past the car and the bus stop and pointed him townward. There was plenty of houses up that way, in case he got lost. He started off in that direction and didn't look back. Like a little dynamo, that old cunt were.

'Blake, you can't just…'

She were trying to go after him, but I put me arms around her and held her firm. 'Rache, you don't—'

She tried twisting round and planting a knee in me bollocks, but I got me thigh up in time and held her a bit firmer.

'Let me go, you—'

I had to put a paw over her gob to shut her up. Little wildcat, she were.

'*Listen*, Rache. That feller…that old man you cares so much about…do you know what he is? Do you know what he done? *Do you? Eh?*'

Her eyes told us she didn't, then went on blazing at us.

'Well, I'll tell yer…'

21

I pulled up outside the Bonehill flats and went to open me door.

'It's OK, Blake,' she says. 'You don't have to come up.'

'You sure? Cos—'

'I'm sure. Thanks, though.'

'I can carry the lad upstairs, if you likes.'

'He can walk, Blake. He's deaf, not lame.'

'I'm just tryin' to help.'

'I know. It's very…sensitive of you.'

'Sensitive? Woss that meant to mean?'

'Nuthin', just—'

'You takin' the piss?'

'No, I'm just sayin' that…look, sensitive is a good thing, OK? Take it from me, a woman likes sensitive in a man. Maybe not all the time, but sometimes.'

'I am actually very sensitive.'

'I know, Blake. I know.'

'Maybe not all the time, but sometimes. Do you know what I mean?'

'I do. Blake?'

'What?'

'Is it really true?'

'About me being sensitive sometimes?'

'No, I mean about that old man.'

I made a grave face at her. It were a grave matter. 'It's fuckin' gospel, Rache.'

'And he really did do that to those children?'

186

'I ain't makin' none of it up, Rache. He's a proper paedophil-iac. I didn't wanna tell yers, but…well…'

'No, I'm glad you told me. I just…I can't believe an old man like that…'

'You can't judge folks on appearance, Rache. You just cannot.'

'And *disabled* children as well. How could he?'

'You knows it goes on, Rache.'

She frowned and shook her head. 'What sort of a world are we living in?'

'A bad one, Rache. A fuckin' shite one in some ways. But do you know what?'

'What?'

'I'm aimin' to make it better. You just watch.'

I winked at her.

She reached for the door handle.

'Hold up,' I says. 'You still owes us that favour.'

'Oh yeah. What is it?'

'You promised to do it, remember.'

'Yeah, I know.'

'On your lad's life.'

'All right. Just tell us what it is.'

I leaned over and whispered in her ear. I were being a bit cheeky but, well, sometimes you got to spin them dice. And I'd always fancied Rache.

Without flinching she goes: 'All right.'

'Honest?'

'Yeah. Whatever.'

'Cos I were only sort of jokin', like. I mean, I knows it's a bit cheeky to just, you know—'

'Look, I promised, didn't I? Come on then.'

'What, here in the motor?'

'Yeah, Come on, let's get it over with.'

'Well, can't I come back later? It's broad fuckin' daylight, and—'

'I'm busy later.'

'Woss you doin' later?'

'Never you mind. Come on.'

'All right…but what about him?' I says, nodding at the lad on the back seat.

'He's asleep.'

'I know but he's still there. I can't perform if he's there.'

'Perform?'

'You knows what I mean.'

'He won't wake up.'

'Well…can't we go up to your flat?'

'No. That's my home and I share it with little Roy and no one else. You want this favour of yours, we do it in your car. Now. Come on.'

'But there's folks about.'

'Where?'

'That old feller there, with his dog.'

'He's miles away.'

'And them lads over there. And there's cars going past. Come on, Rache, I can't do it here. Have some class, girl.'

I felt her looking askew at us, and turned to face her, expecting a dark look like no other. But she just looked bored. And a bit sad, truth to tell.

'Drive round the back, by the garages,' she says. 'There's never no one about down there. But I ain't getting out of this car. We do it in here or not at all. Understand?'

I drove round the back and parked where she said. It were a good spot, I had to agree. There were no one about and no windows overlooking, not even from the flats. You couldn't even see the lad on the back seat when you turned sideways, which I were doing just then. I unzipped meself and placed a paw on her knee.

'Get off,' she says, brushing it off.

'I'm just tryin' to…you know…get meself ready.'

'That's your business. I'm doin' what I said I'd do, and no more. You tell me when you're ready. I've not got all day.'

'Fuck sake.'

I closed me peepers and thought about Rache with no kit on. I hadn't ever actually seen her in that state, but I'd pictured it enough times and the sight were well familiar to us. But it weren't right this time. I had her with her baps out and that, but her face weren't smiling and licking her lips like it normally did. It had that bored and sad look like just now. And quite frankly I found it off-putting.

'Look, Rache,' I says. 'Couldn't you just warm us up a bit? Give us a kiss and feel us up with yer paw, like?'

'No. I'll do what I said and no more.'

'But, Rache, don't you fancy us? You used to fancy us. I always fancied you.'

She didn't reply to that. After a bit, with me looking out the front window and wondering what to do next, her arm came quietly over and she got to work, kneading us like a long lump of dough. I watched her doing that for a bit, and I noticed she had no rings on her fingers. That didn't look right, for some reason, and I found meself wondering about that and not the matter in hand. So I closed me eyes again and just enjoyed the moment, which were a long-overdue breakthrough in terms of me and Rache. Soon I were up and proud and ready for the next stage, which were the actual favour I'd asked of her. I hoped she didn't have snaggly gnashers. I'd noticed one at the front had gone grey.

I didn't mind grey gnashers but it's a bit sensitive down there and you don't want no snagging.

'All right, Rache,' I says, 'you can...'

But I didn't need to say no more cos she were leaning down anyhow. I felt her hot breath on me knob and couldn't help letting out a little groan. She were teasing us, the dirty cow, making us wait. Then the lad started shouting.

'Who's he, Mam?' he says. 'I heard shoutin'. Who's he, Mam? Mam, who's he? Mam?'

'For fuck's fuckin' sake,' I says, turning about.

'It's all right,' she says. 'He's just sleeptalking.'

Sure enough the lad were lying down, eyes shut.

'Ignore him,' she says. She still hadn't gone down on us but she were using her paw again, trying to get the fire back. 'Just ignore him,' she says again.

'Fuckin' *hell*,' I says, doing meself up. 'Just *forget* it, eh.'

THINKING OUTSIDE MY BOX

Editorial by Malcolm Pigg

Sometimes a challenge comes along. It's a hard challenge and it looks like there's no way around it. But no, it's got to be dealt with or there's hell to pay. Times like that, you need a certain type of man. A man who can rise to the challenge and do what others cannot. A man who can think of clever ways to get the job done, in a similar way to David putting out Goliath's eye with a catapult.

When I was a lad, I used to have a catapult. A "black widow" they called it, and I'd use it for harmless fun—killing birds, shooting nests out of trees and the like. One summer—and it was the longest and hottest summer we've ever had here in Mangel, as I recall—my dear late mother was having trouble keeping food in our kitchen without it going astray. Me being a growing lad, I got the blame, even though it was things like raw vittles and other particulars (such as kippers, and even a whole turkey) going missing.

Now, after one such telling off I was sitting in the garden, feeling sorry for myself and fiddling around with that catapult. Suddenly I spied a ginger tomcat come sneaking under some bushes. Without thinking about it, and with lightning reflexes that would put any tomcat to shame, I located a stone and fired him at that cat. The stone hit him on the head and killed him dead. I buried him in the compost and forgot all about it. Meanwhile, things stopped going missing from our kitchen.

We all know the big challenge that confronts us in this town today. Besides vandalism in our parks, it's young women getting murdered, many of them prostitutes. Now, this challenge is not being met in the right way. You can see that and so can I, and so I'll step in here and offer some help.

I do have a couple theories on this matter, as it happens, and Chief Cadwallader might want to think about them. The first one is the moon. No one has mentioned it yet, but each time a woman gets killed, it seems to me that the moon is gibbous. Surely such a factor as that cannot be glossed over? Everyone knows how a gibbous moon can affect certain types, especially when it's yellow. And it's the patients out at Parpham Mental Asylum I'm referring to here. Are they making sure their gates are locked at nights? I hope so.

22

A bit after that I were driving around town, wearing me smart togs now, thinking about this and trying to forget that. I noticed a copper across the way and it all came back to us, about Jonah and the plan, and all the things he'd promised to do for us. I'd forgot all about that, and it were a nice thing to remember. Especially with me being in a right old mood in terms of my head and the way it felt. I'd go so far as to say it made us happy, and I pulled up and got out, aiming to get the hood down on the Ferrari. I couldn't quite work out how to do it, and I found meself going though the glove box in search of the instructions, which I didn't find.

I knew there were summat I ought to have checked before laying out all that cash for this motor. Filthy Stan were a notorious old cunt in terms of ripping folks off and painting up nails to look like screws. Then I recalled how I hadn't paid a fucking bean for it, and that Filthy Stan had carked it in a tragic accident.

'You all right, Blakey?'

'Oh, all right, Rog. Woss you sayin'?'

'Telled yerself a joke, did yer?'

'Woss you on about?'

'You, stood there laughin' like that.'

'I weren't laughin'.'

'You was. Folks has been walkin' past, starin' at you. I heard you laughin' half a fuckin' mile down the road there. Must of been a funny old joke, eh? Mind you, you is a bit barmy these days, ain't you?'

'You fuckin' startin' on us, Rog?'

192

'Blake, calm down, I just—'

I nutted him. Rog had always been a cunt and I'd only just realised it, so I felt justified in doing that. Also I were gonna be a copper in less than a day, what with Jonah and his contract, and I had to start thinking about cleaning up the local community. Breaking Rog's nose were a good way to start, I thought.

I got back in the Ferrari and drove off, unhappy about the hood not working but feeling a lot better otherwise, even though my sides was aching and me face hurt a bit, like I'd been exercising the muscles there. It were hard to smile, I tells yer, but I did it anyhow on account of the plum hand that life had dealt us, when you thought about Jonah. Not only were I set up as one of the biggest pillars in Mangel, but I were gonna be getting wedded to Mangel's top bit of fluff. I thought about the big diamond ring they was getting for us, and the look on Mandy's face when I gave it her.

Mind you, I did feel a mite guilty. I ain't a bastard like some fellers is, and I does have feelings when it comes to birds and being faithful to em and that. And it's Rache I'm on about here, back there in the motor with her mong lad in the rear. But I never actually did get sucked off in the end, you got to remember. And if Rache went as far as kneading us like a long lump of dough, you got to look at Rache, not me. I never actually touched her. There's a name for birds who wank fellers off in their motors and it ain't a nice one.

I cruised around town for a while with the window down, enjoying the attention. It were fucking smart. Nigh on every bird I went past stopped and stared at us and went moist. You could just tell. I winked at every one of em and went on my merry way. Fellers stopped and all, but you had jealousy from them and not moistness, seeing such an exotic motor in the flesh. At one point

I pulled up at a red light and clocked meself in some big office windows that was like mirrors. I didn't half look like class, and I could see what they was all getting excited about. Mind you, I did feel that summat were missing. Summat to do with meself, not the motor (which were perfect). I stared for a while, wondering what it were, when some fucker parped his horn behind us. I turned about and went to shout fuck off, when I saw that it were a bird. Not only a bird, but Mandy Munton. My fiancée.

Sort of.

I got out.

'All right, Mand?' I says, leaning through her window and checking her ring finger all sly like. Last thing you wants is a big wart on the knuckle, but there were none of that with Mand. She were quality. And she had dark glasses on, which made her look well glamorous.

'Yeah. How are you?' she says, beaming up at us like she could see our future life together reflected in me eyes. I beamed back at her, and saw my handsome mug reflected in her dark glasses. 'But look, we can't talk here. There's a queue of cars behind me, and—'

'Look, I just wanted to apologize.'

'For what?'

'For the varmint.'

'The what?'

'The varmint. The one you seen at my house yesterday, and gave you a fright and made you hare off. I wanted to say how it's just a one-off, like. There ain't loads of varmints in the house, just the one. It's a clean house, apart from that varmint. I think he must of got in the back door or summat. They can squash their bones flat, you know.'

'What can?'

'Varmints.'

'What is a varmint, Blake? Look, the lights have changed, and—'

'It's a varmint, ennit. You know, rats and that. Little furry wossnames that get where they ain't welcome.'

'Blake, I dunno nuthin' about rats. If you've got rats, that's news to me. Look, there's cars behind me and they—'

'Ah, fuck em. You all right, though? Eh, you want a cup o' tea or summat? It's on me, to make up for the varmint, like. I got wedge, see.' I were referring to the thirty-five notes that Mike from the paper shop had gave us. I got em out and showed em her.

'Oh, nice. Yeah, all right…a cup of tea. Look, we'd better park properly, and—'

'This your motor, then, is it?'

'Of course it's mine. You think I stole it?'

'Nah, I'm just askin', like. Nice little motor.'

'Well, I like it. But we—'

'For birds, like. It's a nice motor for birds. You don't see many of these around Mangel. New ones like this, I mean. Shiny uns.'

'We've really got to m—'

'You got a bit of wedge, then, have you? What'd you say you was in the city? Shop girl, were it?'

'What? Oh, er…yeah, I worked in a—'

'Eh? I can't hear yer.'

'Look, I really am blocking the road. I need to park, if you wanna—'

It were no fucking use. There were a long line of motors behind Mandy and it seemed like every one of em were parping their horn and shouting out the window. We was in one of the quieter streets in Mangel at that moment and I took umbrage to the racket. In future all I'd have to do is flash me badge and tell em all to shut it, but I didn't have a badge yet. And I knew I couldn't go using one as a crutch. Crutches is for cowards and cripples, and I weren't neither of them.

No, if I were gonna be the copper I intended on being, I had to rely on my own powers of wossname.

'You,' I says to the first driver in the line, a lanky lad wearing a baseball cap and dark glasses. 'Get the fuck out of...'

I stopped there cos I'd just realised what I'd noticed wrong back there, when I'd been admiring meself in that window and thinking there were summat missing. It's funny how things come to you at odd moments, like this one here. Another thing coming at us were Mandy's motor. She were pulling out just then and not able to make it around my Ferrari without touching bumper, so she started backing up. I jumped out of the way sharpish, making a mental note to try and get reversing made illegal for birds, them being a bloody menace in that gear. The lanky lad were getting out of his motor just then so I punched him in the face and picked his glasses up when they fell off. Luckily they didn't seem scratched, and they fit perfect when I put em on. A quick glance in the feller's wing mirror and I knew that the look were complete, in terms of me looking like a very stylish and pillarish copper.

I tossed the mirror and got into the Ferrari. Mandy's posh new motor were away by now and turning into the Wall Road. I gave the Ferrari a gentle coax and roared after her, stalling on the corner but getting going again no problem, it being the ultimate in Italian engineering. End of Wall Road she went into Friar Street, sailing past the Porter Centre and turning left again into the multi-storey there, where you got to go round and round on your way up and it's well tight. I found it a bit hairy, me having such a long bonnet, and I think I might have scraped the front and rear once or twice. I felt a bit sick the first time. When you got a rare and beautiful motor like mine, you got a responsibility to look after her and keep her scrape-free. But then you got to consider how this is a cop car, and a couple of scrapes would make her look more hard. That made us feel a bit better.

On the top level, which is open to the air, Mandy parked in the far corner. I pulled up alongside and gave her a wink and a big smile, waggling me eyebrows. I knew how handsome I looked in me new shades, and I wanted to dazzle her with it all. This is what she'd be getting, in terms of husband material, and I wanted her to know how fucking fortunate she were. I don't think she seen us though, cos she frowned and looked down.

I got out and opened her door for her. She got out and went to the edge, looking at the town down there. It were a nice view from here and you got a clear view of the Deblin Hills over there in the west, and the woods to the north and east. Mandy were looking south, though.

'Hey,' I says, putting an arm around her. 'I can read your mind, you know.'

'Can you?'

'Aye. I can read it like a glove. You're thinkin' about the big city over yonder, and the life you left behind. You're finding yerself here in Mangel, and perhaps missin' some of the style and glamour you was used to in the city. Well, I got some good news on that score, cos I were thinkin' about askin' you to be my w—'

'No,' she says, shrugging my arm off.

'No?'

'No.'

I couldn't fucking believe it. You'd think she'd at least promise to think about it for a while. 'You could at least pr—'

'No, I've got summat else on my mind, Blake. It's…um…' She chewed a fingernail and looked at the floor, then at me with a nice smile on her face. 'It's nuthin', Blake. I'll…I'll be all right.'

'No, come on. There's summat up, and you ain't happy. Spill the beans to old Blakey here. Me, I can get things done. I can make you happy.'

'Well, it's awkward. I mean, you won't like it. You won't like it because it might make you feel jealous, or angry. But you're the man in my life now, and you've got a *right* to feel those emotions.'

The man in her life? I liked that. 'But what is it, Mand?'

'I dunno…I…'

'*Mand.*'

'There's a feller. A man I knew in the city. We was sort of seeing each other, and—'

'Who?'

'Just let me tell you about the—'

'Who the *fuck* is he, Mand?'

'Blake, you're scaring me. Your face has gone all…let go my arm, Blake…*Blake*…'

I let go her arm. I couldn't see right. The sky had gone dark and it were night already, even though…even…

'Just listen, Blake, OK?'

Mandy stroked my cheek and kissed my ear, and I felt the lightness coming back. I even relaxed a little bit, although I had cramp in me jaw hinges.

'It's just someone I was sort of seeing for a while. But it was nuthin' serious, and we never really done much. You gotta believe that, Blake.'

I were trying. I were truly fucking trying hard. The sky were neither light nor dark but a sort of grey, and looked like going either way. I felt her warm breath in my ear, and the sky went the way of lightness.

'I mean, we weren't really…Ah, never mind. What I wanted to say is that he's here in Mangel now. He's, um…followed me here. He follows me around, yeah. He tries to hide, but sometimes I see him. It's creepy, Blake. He's stalking me.'

'Why?'

'Why what?'

'I mean, you got to look at the two sides in a case like this. Have you spoke to him, have yer? Maybe you got summat of his and he wants it back. A spare key, or summat.'

Cos I didn't want the darkness. Not just now. I knew she could make it go away with a stroke or a bit of breath in me ear, but I didn't want to risk that. What if that stopped working? What if I hurt her?

No, Blakey. It *ain't* her fault. It's this fucking feller, and she's just...she's...

'Blake, he's *obsessed* with me. But there's more. This mornin', well, I did finally confront him. It was, um...in the supermarket. I saw him in the next aisle and ran around and caught up with him in the frozen foods section. He wanted us to get back together, and said he loves me and all that. I told him about you.'

'What about me?'

'I just told him that there's someone else, and that I'm no longer available. I told him how I feel about you...how you were the first man to love me right, long before I ever met him, and that no man could compare to you.'

'I know what you mean.'

'Do you?'

'Yeah, I does.'

'You mean you feel the same way about me?'

'No, I mean I understand how hard it must be for other fellers, goin' out with birds after I've shagged em. I'm a hard act to follow, you know. I mean, I do actually feel sorry for them fellers.' And I truly did, at that moment. Feeling sorry for em were the only way to keep meself normal, and hold the feelings at bay. 'Do you know what I mean? I'm actually quite sensitive, in some ways. Did you notice that about us?'

She started crying. Least, I think she were crying, although it could have been the wind in her eyes. I put an arm around her. It went all the way around until I could feel the edge of her far tit. I gave it a squeeze and says: 'Shall we get in the motor now? Bit parky up here, eh.'

I were feeling all right now, personally. And I were proud of meself for it. If you're gonna be a copper, you got to be able to control your emotions. You got to keep the darkness at bay.

I led her over to the motor and opened the door for her. This'd be the first time she'd ever parked arse in a Ferrari and I knew it'd cheer her up. Sitting inside a car like that is a magical experience for everyone. I got in the driver side and shut the door, then leaned in and started snogging her.

'No, Blake,' she says, pushing us off.

'What?'

'You don't understand, do you? You *hear* but you don't *listen*. Sometimes I think you need a jolt, Blake…something to wake you up, click your brain into gear. A bump on the head, maybe. Or a baseball bat.'

I felt summat click in me swede. The feller with the baseball bat. In the park last night. And in the cell next to mine at the copper station, calling us ten kinds of cunt and Aunty Myra. That's her stalker feller, that is. I wished I'd clicked earlier. I'd have saved myself all that struggling between the light and the dark.

'I knows him,' I says to Mand.

'What?'

'Aye, he were at the station the other night, when they brung us in about the satellite. Or the dead bird, or summat. Anyhow, that's where I come across your stalker feller. Had a few gentle words with us, you could say, heh heh. Fuckin' twat.'

'Well, yeah, you probably did see him there, I suppose. But maybe I should give you a photo of him, in case you got the wrong—'

'Don't need it, Mand. I knows him all right. And don't you fret over it. He's harmless, I truly does believe. Feller like that, he's all mouth and no strides. Know what I mean? He's nuthin', Mand, pure fuck all. I'm surprised you ever even went out with him.'

Aye, so I were feeling much better now. I looked out the windscreen and found meself able to think about other, more important matters. I couldn't think what they was just then but I found meself able to think about em, if I could just recall em. Meanwhile Mandy were staring at us sideways.

'What?' I says.

She stayed quiet, so I leaned in again, but stopping short of the snog. I wanted to smell her perfume, and her to smell mine. My aftershave, I mean, not perfume. Actually I weren't even wearing no aftershave, but I wanted her to smell us anyhow, cos that's how animals lets each other know how they feels, when they wants a shag and that. I'd seen it on telly. I took her sunglasses off, cos they was big ones and in the way. Then I pulled away from her, opening and closing me gob and not knowing what to say.

'Harmless, is he?' she says. The skin around her right eye were red and swelled up, and she could hardly open it. 'A harmless man does this to me, does he?'

The darkness were coming down sharpish now. But I couldn't move. I couldn't speak nor breathe nor do nothing. It were like someone had bound us up in a black blanket and launched us into space, where I floated and turned and spun, surrounded by nothingness and getting ate up by the pure rage that were inside us.

'I'll…I'll fuckin' kill him, Mand. I'll fuckin'…fuck…'

'I know,' she says, reaching her arm between me legs and undoing me zip. 'I know you will.'

She pulled us back down to Earth, using only her lips and tongue and the power of suction. When I got there, the dark sky exploded in a bright shower of shooting stars and fireworks, and I spunked in her mouth.

23

After Mandy pissed off I had a little nap in the motor. It were amazing when I woke up. I done it slow, opening me eyes gradual and not knowing where I were for a bit. I had the blue sky in front of us and the whole of Mangel below us, and the plush confines of a genuine Ferrari all around us. I truly did feel on top of the world. And I were, when you looked at it. There weren't no other higher spot in Mangel, and here I were.

After that I done me strides up and got out of the motor, choosing to go for a walk. I had time to kill before me evening appointment with Jonah and his cohorts, and I were feeling well peckish. In time I'd pay a visit to all the restaurants in town and flash me badge at em, let em know who's in charge here. It's a common fact how coppers can get their scran for free, and I weren't about to miss out on that perk.

'All right, love,' I says to an old granny, holding the door open for her.

She croaked summat back and it sounded a bit rude, but she were barmy in the head like as not and you couldn't blame her. I gave her a pat on her bony arse to show no hard feelings, but she went over on her walking stick and hit the marble floor with a crack. No one were looking so I fucked off.

Walking down Cutler Road I noticed the offy there and decided to go in it.

'Ah, it's you, is it?' says the feller there. Gromer, his name were.

'Aye, it is me, actually. Giz twenty Number One, eh.'

'Twenty Number One?'

'Aye. Embassy. They're there, behind you. Box o' matches as well.'

I thought he'd bristle at that, but he never. He just turned and got em off the shelf. 'I been waitin' on you,' he says a moment later, still holding my Embos and matches.

'Oh,' I says, putting a fiver atop the counter. 'That so?'

'Aye. Waitin' on you to come in here. And you did. You came in here, thereby fulfilling the prophecy.'

'Eh?'

'Never mind eh. Just get yerself down the Paul Pry. Nathan wants a word.' He gave us the fags and matches but left the fiver.

Before he could change his mind, I headed doorward. 'Nathan can fuck off,' I says over me shoulder. Outside I lit one up. It were pure heaven, it surely were. Nothing that good can be bad for you, I telled meself. And if I started coughing up blood again I'd just stop smoking again. But in the meantime I were a copper, and I needed things like fags.

I walked down the High Street, quite enjoying meself in a quiet way. It were a good feeling, knowing how this were my town and I were in charge of it. Things looked different, when you looked at em as a pillar. Before, in the old days when I'd been getting meself into scrapes all the while, town hadn't looked like much at all. And then you got the more recent times whereby I'd been keeping me profile low, and town had seemed to us like a scary and confusing place, I don't mind telling you. But now it were like opening me eyes to it. I could see the dodgy things that had troubled us a while back, but I could also see how to set em straight and make em good. Like them little fuckers over there, coming out of Burger City and tossing their wrappers all over the place.

'Hoy,' I shouts.

There was four or five of em, including a bird or two, and they all looked up and clocked us, stopping what they was doing and giving us their full and undivided.

I liked that. It meant that I had a natural authority, and that folks would hark us and do what I says whether I were a copper or no. Course, I knew all this from me dooring days, but it were nice to see it in action once again. 'Pick that fuckin' litter up,' I says, crossing the road towards em. 'This is a decent town, with decent folks in it. We can do without cunts like you messin' it all up. Now go on.'

Like a good boy, the one at the front bent down and picked up his screwed-up burger bag. Then he shouts: 'Fuck off, you weird fucker,' and lobs the wrapper at us. Hard.

I think there were still some burger in it cos it felt quite heavy, pinging off me shoulder and breaking apart. The younguns started laughing and chucking more litter at us.

I couldn't believe it. Did they enjoy losing teeth and getting bust jaws? I stepped forward, hoping it wouldn't come to that, and that they'd pick up their shite and say sorry before it did. Three of them was male—two on me right and the other by the bin. None looked hard but the bin one would have a go, like as not, so I headed for him. You couldn't tell with the other two so I kept eyes on them as well. And the birds, cos you can't leave yerself open to kicks in the bollocks and fingernails in the eyeballs.

'Come on, weirdy,' says the bin lad, assuming the stance. He had a sort of brown tartan scarf on and he pulled it up over his trap like there were a gas attack. Behind him the Burger City doors opened and three more piled out and stood behind him, all of em bigger than him. And two of em bigger than me.

'I said come *on*, cunt.'

Bin lad came at us, followed by his pals.

Being a copper, you got to make wise decisions and not fret over honour and pride and saving face. Them matters is a luxury that a copper cannot afford, him being a public servant. He's got to look after his own arse a bit more and make sure he turns up for his shift the next day. So I pegged it.

Over twenty yard or so no one beats us. You knows that. If they had twenty yard races I'd be world fucking champion, no problem. I'd have the world record and everything, and I'd be rich and famous and the lot of it. As it stood, the bin lad almost had a paw on me jacket after thirty yard. A black BMW were coming and I crossed the road just before it, hoping that bin lad and his mates would stay their side and get bored and pack it in, but the car slowed and pulled up, and they came on after us with nary a pause. I were in a fairly fucked situation, with no alleys to hare down nor turnings nor nothing, and I wished I had a gun on us like yank coppers does. Sonny Wossname wouldn't have to put up with being run down the street by a mob of neds in trackies and trainers.

I slowed up just before the bus stop and prepared to fight. But before I could turn about I had to quickly bend over and chuck me guts there on the pavement. I dunno what had come over us. When I finished, I looked up, expecting a smack in the face. But the neds was way off up the road, sloping back towards Burger City, heads down and tails between their tracky bottoms. The Beemer were still stopped there in the road and the driver of it were stomping Blakeward.

'All right, DI Dave,' I says. Cos it were him.

'What? You takin' the piss?'

'No, I'm just—'

'Those little herberts are a fuckin' menace, Blake. You don't wanna mess. I know they carry blades, and if I wasn't feeling so stressed I'd search em all now and bring em in. See the one with the scarf? I've had him down the station fuck knows how many times. We've got a deal, see. That's how you got to control these cunts, Blake. You got to strike deals with them. You all right, mate?'

'Aye, I just…'

'Only you've got some puke on your chin there. Here, you want a lift? Better wipe that puke off first, mate.'

DI Dave had a nice motor. You never saw too many Beemers in Mangel, and never one as new and posh as this one here. I spent a moment or two admiring the flawless black paintwork and the sleek lines, then climbed aboard. The interior were fucking plush. Especially the seats. I'd compare em to the ones in a Granada or your Rover P6, but a bit newer and more perfectly suited to my arse, which were pure chance and not summat to impress the average punter necessarily, unless he's lucky and he's got a powerful arse same as mine.

'This ain't a bad motor,' I says. 'Yours, is it? Or is it like a squad car, or summat?'

'The latter.'

'Oh aye?' I says, looking at him funny. 'Woss a latter, then?'

Dave looked at us funny in return.

'Do you know what I reckon?' I says, letting the matter pass. 'I reckon Beemers is one of the best British motors on the road, after yer Capri 2.8i and your Grana—'

'German,' he says, pulling up at some lights. 'Beemers are German.'

'Eh? Don't be a twat, DI Dave. Everyone knows Beemers is British. Look, just think about it—BMW…British Motor…erm… wossname. Aye, that's it—British Motor Wossname.'

He seemed to find that amusing, which narked us a bit. Mind you, I did see where he were coming from. 'All right,' I says, 'all

right, I knows it can't be "Wossname". Very fuckin' amusing, aye.
British Motor W…'

'Ah, never mind that,' he says, pulling away at the lights.
'Look, I got a problem. I got bird trouble. You ever have bird trouble? Me, I was fuckin' born with bird trouble.'

I were shaking me swede, thinking about the general subject
of bird trouble and not knowing where to start. So I had a chuckle
first, still shaking the swede.

'No, honest,' he says. 'I honestly did have bird trouble as I was
being born. My mum died on the table, see. They say I was too
big for her.'

He turned and laughed, sending little drops of flob at my ear,
so small you'd not see em, but I always knows these things.

Personally I weren't laughing. 'You sayin' your mam died
bornin' you? That's the honest gospel truth?'

'Well, I was just havin' a joke there,' he says, not laughing no
longer himself. 'But yeah, she did die giving birth to the sprog
who grew up to be me. And yeah, as far as I know it's because I
was too big and she couldn't get me out in time, the silly cow.'

From the angle I were at, and if I tilted me swede back a mite,
I could get a clock of his eyes in the rear-view. I looked at him,
wondering what kind of a cunt laughs about his mam carking it
like that, and calls her a silly cow. I thought about setting him
straight, but I couldn't seem to line up me thoughts on the matter.
And while I were still working on it, he were moving on:

'But no, birds…fucking birds, eh? You ever been in a long-
term relationship, Blakey?'

'Actually, I—'

'Let me tell you—don't go down that road. Those sorts of
arrangements, they're a fucking nightmare from the moment she
moves in. I dunno how I've lasted, I really don't.'

'Well, I were once marr—'

'Actually, I do know how I've lasted. *Extracurricular*, Blakey. Know what I mean? It's the only fucking way.'

'Oh aye,' I says. 'It is a good one. Especially when the space-ship comes back and he goes home at the end. I couldn't hold the tears back, DI Dave. I freely admit that.'

'Well, yeah. But yeah, birds. *Birds*. Why do we fucking put up with em, Blakey? You tell me that. Eh?'

'It's because—'

'But I'll tell you summin—you do need a woman. At home, you know? You just need it…especially if you got a busy lifestyle, like me. But, ah…it's a constant struggle, mate. Do you know what? I give her everything. Money, lodging, protection…and she still ain't happy with it. She still insists on going out to work. And that's where the root of it is, Blakey mate.'

I were shaking my head. 'That's fuckin' terrible,' I says. 'What do she do? Work-wise, I mean.'

He frowned like he couldn't remember. 'Er…that ain't impor-tant. What's important is that she don't have to work, and her fel-ler don't want her to. Do you know, we met through work, in a roundabout way. We had a business relationship at one time, you might say. But when I told her we could get together, it was meant to be so she could stop all that. I wanted to lift her out of it, and let her live like a proper lady. *My* proper lady. It meant she was different from the others. Do you know what I mean, Blakey? No, I guess you don't.'

'Well, personally I were happy to let mine carry on at the spud factory, once we'd—'

'You know what? If she was happy in her life—I mean *prop-erly* happy—I just know that she'd pack in the whole working girl bit. But I just can't seem to make her happy. Do you know what makes em happy? In the long term, I mean, not just for a couple of hours.'

I held back for a minute in case he wanted to add summat. Then I goes: 'The best thing you can do for a woman, I've found, is to give her a ring. And it's diamonds I'm on about here. Diamonds is forever, see, and women knows it. And every time they looks at their finger, and sees how sparkly it is, it stops em being sad. A man, he can't keep a bird happy all the time. But a diamond will.'

It were quiet for a bit while we both thought about that, turning it over in our swedes like an omelette that is coming along nicely. I were fucking starving, thinking about that omelette, and I wished Mandy had come for a cuppa like I'd asked her. I'd have took her down to Burt's Caff and ordered an all-day brekky with a couple of pies lobbed in cos it were lunchtime. I were thinking about proposing that to DI Dave, him being so pally with us just then, when he stops the motor.

Only a few yards along from Burt's Caff.

'Fuckin' hell,' I says, getting out and shaking me swede at the pure wonder of it. 'You just been readin' my mind, ain't you? Do you know, I seen a program on that once, on the telly, and—'

'You're a fuckin' genius, Blake,' he says, getting out his side and beaming at us. 'And I don't care what they say about you.'

'Hold up,' I says. Cos he were off across the road, which is the wrong direction for Burt's Caff. 'The caff, it's just…'

I think he had a problem with his hearing, like Rache's lad. It's a shame cos he were a fucking superb copper otherwise. He stepped up on the pavement and I thought he were headed for *Margaret Hurge Twentieth Century Hair Design* for a minute, which I couldn't understand at all. But he went past that and into the one next door, a new one I hadn't seen before, which were called *Cash 4 U*. The window were full of bits and bobs like tellies and stereos and lamps and the like, with a display of nice watches over the one side. I stood there, having a look at em. There were a well nice one there made out of solid gold, by the looks of him, and with a blue round bit. It were easily the biggest one there, and you could tell the class from a mile off. I could see it on my wrist, no problem.

'Hey,' says DI Dave. He were back on the pavement and waving a little box at us.

'Woss you got there, DI Dave?' I says.

'Come on,' he says, getting into the motor. I got in as well and he opened the box, showing us the diamond ring inside it. Looked like quite a nice one.

'Looks like quite a nice one,' I says. 'How much he cost?'

'Fuck all.'

'Eh?'

'Not a fucking penny, Blakey my friend. I got an arrangement in there, see. There's all kinds of stuff I could bring em in for, but I don't. It's better to have arrangements.'

'Oh,' I says, looking over his shoulder at the watches in the window. 'Arrangements, eh?'

'That's right, Blakey. Arrangements are what community policing is all…hang a minute.' He got his phone out and started talking into it, saying: 'Yeah? Oh, Shitface. What the fuck do you want? I'm busy, so…'

I looked out the window while he yakked, counting all the shops along that stretch and how many of em I could have "arrangements" with. Being a copper were gonna be well fucking smart, and I couldn't wait. Mind you, I wouldn't have to wait. Only a few hours and I'd be official. I'd get one of them mobile blowers and I'd be able to swear at people down it, calling em shitface and the like.

'Nine, you say? You wanna meet at nine, by the…No, I won't bring anyone. Do I ever fucking bring anyone? I'm a maverick, Shitface, and don't they all know it. Now *you* listen to *me*, you little cunt: this'd better be fuckin' good. If it ain't good, I ain't payin' you. Plus you'll get a punch in the guts. Do you see what I'm sayin', Shitface?' He hung up and put away his blower, saying: 'Her indoors.'

After a bit I goes: 'Dave, you really wanna look at how you're addressin' her. I mean, there's ways and there's—'

'I'm jokin', you twat. Shitface is an informant friend of mine. Code name, you know? If he comes through with what he says he will, I'll be set up. It's *arrangements* again, Blakey. You make a relationship and then you *milk* it until it's dry.'

'Arrangements.'

'You what?'

'I knows about arrangements,' I says. Like I says there, me and DI Dave was like best mates now. I felt like I could spill the beans to him on any matter. Thinking about beans got me guts rumbling again, but I put em aside and said me piece to DI Dave, telling him all about Jonah and the arrangement we had whereby I turned up and caught the Reaper and he made us a copper in return. I even told him about the contract and the extras, and where I were turning up for the job and at what time. 'So, you see,' I says in conclusion, 'me and you, we'll be on the same team. We might even be partners, like Starsky and…Er, why's we goin' so fast, Dave?'

Questioning a man's driving is a bad thing and I don't normally do it, but eighty mile an hour along the Wall Road weren't normal, and I didn't feel out of order in bringing it up. Especially with us nigh on tail-ending a bus before he slammed the brakes.

'Blake,' he says, pulling over. You cannot pull over on the Wall Road but I thought I'd let that one go, him being a copper. He seemed a bit out of sorts as well, breathing hard and clenching the wheel. After a bit his knuckles loosened and he started breathing slower. Then he pulled away. 'I owe you one, Blake. You're a true pal and I won't forget it. First the ring idea, now this information. I swear, I could kiss you.'

'What inf—?'

'But all I'll say to you right now is this…Sometimes you gotta look close-up at who you're dealing with. See what I'm sayin'? There's three sorts of people in this world: those you can't trust, those you don't need to trust cos you got em over a barrel, and those who are just thick.'

He pulled up on the curb and turned off the engine. Double yellow lines here but I knew how it worked for coppers like DI Dave by now. We got out and he slapped us on the shoulder, saying: 'Oh, before I fuck off…you want a bit of action, Blakey?'

'Wuh?'

'Action, mate. *Birds*, you know? I can set you up, my friend. Any time you want a service, just give us a bell and I'll get someone round your place. On me.'

'Service?'

'Yeah. Mate, the service industry in this town, I got it *cornered*. It's like I said before: *arrangements*, mate. Blonde/brunette, buxom/skinny…you give us a ring and place your order, eh? But now I gotta give a little someone a ring.'

He winked and went off up Cutler Road. I watched his back getting smaller for a bit, feeling confused about summat but not knowing what. Sometimes I just wished I had a normal job to do, like the old days when I were on the doors at Hoppers. With normal jobs, you always knows where you're meant to be. At that moment, stood there in the gutter, I didn't have the first fucking clue where I were meant to be. I had to think hard to recall who

I were. And even then, all I could come up with were Sonny Wossname, but with the head of Clint Eastwood and the body of Ivan Drago out of *Rocky IV*.

I went up Cutler Road. I weren't following DI Dave, just not knowing what else to do. I were sure it would all come back to us in a minute and I'd give meself a kick in the nuts for being so thick. But until then I wanted to stay near someone I could trust, namely DI Dave. Just in case summat happened, you see. Cos I felt like summat were gonna happen. And fairly fucking shortly as well.

DI Dave turned right at the top and into Monk Lane. I were getting closer now but I knew he wouldn't turn and clock us. It were plain to see he had his mind on other matters, them being his young lady. Halfway along there he went into the back entrance of a place called Tubthumpers, which I could have sweared used to be a church. I hung around the door there for a bit, smoking a fag. A minute later, and sparking up another one, I pushed the door open and went in.

I weren't spying nor nothing. And I didn't have no ideas about barging in on DI Dave and his intimate little wossname with his bird. I just…

I just wanted to see her. From a distance, like. I wanted to see what it were like for a feller, having a woman of his own and giving her a ring. I'd be doing it soon meself, see. I wanted a taster of it. And I did get me taster. Only it weren't a good taster. It were a rotten taster and it made us sick to the pit of me guts. See, DI Dave were sat over in the corner there.

With Mandy Munton.

She looked down at her new ring, and then up at DI Dave with a big smile across her filthy, cheating face.

CHIEF BACKTRACKS ON REAPER

Police Chief Cadwallader called a press conference earlier today to announce new developments in the hunt for the Reaper. Formerly he had said they were looking for a weedy, pockmarked man with thick-rimmed glasses. 'We're not after him anymore,' he said this morning between sips from a glass of water. 'What we're after now is a different animal entirely. We have reason to believe that this so-called "Reaper" character is in fact two characters, working in tandem. One of them is a large man with close-cropped, thinning hair and a lot of scars. The other is of medium build, well-dressed and with a full head of hair and a sun-bed tan.'

Asked to explain this sudden turnaround, the chief said: 'We don't have to explain anything to you. Our job is to catch villains, and catching villains is what we're doing. I called you here today to let you know what we're up to, because I believe the public has a right to know. I'd also like to point out that I stated to you awhile back about the prospect of it being two murderers. If you reporters were paying attention instead of just trying to pick faults, you might have took notice. That's what I mean about everyone pulling together. It's all very well me and my men working night and day to catch the killer...I mean, er, killers...but if someone fails to pull their weight, lives will be lost. And it's you reporters I'm looking at now. It's about time you did some good for a change.'

24

'Hoy, you.'

I went on walking. I were planning on walking for a long time, out to East Bloater Road and beyond. Actually I'd drive out there in my Ferrari. Only I couldn't recall where I'd left her. Not that I gave a toss. I didn't give a toss about nothing, me. Only walking. Mind you, the toes of me right foot was aching summat chronic. Espadrilles is all right for coppering, but not kicking rear headlights in.

'Come back here, you,' says the feller. 'You're payin' for this, you bloody maniac.'

I done like he were asking, going back there. He were about my height but not half as built. I took a swing at him but slipped on summat and went down without connecting. I got on me arse and looked at my espadrille, which were red instead of white, and with a bit of headlight glass sticking out of it. Blood trickled down the one side and onto the hard stuff. I pulled the glass out.

The feller were behind the motor now, saying: 'Now hey, don't make it worse for yerself. Vandalising a man's car is one thing, but assaulting...'

He stopped there cos I were up and at him again, limping on me bad foot. I had a nice headbutt lined up for him but he were shifting fast and getting away, down that wide alley that takes you to the High Street. I hared after him like a hare with only the one foot. I mean, how the fuck could she do it to us? And why, for fuck sake? And...and...

And I didn't know what. I just didn't know.

I hared for a bit and then slowed to a walk, thinking about how much I didn't know and trying to put me finger on some of them things. But they kept slipping away, like the last couple of pickled onions in a jar. I closed me eyes, hoping for darkness to befall us. But there she were, beaming at DI fucking Dave and licking her lips at him. Under the table her paw crept over and up his thigh. I tried closing me eyes again but they was already shut, so I opened em again. There was noises and goings-on all around, beepings and roarings and honkings and many more wossnames along them lines. I were surrounded by em, them big roaring wossnames. They was bearing down on us and aiming to knock us down and gobble us up, I just knew it.

'Get out of the flamin' way, you ruddy fool,' one of em were shouting.

But I couldn't see how. I couldn't see how come they was there, trying to knacker us and kill us.

'I fuckin' trusted you,' I says to one of em, the one with long brown hair and dark eyes and long lashes and…and soft white tits that seemed just a mite too big for the rest of her. 'You was meant to…we was…'

'I said shift, you ruddy fool, else I'm callin' the police.'

'The police…' I says, moving again. Actually I were running, away from them roaring bastards and their soft white tits. I wanted em, but I didn't want em. I wanted em to want me, not him. And I didn't want em to lie to us. I wanted soft white tits that I could trust, and that didn't lead us down hill and up dale without a paddle. White tits that I could get wedded to and who would appreciate the kind of man I am, which is a very classy and sophisticated one but also hard as nails, and one of Mangel's premier pillars, community-wise. White tits that was soft, and didn't go off getting hitched up with other bastards. Soft white tits, with nice nipples on the end, that will bear us a couple of sprogs and—

'We don't do em,' he says. And it didn't half sound like Nathan the barman. 'We got some pickled eggs, though. Bob Gretchum swears by em. Don't you, Bob?'

'Aye. Fuck.'

'Says they keeps him regular. No swearin' in here, please, Bob.'

I looked around the Paul Pry, wondering how I got there and why. Seemed like I might be dreaming, and that I were fast akip somewhere and not truly here at all. And I hadn't really seen Mandy with DI Dave, nor none of the bad matters that had befell us of late. I tried casting me swede back, working out exactly when I'd nodded off.

'You ain't sleepin',' says Nathan, plonking a nice pint of lager in front of us. 'This in here is true reality. There's more reality in here than in all the rest of the world rolled together. Right where you're stood, but a couple of levels below, that there is the centre of the universe as we knows it. I'm talkin' about covert machinations. It all goes on down there. Ain't that right, Bob?'

'Oh aye.'

'Aye.'

I sank my lager and lit a smoke. Nathan put another pint in front of us, which I also sank. He put another one there. I were starting to see how it weren't so bad, being back in the Paul Pry. Thinking about it, I couldn't recall why I'd stayed away so long.

'I knows why you stayed away so long.'

'I never asked you.'

'Aye, but I do know.'

'Fuck sake, Nathe, this is one of the reasons I stayed away so long, you, harkin' in on my thoughts the whole while.'

'That, yes, but also other reasons. And it's one in particular I'm inchin' towards. It's this town, Blake. You got scared of it, didn't you? You got so you couldn't even open yer front door, didn't you?'

'I ain't scared.'

'Maybe so, but you was. Wasn't you?'

'I just didn't like the way things was gettin'. And it ain't just in Mangel, Nathan. It's the whole fuckin' world over. You can't trust your fellow man no more. Nor your fellow bird.'

'I don't care about the world over, Blakey. It's Mangel that counts. Mangel is the only place in the world, the pole around which it all spins.'

'You know what I think about Mangel, Nathan? You can shove Mangel up yer filthy arse. I've had enough of the place. And I ain't scaredy of it, neither. I've just plain had enough. You know what I'm thinkin' on doing, Nathe? Gettin' out. Leavin' this fuckin' shite-hole of a town.'

Nathan picked up a tankard and polished it. He polished it so hard the metal appeared to turn red in his hands, and you could almost smell the melting pewter. After a bit the red went down, along with the rate of his polishing. He put the tankard down.

'Mangel is special,' he says. 'I'll let you in on a secret, Blakey. The whole world were once special, going back some time. The true ways of the world was known to the right people, and them people acted upon that knowledge and administered to matters as required. And I'm talking about arcane knowledge here, things that yer common man need not bother himself with. It's all about keeping the *balance* right, you see, and not upsetting the natural order.

'And then the new ways came in, and balance went out the window. No one cares about balance no more, out there on the outside. That is the great ailment of our times. And it's creeping like a plague into our town, right under our very own hooters. However, it won't get a foothold here. Not while there's me and others like me here. And do you know why? Because we knows what to do, that's why. Now, the time has come to initiate you unto our ways.'

He stepped towards the door behind the bar. I didn't like that door and never had done, and I felt myself pulling upright and getting set to peg it.

'Fret not,' says Nathan. 'I knows how you feels about this here door. So we've took measures.'

'What fuckin' measures?'

'Bob Jr, there.'

I looked behind us and sure enough there were Bob Jr, a lairy look and about two dozen stitches on his face. In his hands he held an axe. A very big axe. I don't reckon I'd ever seen one so big. He had on an old butcher's apron, judging by the stains down it.

'It's not a bad measure, is it?' says Nathan. 'I mean, you won't have no trouble comin' through this door and down these stairs now. You do have trouble, and Bob Jr, with his axe, he'll—'

'You got a fuckin' problem with me, Bob Jr?' I says, ignoring Nathan. ''Cos you got some sort of attitude towards us. I can sense it. Eh?'

He took a step forward, baring his gnashers at us. Like I says, the axe were a big one and I knew he were too close now to make much use of it, so I moved to take a swing at him. Tag him on his left cheekbone and all them stitches'd pop.

'Like I says, Blakey,' says Nathan, '*measures*, not measure.'

And, with that, Bob Sr poked us in the ribs with the end of a shotgun.

The Gretchums and their weapons behind us, I went behind
the bar and followed Nathan through the door at the back. There
were a small area there with boxes and bottles and the like stacked
up against the dirty white walls, lit overhead by a bare bulb that
made a slight humming sound. I'd clocked all this from out there
in the pub, and it weren't what bothered us. It were the dark stairway beyond it. No one had been down there besides Nathan, far
as I knowed. And no one talked much of that place. I'd heard one
or two mutterings over the years, mind. I'd heard talk of a wind-
ing tunnel that keeps on going down until you gets knackered or
cacks yer pants and have to go back. I'd heard say that there's only
one place that them stairs under the Paul Pry leads, and that's hell.
And Nathan, him being the only one goes down there, he's got a
pact with the devil. They says he started here as a young barman
many a year ago, and one night he wandered down there in search
of a box of pork scratchings. He didn't find no scratchings nor no
other bar vittles, but he did follow the downward path all the way
to the end and came conk to conk with the devil himself. Satan
and Nathan went on to strike a deal involving him being lord and
master of all what he surveyeth, handing over his soul in return.
That's what I heard.

'Don't talk yer nonsense,' says Nathan, looking over his slopey
shoulder.

'I never said nuthin.'

'All right, well don't *think* yer nonsense. There's no devil down
here, only three barrels of mild and four of bitter. And some pork
scratchin's.'

'You out of lager, then?' I says.

'No. Lager comes from a special place.'

And with that he marched on and downwards, me following and the Gretchums pulling up the rear. I think it were Bob

Jr directly behind us cos I could smell his apron and sense the hatred he harboured for us. I couldn't understand how come he hated us so much, but I weren't overly bothered about that just now. I didn't care about much besides these stairs we was going down. They was hewn of very old stone and worn smooth by the passing of feet. I wondered how many different pairs had passed down here over the years.

'Not many,' says Nathan without turning.

'Oh,' I says.

'Not many human ones at all.'

The walls was put together from brick and mortar on each side, curving inwards and meeting at the top to form a dome. It were an all right dome at first and I could walk tall and keep me chin up, but after a while it started getting lower and lower and I had to stoop, while Nathan in front didn't seem the littlest bit hindered. It were getting darker as well, and I really could have done with a torch. But summat about the place took my words away before I could ask em, so I just kept on walking and looking down and ducking me swede. Every now and then I'd get a poke from behind, letting us know who were where and what he were armed with. It hurt quite a bit, getting a big old axe blade in my back, and normally I'd have summat to say about it and possibly a thump or two to dole, but down here I didn't have it in us. I had fuck all inside meself besides the fear.

And I don't mind admitting that to you.

As someone who ain't ever been scaredy of nothing during his entire time, I don't mind telling you that it got to us, down that there tunnel. And it *were* a proper old tunnel now, cos the steps had worn flat and the ground were sloping down like the side of a hill, and it were pitch-black and the ceiling were low and I had a bastard to the fore and two cunts to the rear. And I were trapped.

It were all too much, of a sudden like, and I wanted to wail. I had a wail the size of a whale inside us, and the fucker were starting to spout water and wanted out sharpish. It's like Jonah… not the copper one but the one who swallows the whale. Actually I dunno if that's right, but it were near enough like that. But it don't matter cos I couldn't get the wail out anyhow. It's like back there, with the words getting took away before I could say em—I opened me gob to let rip and the fucking wail were torn out of us silent and violent, like a big gnarly paw reaching down and stripping out me spine. And it truly were like that cos I couldn't stand up no more.

I went down.

I were waiting for the axe blade in the back. Or a shotgun barrel in the neck. Or a harsh word from Nathan at the very fucking slightest. But I got none of that. What I got were…were…

25

Actually I'm just fucking you about. I didn't get very much at all, only the light coming on overhead (another bare and humming bulb), revealing a sort of clearing. The tunnel went out the other side and on downwards, but this little patch were about twelve by fifteen and no more generous headroom-wise, and I could tell we was at our destination. I could tell that cos Nathan cleared his windpipe and goes:

'Here we are, at our destination.'

The place were empty except for one corner, where there were quite a large summat set up there and draped in a red sheet. I didn't like the look of it, in terms of the bits jutting out here and there under the sheet, but I could tell it were the reason for us being brung down here. The Gretchums were still behind us, holding their weapons and looking filthy at us. While I were giving em some of the same back, Nathan says:

'Prostrate thyselves.'

The Gretchums got down on their knees, sending us a last bit of eye piss before looking at the ground. Bob Sr kept his barrels trained on us.

'You get down as well,' roars Nathan, addressing us.

'I am down.'

'On your knees, not yer backside.'

'Oh.'

Nathan pulled the red sheet off, revealing summat or other. 'Do you know what this is?' he says.

'Looks like a bit of concrete,' I says. 'There's some old girder stickin' out there and…er…'

…stuck in this rock, and you can't pull it out…

'What?' says Nathan. 'Woss you sayin'?'

'Eh? Oh, I, er…I'd say it's off a demolition site. Them old bogs in Frotfield Way, perhaps.'

'First off, it ain't bloody concrete,' he says, roaring again. I didn't like him roaring cos it bounced off the walls and went up the tunnels and back at us again. 'It's stone, you bloody fool. This here is ancient stone, the oldest bit of stone in the world. And that there—that "girder", as you terms it—that is the Horn of Gerontius, the holy cypher via which the stone sends his magic unto the world. This here is what it's all about, Blakey. This is the Mangel Stone, and all order and balance in the world emanates herefrom. That is why you are rightfully supplicatin' yourself before it.'

In front of the stone (although I still reckoned it concrete—especially with that half brick stuck on the side), lying in a row on the deck, was six round things wrapped in big leaves, or summat, each one of em about the size of a swede. On most of em the leaves was dead and brown. Two still had em green and shiny.

'What do you reckon to that?' says Nathan.

'I don't fuckin' know, do I?'

Nathan smiled. It took us back to a school day where the teacher had smiled the same way after I'd answered a question wrong. I waited for that teacher after school and sparked him in the car park, then drove off in his motor with Legs and Finney and dumped it on the river. I didn't feel I could do that with Nathan, though.

'Touch the stone,' he says. 'Go on an' touch him. All will be revealed unto you.'

'It's just a bit of—'

'Touch it.'

'Nathan, it's a lump of bloody conc—'

'Touch the flamin' stone!'

'I don't wanna!'

A poke in the back had us moving towards it anyhow. I weren't sure why I didn't want to, but I didn't want to and that's all I knowed. I stumbled on, fighting the mental fight and losing it.

…the Sword of Excrement…

'And watch them offerings,' snaps Nathan as I almost tripped over one of the round wossnames wrapped up in leaves. 'It's took Bob Jr there nearly a year to reap them. Ain't it, Bob Jr?'

I were stood next to the stone now, getting me right paw ready to do what it didn't want to. I felt well dodgy about it and shook up inside, like two dozen ghosts from the past was tearing up me guts and going barmy at the thing I were all set to do.

…no one can pull him out, they says, except for one very special feller…

'That's it,' says Nathan, rubbing his paws. The bulb seemed dimmer now and his fleshy face looked like it were made of wax. 'At last you'll be joinin' us, Blake. I tell yer, I been campaignin' fer this fer years and you wouldn't believe the opposition I came up against. Mind you, you never really helped matters, eh? With your behaviour. But we're here now, and if you'll just go on and do the honours, we'll…'

Me paw were hovering over the stone. I could feel the heat off it, and it weren't a nice heat. I closed my eyes and me swede emptied, and then filled up again with the darkness.

…all I knows is that the special feller ain't meself, and it ain't no one else what I knows of. And shall I tell you summat else, Blakey?

What?

…it fuckin' ain't you, neither…

'Not the Horn of Gerontius, Blakey. You don't touch that bit. The Stone, Blakey…touch the…Hoy, woss you doing? Get off that Horn, for fuck sake!'

The black inside my brain filled up with red. I knew that red. There were a roaring, too, and it were coming from my lungs. I roared and I saw red, and I pulled. I pulled like no other, thinking about how everyone had always took us for a cunt and not gave us chance to show me true colours. Well, I were showing em here. And they was red and black, like I says. And white. Everything went white.

'Blakey!'

'Flamin' hell, Nathe! Woss he done?'

'Blakey, woss you gone an' done?'

'He's knacked the flamin' Stone, Nathe!'

'*Woss you gone an' done? Woss you—*'

Bob Jr took a swing at us with his big axe. I were stumbling backward just then and he missed. I hit the wall and slid down, pushing meself up again with the Sword of Excrement. I didn't know what sort of sword it were and didn't have time to look, but it felt good in me paw. Bob Jr took another swing and I ducked this time. Nathan, who had been shouting all along about me and what I gone and done, started screaming. Bob Jr were gearing up for another swing. I backed off and tripped over a bit of the stone, or whatever it were. It were in eight or nine bits now and I fell on em, and it fucking hurt. Nathan were still screaming. The shotgun went off and summat large hit the wall behind us, and I felt warm rain on me face. It were hard to tell what were going on, really. I lobbed the Sword hard and it hit Bob Sr in the face.

He went down.

Bob Jr were bent over, trying to get a grip on his fallen axe, but summat were wrong with him and I couldn't see what it were straight off. He got hold of the axe in his left and stood up. His right arm were missing and half the shoulder. He held the axe out wide, roaring, and charged at us. I were in the corner with nowhere to go, and didn't have the Sword no more. Nathan were screaming. I scrabbled around, keeping my peepers on the one-armed Gretchum lad and me fingers curled around summat. He went to close the last couple of yards, starting to bring his axe down. I went forward, keeping low, and smacked him in the face with the thing I had, which seemed to be his fallen arm. He toppled, dropping the axe and going down on the rubble. Nathan were still screaming and starting to do my head in, so I lobbed the arm at him and it shut him up a bit.

I went over and got the Sword of Excrement, which were next to Bob Sr, who were lying down just then and bleeding from his mashed eye socket. To look at, you'd think the Sword were a length of rusty iron with a lump of concrete on the end. But I knew it were the Sword. It felt good to be holding it, and I felt like the Chosen One. I *were* the Chosen One, cos I'd pulled the fucker out when no one else had. Not only that, but I'd done it while these three cunts here was doing their best to halt destiny. I didn't begrudge em it, really. Every hero needs his obstacles, and Nathan and the Gretchums was mine.

I lifted the Sword and twocked Bob Sr on the head.

In practice, I found it more like a mace. Or a very large hammer. The concrete lump on the end made quite an impression on the top of Bob Sr's skull, and I knew I wouldn't be hearing from him no more. I went over to his lad and done the same to him. I were getting into it now. I felt like Jason and the Astronauts. Bob Sr were a cyclops, his lad here were some sort of one-armed wossname, and Nathan over there were...actually I weren't sure what

Nathan could be, so I finished with the Gretchum lad and went over to him for a look.

I could see what Nathan's screaming were about now. The lad had put a big slice in his thigh with his reckless axe-swinging, leaving him deck-wise and bleeding a lot. But he still had it in him to flash fire at us.

'I stood up fer you,' he says. 'I telled em aye when they says nay. And look how you repays us. I works meself sore to welcome you into our cabal, and you've…you've gone and ruined it all!'

I knew what Nathan were now. He were a banshee, which is a sort of monster who screams a lot and gets up to other things that I can't recall just now.

I lifted the Sword.

But there's summat about Nathan that makes a man reluctant. Do you know what I mean? You just don't want to cross him too much, or ping him with the Sword of Excrement, in case…I weren't sure what. But you never knows, does you?

'Look…' he says, coming to his senses of a sudden. 'Look, Blakey, I don't begrudge you for what you done here to the Gretchum kin. Young Bob shouldn't of tried implicatin' you, and his dad just never liked you anyhow. And the Stone, well, I think I might be able to—'

'Woss you on about?' I says. 'Implicatin'? Implicatin' us on what?'

'Implicatin' you on his reaping, o' course. I knows what he done, leavin' bits and bobs behind your house, and trying to get you fingered for summat you never done. He always bored a grudge towards you, see. Says you slapped him once, a few year back, and—'

'Woss this reapin'? You mean like farming? The Gretchums been doing some farmin'? Woss you on about? I don't understand…I don't…'

'Fret not, Blakey. I'll explain it all to yers. All you got to do is help us acquire the last and final offerin', and perhaps get a cement mixer down here so we can put old Humpty back together again, and…'

He were going on like that, yakking about all kinds of shite and I knowed not what else. I were confused, you see, and it were sinking through to us that it might not be regarding just this one case, with Nathan and the Gretchums and their barmy goings-on. I were starting to wonder if I didn't know much about matters in general, and that I weren't the genius everyone made us out to be. I felt the reality I knew and loved come crashing down around me lugholes, and heard Nathan still going on about his matters, and I didn't know what to do.

So I pegged it. I didn't care how low and dark the tunnel were, I wanted out of there sharpish. I hared, swede bumping off the bricks overhead and Nathan's bleating roar still going on behind us. When I got to the bar area I pulled meself a pint and stood with a wet bar towel atop me swede, just taking it easy and calming down. In a short while, and after another few pints, I felt meself come normal again. I were hurting here and there and I'd had a wasted couple of hours, but I knowed where I were headed, and for why.

MANGEL TODAY—PROSTITUTION (PART TWO)

Russell Pank

She was the one who talked, the lady of the night who dared speak her mind and reveal the secrets of the sex trade. I sensed that I had caught her at the right moment. Any other time and she would have been as inaccessible as the others…unless it was about business. And I knew that I had to get straight to the point, because in five minutes' time the moment would be gone.

Her answers came thick and fast, like the punters she serviced every day.

'How did you get started in this profession?'

'Profession? You call this profession? It ain't a profession, right? It's just a thing I do. It's exploitation. Exploitation ain't a profession, is it? I'm exploiting what I have. That's the way the money goes round. How did I get started? I was in the city. I come from this town but I went to the city. Big mistake, I suppose, but I…I had no choice. Anyway, I was there and I had nothing. It didn't take much to get something, though. Know what I mean?'

But why did she still do it?

'Because I need to. Not for money. I'm all right for money now. Most of the girls do it for money, because they need drugs. But I don't do drugs. I'm not stupid like them, What I do it for is control. Control over men. Men come to me, I can take them or leave them. I'm not afraid of them. I've never been afraid of men but I've always felt…'

The line went quiet. I wanted to prompt her, but I didn't know what to say. I was out of my depth. No words were coming from her, but I didn't feel that the moment had gone. I could feel her struggle. She was treading unknown territory, facing new demons.

'It always comes back to men, don't it? You can't do nothing without a man's say-so. They've always got to feel like they're the boss, that they're looking after you and you ought to be grateful. Well, I'm not grateful. No one needs to look after me. Not that way, anyway. I need something else, summat that…Oh, what's the use in talking about it? You don't understand because you're a man. And

don't try and tell me no different. You know what I think, deep in my heart? There's not a man on this earth who'll give me what I need. And do you know what else? I need it. But I don't get it, and I won't. How's that for an interview?'

The line went dead.

So many questions unanswered. I wanted to ask her if she didn't feel any shame, doing what she did. Did her family know about it? I wanted to ask her how she felt, walking the streets of Mangel and knowing that she brought vice to those streets. But underneath it all, when I put aside the questions and answers and theories and conclusions, I was left with her voice. I could not get it out of my head. And I knew that never, no matter how hard I thought about it, never would I ever understand it.

I walked away from the phone box. I felt like something had been wrenched out of me. Or perhaps it had never been inside me, that thing, and I just hadn't felt its absence until now.

I went to file a story.

26

And I'll tell you where that place were that I were headed, and for why.

It's Alvin's Kebab Shop & Chippy.

Cos I were fucking starving.

It were only a short walk from the Paul Pry to there, but I done it slow and took the time to get other matters sorted, like what I had planned after the scran. And it's Jonah I'm on about here, and his plans to catch the Reaper that involved meself. I looked at my watch and found it to be knackered. Glass were smashed and the hands all bent and buggered, which I suppose must have happened in the rumble with the Gretchums back there. Mind you, could have been worse than a bust watch. I knowed how close I'd come to carking it, and were grateful to the gods for saving my arse. But I knowed why they'd done it, see, and it weren't all about doing Royston Blake a favour. No, it's about Royston Blake doing *them* a favour.

Namely turning copper, and making meself useful.

'All right, Alv.'

'All right, Blakey. Woss you been up to? You got red all down yer.'

'Ah, bit o' paintin'.'

'Oh aye?'

'Aye. Paintin' me motor.'

'Oh aye? You got a new motor. Woss it?'

'It's a F…well, it's a surprise, like. You'll soon see. Everyone'll soon see.'

'Hmm…very mysterious, I must say. And did you swaller yer pride and go see Nathan, eh? Go on—tell us you did.'

'Look, just do us chips, eh? Large. Two large chips and a couple of saveloys. And one or two pies.'

'Well, I dunno. You still owes us two pound and sixty-five from last time.'

'Eh? Oh, aye.'

'You gonna pay us now?'

'Aye.'

'Go on, then.'

'Just giz me scran first and I'll pay yers for both. I ain't gettin' me wedge out twice.'

Alvin sighed and shook his swede, then goes: 'One or two pies, you say?'

'Aye. Four.'

'And how many saveloys?'

'I says a couple.'

'Two?'

'No, a couple means *about* two.'

'How many, then?'

'Six.'

'Right you is, Blakey.'

'And some fish.'

'We only got fishcakes and fishfingers.'

'I'll have the fishcakes.'

'How many?'

'All of em.'

'All me fishcakes? What if someone else comes in here wantin' fish?'

'Oh aye, I hadn't thought o' that.'

'Exactly.'

'I'll have the fishfingers as well.'

'Eh? You don't even like fishfingers.'

'How'd you know?'

'Cos you telled us once.'

'When?'

'I dunno. Eleven year ago, I think. You was in here after work at Hoppers one night and you says that, about not likin' fishfingers.'

'Well, I changed me mind. I wants all the fingers and all the fishcakes. All right?'

'But, Blakey...'

'You hear us?'

'Aye...aye, er...right you is, Blakey.'

'And a kebab.'

I waited for me scran, looking out the window. It were all steamed up and I had to rub a hole in it to see through. I quite liked doing that and I started doing some patterns. It were a big old window and I had loads of space, so kept on doing that for quite a while. As I drew, and the shape of a face and long dark hair well-known to us started coming clear in the fogged-up window, my mind started drifting to matters of the heart. And it's birds I'm on about here. Mandy Munton in particular, and the way she'd treated us. It still made us sick to just think about it, her with DI Dave. Even after all this time, and it had been at least a couple of hours, I reckoned. Mind you, it weren't so much of a surprise as you'd think. See, I'd been let down by every single bird I'd got meself tangled up with. They sees us as a pushover, see. They uses us for me body and tosses us aside, limp and used up.

Well, I weren't having it no more.

Once I got me badge, I'd show em all how much of a soft touch I were. Birds was gonna get it just like the fellers. Everyone knows how much lifting birds does in the shops. And then there's all the pubs in town full up of underage slags. Plus the prozzies. Mangel just weren't a nice town to live in and bring up younguns in no more. And it's all cos of birds.

As I were rubbing another big hole in the steam, I clocked someone going past outside. I ran out after her. 'Rache,' I shouted. She had her head down and shifting her pins fast, but I weren't letting her get away. It's like I says just now—no more shite from birds. 'Hoy, Rache,' I yells, catching up and grabbing her arm.

'Ow,' she says. 'You're hurtin' me.'

'Soz. Look, I just wanted to say—'

'Blake, I'm in a hurry.'

'I know but I just wanted a quick word, like. About a certain matter.'

'It can wait, Blake. I've really got to—'

'Look, you ain't goin' no place, right? This is fuckin' important. And I ain't takin' no more shite off of…erm…'

'Go on,' she says, pursing her lips.

'Well, I just really and truly does need a word. I can't go on without it, Rache. Come on, hear us out.'

'Hmm…' she says, looking at her watch. 'Maybe I can spare five minutes, at a push. Go on then.'

'What, here?'

'Yeah. Where else?'

'Well, I were thinkin' we could go for a quick—'

'Hoy, Blakey. You're payin' for this scran, you know.'

'Fuck off, Alv. I never says I weren't payin' for it. Go on—fuck off back inside.'

Alvin went in, giving us a shite stare first.

'Eh, Rache,' I says. 'Fancy some fishfingers?'

• • •

We sat on a wall, down by the old market, which was now a furniture shop. I got a bit of chip paper and put all the fishfingers into it, and gave it to Rache.

'Ta for that, Rache,' I says, popping a pie in me gob. 'I'll pay you back tomorrer.'

'Well, I do need it, Blake.'

'Aye, aye. Giz it a fuckin' rest, eh? Fuck sake…'

We went quiet for a bit while we enjoyed our food. After finishing me dinner I moved onto pudding, which were the kebab. Rache were still on her first fishfinger.

'Look, Rache…' I says, chewing doner, 'about earlier on, when you was…I mean, in the motor, when I were gettin' you to…'

'When you asked me to suck your dick?'

'I never meant it like that, Rache, it's…'

'No.'

'…it's just, well, I were a bit lonely, and…'

'And you're not lonely no more? Cos you got a blowjob off someone else?'

'Aye, actually. I mean no, I ain't lonely no more. I mean, I am, but…Ah, fuckin' hell, Rache. I'm just tellin' you no hard feelin's, like. Eh? I respect you as a bird, and I only asked you to do that thing cos I fancies you. You knows I always fancied you.'

She looked at her fishfingers and kept quiet. That were all right, I thought. Better than another snide remark from her anyhow.

'Look, Rache, I were thinkin' just now about birds, and how they'm all bitches. And then I seen you goin' past, and I realised that all of em ain't like that. There's one or two who's all right, and who's been fair to us over the years. And it's you I'm on about here.

And, realisin' that, it made us think about the blowj…the thing in the motor there, and how wrong it were. That's all I meant to say, eh.'

She looked up and took a deep one. I watched her tits rise and fall under the big coat she were wearing. She were a bit rough them days, it's true, but she still had a good shape to her.

'Well, all right,' she says, looking at us finally and even putting out a little smile. 'But I really do have to go now. I got work.'

'Oh aye? Woss you doin' these days, then?'

'It's nuthin'…just a little one-off job is all.'

'What little job? You pullin' pints again, eh? Ah, me and you at Hoppers, eh? You was the best fuckin' barmaid in town, I fuckin' swear. One of the best anyhow. And me, I were the hardest pound-for-pound doorman in the whole of the Mangel area. Weren't I? I still am, actually, only—'

'Blake, a lot's changed since them days.'

I looked at her and she had tears in her eyes. I put me arm around her and pulled her close, saying: 'I knows it, I knows it,' and making cooing noises in her ear. She were talking about me, see. She could see I'd fell on hard times, and were feeling sad about that. Poor lass had forgot all about me being a copper. I didn't remind her straight off, though. I quite enjoyed having a bird cry over us for a change. Mind you, I thought she were going a bit too far. Especially when she started wailing like sprog with a dirty nappy.

'Hey,' I says, 's'all right, babe. I'm here now.'

'Oh, Blake…I wish you'd of been here *then*, when…'

'Shhh.'

'…wh…when…'

'When what, eh?' I says all gentle, stroking her hair. 'When the cow jumped over the moon? When Jack and Jill ran up the hill? When Little Miss Muffet sat on her wossname, and ate her...what were it? Lemon curd, or summat? Aye, a lemon curd sarnie. I prefers jam meself.' I were quite good at this, I thought, being nice to birds. And I enjoyed it as well. I reached a paw in me pocket and adjusted meself. With the other paw I reached down over her shoulder and into the top of her coat, and found her bra strap. 'You just don't worry about a thing, eh.'

'...when I was a prostitute.'

I took me paw out of her bra, nice and slow. 'A prozzy? You weren't no prozzy, was yer? When was you a fuckin' prozzy?'

'Right up until a couple of weeks ago. I didn't want to get into it, Blakey, but I was in trouble, and there was this bloke who helped me. Seemed like he was helpin' me at the time, anyhow. He was a copper.'

'It is true that coppers is helpful,' I says. 'Only the good ones, mind you. You can rely on them. But many of em is cunts.'

'This one was a...I don't like that word.'

'What word?'

'The C word.'

'Copper?' I says, nodding. 'Aye, it can be a bit confusing cos you might be on about the type of metal, and not actual coppers. But there's other things you can call em. "Policeman", for example. Or "pig". Some of us—I mean, some of *them*—they calls emselves other things as well, like "DI". And "constable". Mind you, that one sounds like "cunt stubble", which is about right in many cases. But you can't call em all cunts. Like I says, some is all right. I knows a very good one and he's a DI.'

'I knows a DI as well, and he's...he's a *cunt*.'

'Hoy,' I says, 'mind yer language.' I don't like it when birds is swearing.

'The DI I knows is the one who got me on the game. Do you know what he did? I got caught for shopliftin'…and it were the third or fourth time, and he said I would definitely go to jail for it. And I couldn't go to jail, cos of little Roy. But this copper offers us a way out of it. It seemed so nice as well, the way he described it. A "hostess"—that's how he put it. If I did the hostess thing for him a couple of times, Mr Copper said he'd make sure I'd never see jail. Plus I'd make money, so I wouldn't have to shoplift no more. You knows what the rest is, Blakey. It's Mr Copper who ends up makin' all the money, and me who ends up stuck on the game. Our little *arrangement*, he called it.'

'Well,' I says, shaking me swede and looking at the pavement, 'it don't surprise us, coppers like that. But do you know what? Me, I'm gonna clean it all up. When I gets me badge, I'm g—'

'You can guess what happened when I told him no, I ain't gonna be his "hostess" no more. All of a sudden I get picked up by his mates in uniform, and I'm facing jail again. Bastard. Bastards.'

'Fuckin' hell, Rache. So who's gonna watch your lad? He goin' into care, is he? Actually it ain't so bad. I were in a home for a little while when I were—'

'But no, I ain't, Blakey. I ain't goin' down. I struck a deal with em, see. They asked me to do a job for em, and in return I gets off the charges. So that's what I'm doin' tonight, since you was askin'.'

'Fuck me,' I says. Cos it weren't half a coincidence. 'You're doin' a police job tonight?'

'Yeah.'

I opened me gob to tell her that I were as well, and spill the beans about how I've been specially recruited as the only man in town capable of catching the Reaper, but I shut it again without spilling not even one drop of tomato sauce. See, hers might be a spot of light police work, but mine were a *secret mission*. And

I really oughtn't to be yakking about it to prozzies like her. Pillow talk, see.

'Yeah,' she goes on, 'I won't lie and tell you I ain't a bit nervous. They wants us to act as bait, cos they're plannin' on catchin' two fellers for some crime or other. Course, they won't tell us what the crime is. They won't tell us fuck all, Blakey. Mind you, I ain't surprised. You should hear how they talks to me. You should hear how everyone talks to me now, them that still does. Everyone knows now, see. I'm the tainted lady. I've brought shame on the neighbourhood, and…and…Oh, Blake…you don't blame me, do you? I had no choice, I honestly…Do you think I'd do summat like that unless I had no other way?'

'Eh? What?' I hadn't been listening. A man like me, he's got to follow his trains of thoughts and concentrate on matters in hand. I didn't have time to fuck about listening to Rache carp on about her problems. There was much bigger problems than hers in this town, and I were the feller to fix em. Plus I weren't so keen on Rache now anyhow.

'I said,' she says, 'do you think I'd do s—'

'Aye aye. Look, I gotta make tracks.'

'Make tracks? But—'

'Look, some of us has got important shite on their hands. Do you know what I mean? No, I don't reckon you do.'

'Eh? Woss up with you all of a sudden?'

'Fuck all's up with me. It's you, not me. Don't go blamin' me.'

'Me?'

'Aye, *you.*'

'Woss I done?'

'You knows what you done. Or never done, more like.'

'What?'

'Don't come the ignorant. I'm on about in the motor back there, you goin' all high and mighty, turnin' yer nose up at me knob like that. And all the while you been…er…'

She looked back at us, trying to put us off. It were getting dark now and the moon shining overhead, marking out a little tear working his way down her face. Birds always does that when they ain't got no proper answer, and I couldn't be doing with it no more.

'Ah,' I says, turning, 'just fuckin' *forget* it, right?' Halfway up the road I stops and turns back. 'Hey, Rache,' I says. 'You got a spare tenner?'

27

I were on a bench down by the river, smoking. Also I had a half bottle of whisky to keep us warm and focussed, and I were sucking on that.

I weren't thinking about nothing. There were nothing to be thought about no more. It were all set, see, fate-wise, and nothing left to be sorted out in the swede. Jonah had said half eight for me secret mission, and it were fifteen minutes to go still. I knew where to go, and I knew what to do. There was things I didn't know, course. Like who this Reaper feller were. But I didn't need to know that. All I knowed were that he were a big one, like as not, and Royston Blake had been handpicked as the only man to bring him down.

Well, I could do that all right.

I stood up and boxed the night air for a bit, hissing between me teeth as I jabbed and hooked. I were in good shape, no doubt about it. I sat down and had another smoke, lighting it off the last one. The thoughts was getting too hard to keep out, and after a bit I gave in and let one in. It were about DI Dave and Mandy, sitting all cosy in that pub back there. But it weren't like when I'd thought about it before. I'd got over Mandy now, and had her down as a common slag and not to be fretted over. No, I were thinking about Dave now, and how it would be with me and him as partners, once I got me badge. See, it weren't his fault that he were going out with Mandy. He didn't know about me and her. He didn't even know about her, and the things she'd got up to in the dim and distant. You had to feel sorry for the feller, and I found

meself struggling over whether or no I ought to spill the beans
to him about his dearly devoted bird and her true nature, which
were that of a lying bitch who murdered her own kin. He were a
mate, see, and I didn't want him made a cunt of like this. Plus it'd
be awkward, me and him driving around, nicking crooks every
day and me knowing that I shagged his wife. Not only shagged
her, but gave her a time like no other. It'd be like *I* were making a
cunt of him as well, just like Mandy had. So I had to tell.

But in a nice way, whereby me and him was still best mates,
and our friendship were strengthened all the more on account of
our both being taken for a cunt by the same lass.

I thought about that and smoked a fag as I walked to the
secret mission. It were down by the hairy factory. Jonah had said
to go down that alley over the far side and I'll find a bird there,
and a feller getting ready to kill her. All I had to do were jump the
fucker and bring him down. I could break his swede if I wanted,
so long as I didn't let the bastard go.

I flexed me paws and went round there, skirting the wire
fence that kept folks out of the hairy factory. Or kept the hairiness
in, perhaps. I lit another smoke as I walked and finished off the
whisky. I hadn't been down here much since being a youngun.
There were a hot air blower out the back and you could sit by it all
night and keep warm, if you had to. Sometimes I used to sit there
with a young Legs and Fin, and we'd do the innocent things that
young lads does, like smoke fags and neck cider, and sniff glue.
Legs and Fin never really liked the place beyond the hot air and
the privacy, but I always liked going there. It were where me mam
used to work, see. I used to feel like she were still there, watching
over us as I held the placcy bag to me face and inhaled. If I held
the fumes in long enough I could almost see her, though she were
a bit blurry. She'd be stood over there, by them skips, wearing

a pink dressing gown and with her hair up in rollers and a fag hanging out of her mouth. Mam had always been a cut above, see, and I felt ashamed to be with Fin and Legsy when she turned up, them being a bit pikey, the both of em. Actually I weren't really ashamed of em, but I still wanted em gone. I wanted to be alone with me mam. But one time I went down there on me todd and she never turned up. Everything seemed wrong about the place, and I knowed from the moment I jumped over the fence that I'd be disappointed. In the end I passed out, waking up at first light with puke down me front and the bag stuck to me chin.

I were at the corner of the alley now, and I stopped and had a peer around it. Didn't look to be much going on down there. I started walking. As I walked I took a lot of deep breaths, getting me body full up of puff. I didn't know me opponent or how big he were, so I had to be ready for a long and lasting rumble if need be. I didn't fancy that. In terms of fighting styles, I'm a knock-out artist. Box us for three minutes and I don't know what. Mind you, I don't know what because no cunt's got that far. I stopped and felt me pockets.

Monkey wrench.

Why didn't I have no monkey wrench? I used to always have a monkey wrench in days of yore. Course, I knew why I didn't have one now. It's cos of me being all set for coppering. A copper can't hardly twock a cunt with a wrench and explain that in court. No, he's got a truncheon for that, and soon I'd have mine. But I didn't have one yet. I breathed deep a bit more. I flexed a bit more of me paws and laid a couple more jabs on the cold night air.

Up yonder, just a few short yards off, were a little wossname. And by wossname I means a little alcove, cutting into the brick and providing a smart place for a cunt to hide and prosper. Other side of the alley were a fence too high to scale, so the bird and the bad feller had to be in the alcove. I rubbed my nose and slied up on em like a ninja, keeping low and close to the wall. There were no chance anyone would know I were creeping up on em. When I got right next to the alcove I put my fag out and flexed me muscles one final time, getting cramp in me right calf and having to wait a few minutes until it got better. Then I jumped out.

I grabbed him, getting his swede tight under my right arm and knacking it with me left. Maybe I'd knock him out or maybe I'd strangle him. Either way, he were going down. I loosed me grip for a sec so I could get a better hold of him. '*Blake,*' he yelps during that sec. And it didn't half sound like a weakened Jonah. I loosed him again. 'Blake, it's…it's…'

'Jonah, I knows it,' I says, letting him go. He went down. 'But why the fuck's you—?'

'I were waitin' on you,' he says, on all fours now. 'I wanted to…to de…'

'What?'

'…to debrief you, before you…'

He chucked his guts.

'Ah, fuckin' hell,' I says, stepping out of the stench zone and lighting one up. I looked through the fence at the tangle of trees and brambles there. Beyond it were the river, if you kept going down through the wasteland. I could see a tiny light through the thicket, moving slightly and flickering. I wondered if it might be a boat on the river, making headways for some place other than Mangel. I wondered how it would be to get a berth on that boat, leave all this behind, and work in a shop in the big city, like Mandy had. Mind you, that were bollocks, like as not. If she'd kept it from us about being married to DI Dave, she'd lie about anything. The light in the thicket seemed to be getting stronger and clearer, like it were a little fairy light nearby and not a big faraway light on a boat at all. I scratched my head.

Jonah had stopped his upchucking and were stood tall again, holding his belly. Blood were coming from his hooter, and one side of his forehead were a bit blue and bumpy.

'Soz about the hooter,' I says. 'And the forehead.'

'You flamin' ought to be.'

'Actually, no, I ain't.'

'What d'you mean, you ain't?'

'I takes it back. I ain't sorry. It were your fault. You shouldn't of been here. Right here is where you says I got to knack that bloke, so—'

'Look, you're over twenty minutes late. I said be here at—'

'Me watch is bust.'

'That ain't my fault. But look, there's still time. I asked you to come here early cos I knew you'd be late.'

'So I ain't late then, really?'

'Well, not in actual f—'

'Fuck off then.'

'It's only my foresight that...Ah, just shut up about it. Look, y—'

'Don't tell me to shut up. You got all them things on the contract sorted, have you?'

'Er, yeah. That's all been took care of, aye.'

'You don't have to worry about the ring, though. I don't need no ring no more.'

'Oh, no? Well, we'll send it back then, heh heh.'

'Actually, no, I still wants it. I can flog it, see.'

'True, true. Look, you—'

'But you sorted all them other matters, right? I can join the force straight away, and I don't have to wear no uniform?'

'Oh aye. We got you yer own office and everything. All the lads, they can't wait to meet you.'

'Honest? Fuckin' hell…You know what? I almost feel a bit nervous about it. It's like I'm finally gettin' somewhere in me life. D'you know what I—?'

'Look, Blakey, you won't be going no place unless you gets a move on. Round the back of here there's some tall conifers, and a path leading through em down to the river. The lass is waitin' down there on a bench, and if you times it right you'll be coming along just as the Reaper is turnin' nasty on her.'

'Will he be choppin' her head off?'

'No. He subdues em first, then takes em somewhere more quiet where he does the deed. So he'll be subduing her.'

'Oh aye?'

'Aye.'

'When you says "subduing", woss you mean, exactly?'

'You dunno what "subduing" means?'

'Course I fuckin' knows it. I just mean, you know, I needs a few more details.'

'Well, he could be doing anything. He might just be talkin' to her, see, chattin' her up. But make no mistake—it is him and he is aimin' to commit a murder.'

'So he won't have no axe?'

'No, he don't walk around with an axe.'

'What about a saw, or summat?'

'He won't have nuthin' much at all, Blakey. You'll be all right using your bare fists on him, no problem. But just in case, I brung you this.' He reached inside his jacket and brung out a monkey wrench.

'Fuckin' hell,' I says, taking it, 'this is me old monkey wrench. How'd you have me old monkey wrench?'

'Ah, it's amazin' what you can turn up if you has a look around. Anyhow, you gotta shift now,' he says, looking at his watch and wiping the blood from his nose. 'Go on—round the back and down the path by the conifers. Nobble the feller and then start shoutin' for police, or "help" or summat. We'll come by anon.'

'Anon?'

'Aye, anon.'

'Fuck's "anon" mean?'

'Blake, we ain't got time. *Go now.*'

'Nah, come on—woss "anon" mean?'

'It…it means "shortly". Or "in a bit". All right? Now please—'

'Why can't you just say "in a bit", then? You tryin' to be clever? You tryin' to make out like I'm thick, and you're more brainier'n me?'

'No! Blakey, you gotta—'

'Say I'm more brainier'n you.'

'Eh?'

'*Say it.*'

'*All right…* You're brainier than me. Happy? Now *go.*'

I stopped to light another smoke as I went down the alley, and looked back over me shoulder before setting off again, catching the tail of Jonah as he pegged it round the corner up the other end. Summat struck us as peculiar about all this, I suddenly realised, although I couldn't put me pointer on what it were. I smoked and walked and wondered, coming up with fuck all besides a length of ash and a limp in me leg (from earlier on under the Paul Pry, like as not). Rounding the corner I spotted them conifers straight off and headed for em. I were walking slow, taking care to step on no twigs. Plus there were a lot of dog shite down there and I didn't want me espadrilles besmirched again. I noticed the shadow of meself come clear on the path before us and looked up, expecting to see the moon full and high in the sky. But it were no moon, only a ball of light hovering about ten foot off the ground, about ten yard behind us. It were a bit like a football and a bit like the sun, but I knowed it were really my mam's head—the one I'd knocked off her statue by accident.

'All right, Mam,' I says.

'You have done well, Royston,' she says, hovering. 'You have done your mam proud. Now go.'

'Mam, I ain't even started yet.'

'You have. You have brung the villains to justice.'

'I ain't. I'm just about to—'

'You followed the path through darkness and many a nasty thing, and destroyed the awful cabal that sits at the heart of Mangel. But evil lives on, Royston. From the ashes of the pyre crawls a charred and battered seed. And that will spawn yet more evil, my son. More harm to women will be committed in the name of madness. More butchery of innocents, and denial of all that is good.'

'Cabal?'

'Now you must go. Go and destroy that which threatens this town yet! But well done on smashin' that cabal.'

'Mam, listen, I ain't sure what you…'

But she were going backwards fast, and I don't think she could hear us. I called her name and ran after her but soon she were gone, and there were no light at all besides the full moon that had broke from cover up there. I headed for them conifers, puffing on me smoke and thinking about Mam. I felt a bit bad, her saying she were proud of us for bringing villains to justice, and me knowing that I hadn't even started yet. I felt like I'd lied to her somehow, and that made us feel even worser.

'I never lied to you, Mam,' I says, looking up at the moon. 'You just got confused, is all. Like old people.'

No one answered, but I didn't mind. I knew she could hear us.

'But you will be proud, Mam. You just keep watchin'. When I gets me badge, you'll see a real man at work. And you'll be well proud, aye. I fuckin' promise.'

I found the path no problem and set off down it. It were well dark down here and I couldn't see me way proper. Summat long and dangly and with thorns brushed me cheek, scratching fuck out of it. Then I trod in some shite. It were a lot of shite, like a Great Dane had been saving up.

Follow the path, though it may be dark and full of nasty things…

I looked up, hoping for a glimpse of moonlight. But she were undercover again and I were on me todd. I knew that's how it were meant to be, though. Just me and my monkey wrench, which I got out and felt the weight of in me paw. It were quite heavy. I wanted another fag. I wanted to be sitting in front of a pint of lager, having a chat with Nathan and the lads down the Paul Pry. Maybe I'd start going back there. Aye, I'd rather be there than here.

…leadin' you to places you don't want to go…

The moon came out again and lit the place up a bit. There were a bend just up ahead. I went through that and into quite a long stretch, which opened out by some steps that went down to the river. But before then, about ten yard in front of us, were a bench. And on it were sat a bird. I couldn't see much of her face. There were no feller nearby and not much of nothing besides the bird and the bench and a lot of dog shite. She were looking at us and I had a feeling she were scaredy about summat, like it were me who were the bad feller and I were holding a big axe. I looked down and saw that I didn't have no axe, but I did have the wrench out and ready. I put it away and smiled at her, and walked up to her slow. I didn't know what else to do. There were meant to be a feller here and I were meant to knack him. I felt like I were fucking it all up, even though it weren't my fault.

About five yards from the bird I got a look at her face, the moon breaking out yet again, and clocked that it were Rache. She were staring right at us and summat were awry with her mouth, opening and closing like that and the jaws working like she'd got cramp in em. I opened me own gob to ask her about that, when I realised that she were actually mouthing words at us.

'What?' I says. Cos I couldn't hear em.

'Just walk on,' she hisses, tucking her head down like she weren't looking at us.

'Eh?'

A rustle in the bushes and someone jumps out at us, aiming to deal us a twock on the swede with the summat or other he were holding. I didn't have time to get a good look up and down him, only to think and react. A bit like a ninja. This were it, you see—my chance to shine, to grab copperdom by the bollocks and make it me own. Never mind that Jonah had told us a fib back there, about the Reaper not having no axe. I could get grumpy about that and have me swede chopped off, or put it by for a later time and duck out the way.

I ducked out the way, thumping the feller in the guts. It were like laying one on a padded wicker chair, and I think I bust a rib or two. I pulled back to bust the rest of em when I felt an arm round me neck. I bent down low and threw the fucker off, surprised at how slippery he were, coming at us from different angles and all. Summat hard and wooden pinged off me ear. It's about then that the darkness started coming down around us. And I don't mean the moon hiding behind another cloud, but the black stuff in my head that always took over when braces was down and the chips was on the pavement. It were the one thing I could rely on, that darkness, and I breathed it in like the first fag of a bad morning.

• • •

'What?'

'You've gotta run. Summat bad has happened, and…'

'What?'

'Blake, they'll take you. They'll lock you up forever. You've gotta *run*.'

'What?'

'Stop sayin' "what", will you?'

'Wh…eh?'

I experienced a sharp pain in my cheek, bringing tears to me peepers and sense to me swede. Rache were stood before us, looking worried and none too happy. Behind her, on the deck, five or six coppers was laid out. The moon came out for a moment or two and showed us that one of em were Jonah. 'But…'

'No buts, just go. *Now*.'

'But there were a feller…the axe…'

'There was them coppers back there, and you. That's all there was. I can't believe you, Blakey. Why'd you follow me here? They…this was a big case that they was workin' on, tryin' to catch the murderer. And you…you've gone and…'

'I never followed you, Rache. I were just—'

'*Go*, before one of em wakes up. *If* one of em wakes up.'

I had another look at em. One of em looked like he were stirring. I turned and went. At the end of the path, by them steps that leads down to the river, I turned and shouted to Rache: 'But…'

'*Go!*'

MAN ARRESTED FOR BEING DRUNK AND DISORDERLY

A man was arrested in Tubthumpers last night after abusing staff members and fellow customers, dropping a pint glass, and vomiting on the floor. Dominic Mouse, of Barkettle, was taken to the police station and detained overnight in the cells, after which he was released with no charge.

'He was in a bit of a state,' said PC Mard of Mangel Constabulary. 'But really, he was no danger to the public. It was more for his own safety. The staff at Tubthumpers just thought he might get himself into trouble, if you know what I mean. He was going on about a satellite dish, as I understand. Someone stole it and he wanted to get even, summat like that. We gave him one of our "Victims of Crime" booklets, which tells you what you should do if you have any property stolen and how you can get counselling for it, and then let him go.'

If you are a victim of crime, you can pick up a 'Victims of Crime' leaflet from the front desk at Mangel Police Station.

28

I'd always liked it down by the water. You can sit there and watch it all go by, coming from somewhere else and going to another place. The sea, like as not. I'd seen it on telly, about all rivers flowing into seas. I looked at the River Clunge, which is the name of the one here in Mangel, and I thought about that. After a bit, and sucking the last bit of baccy out of the long butt I'd found on the ground, I came to a decision. I decided that the River Clunge didn't flow seaward at all, and actually just went round and around, the same water coming in as what had passed out earlier on. A bit like animals drinking their own piss, which they have been known to do. I'd seen that on telly as well, and it means the animal is sick.

I waded into the water. It were well muddy on the banks and hard to stand up, so I threw meself forward and swam out a bit. The current took us and soon I were in the middle, shifting fast away from the place I'd been stood. Little bastards kept knocking into me pins under the dark water, and I took em to be fish. They had twenty-pound barbel in the Clunge, so I'd heard, and it felt like one of them. After a while, and spinning around a bit and not really knowing which way were what, I started going under. I am a good swimmer, I just hadn't done it in a few years. About thirty years. And the togs didn't help. There were a bastard of a current about a foot below breathing level and it got right in me jacket, treating it like a sail and pushing us about like a submarine in an underwater storm.

'I'm sorry, Mam,' I says, looking up at the moon. I noticed that it weren't actually full, although it did seem like it were. It'd be full on the morrer, like as not. 'I'm sorry I...fucked up the copper job there, and...' It were hard to get the words out cos I kept going under. 'I'm sorry I disapp...dis...'

• • •

It were a snail or summat. Summat soft and wet and working across me face like a...a...like a fucking snail, or summat. Or a worm. Aye, a worm. I opened me eyes.

I were blind.

No, it weren't blindness. There were summat in me eyes, and that's how come I couldn't see. I went to rub em but me arms wouldn't lift. It were like they was weighted down under...under... My legs wouldn't move neither. I squeezed me fingers shut and felt what were between em. Mud. Mud and shite. I opened me eyes again and it were more shite and mud. I kicked me legs but they was held down under the weight of all that dirt.

I were buried alive.

Someone had found us and took us for dead, and they'd put us in me grave, planting us there in the soil without even a fucking coffin and...and...

I chucked me guts.

The force of the spew made us roll over and curl into a ball, panting and continuing to honk, although a bit slower now. Tears and what felt like more spew was coming out me eyes, and I rubbed it all off and reached for summat to blow me hooter on. There were nothing.

I lay still like that, in me early grave, and drifted off to kip. Or maybe it were actually death. Maybe I'd gone off to the land of deadfolk after all, and this were how it is in that far and distant land. Maybe all you does there is spew and curl up and want to blow yer hooter, but not have nothing to blow it on. Aye, that were it for surely. I'd carked it, back there in the…the…I couldn't recall quite how I'd come to get here, but I knowed where I were.

So, like I says, I drifted off.

• • •

When I came to again I were on me knees. Paws planted afore us inches deep in the mud, face turned up to the moon, which were a big silver sovereign up there. Made us think of a bird—one of the many birds I'd had in me life—and she were sat nearby with a vodka and summat or other, and a slice of lemon in the glass. She sipped it and looked at us and I didn't know who it were, and I wanted to shout at her and ask her how come she weren't helping us. She were there and I were here, and…

You know what I heard, Blakey?

And then I knowed it.

I heard all the birds who goes out with you carks it in the end. Mysteriously, like…

'Which one is you?' I says to the bird. 'Beth, is it? I never meant it. You knows that, right? Is it Sal? Or…'

But she were gone, her and her vodka and summat or other, and it were just me and the moon and the mud again. I stood up and stepped backwards, planting a shoe in the water. I were on a riverbank and there were trees all about, both sides of the water. I went up the bank and started walking through them trees.

Looked a bit like Hurk Wood.

I found it hard to think but I knew I had to. Hadn't I been dead and planted in the ground not so long back? What had happened to that? How come I were out and walking again now, dirt in me fingernails and paws and all over us? I glanced up at the moon again and it gave us the answer, placing it in me swede without the use of words nor actions nor nothing else. The answer, you see, were that I were like a zombie. This were Hurk Wood and I'd died and been buried here, just like I'd buried them what had come before us and whose dead corpses I'd been lumbered with. But…

But, you see, there were magic at work here. And it's the moon I'm on about. The moon had looked down upon my plight and doled us out a second chance. And not only that, but he were showing us how to pull it off.

You'd have to make a big statement if you wanna win em round. A big fuckin' statement…

I walked through the trees, stumbling here and there and gasping for fags and scran and lager. I didn't have none of them just now but I knew I could have em. I'd be rolling in all the good things I'd ever wanted, along with glory and birds and the respect of the whole community. And Mam could rest at last, knowing how her son done her proud. But…

First I had some graft to do.

• • •

I wished I'd gone and fetched my motor first. There were a spade in her, I think. The boot weren't a large one but big enough for what I needed it for. I couldn't recall where I'd left her, though. And it didn't matter anyhow. I'd found an old pickaxe tangled up in some brambles. And a rusty wheelbarrow, half buried down a little gulley. It seemed lucky that I'd found em, in a way, but I knew it weren't luck. It were the moon, helping us out and leading us to the things I needed. With the moon behind me back, and my heart beating inside of us, there weren't nothing I couldn't do.

That's what I kept telling meself as I dug down into the earth, pulling things out and dropping em in the barrow.

Do summin impressive that they can appreciate...

The moon had showed us where to dig as well. I'd thought I could recall how to get there but I couldn't, as it happened, and ended up lost and wanting to lie down. Then I seen the spot over yonder, plucked out of the darkness by a long finger of silvery light.

I sang a song as I worked. The song were 'Whistle While You Work', by Snow White and the Midgets, or whatever. It were a good and happy tune and it kept us going, and the moon sang along, too.

I'd buried em all a lot shallower than I'd thought, so it didn't take so long as you'd reckon to dig em up. About an hour, perhaps, although time were passing funny on that particular night. And I couldn't find all the bits. Certain parts was missing, and I put that down to the shallow burial and varmints digging em up and having em for tea. But they'd left the most important bits, and I placed the three of em atop the pile in the wheelbarrow and stood back to admire me work. Sun were coming up in the east and it looked like being a beautiful day, and do you know what? I didn't want a fag.

But it'd have to be very, very impressive...

I got hold of the barrowload and wheeled him roadward. No tyre on the barrow but the wheel were round and the axle still turned, which I found remarkable considering the corrosion. When I got roadside it were broad daylight. I parked the barrow and sat on my arse, waiting for the next bit. I knew it'd come. The moon had fucked off now but I knew she hadn't forsook us. And no way would she expect us to wheel a barrow into town, without a tyre and loaded up with the three Munton brothers.

29

I got a shock when I woke up. I didn't know where I were, and I thought I were still in me dream and the face up there were a part of that. But then I thought about it and realised that I hadn't dreamed at all, and that I'd just been kipping hard and too dog-arse knackered to get me dreaming muscles shifting. And when I thought about it again, and reminded meself that the face up there were a real one, I realised that I were in trouble.

And that my hopes and dreams—and them of me mam as well—were looking like turning to shite.

'Mand,' I says. Cos it were Mandy Munton. 'Mand, woss you...er...'

'Woss *you* doin' here, more like. I drove past and saw you lyin' here. What happened? Are you all right? Did you get knocked down?'

'Knocked down?'

'Yeah. You know, a hit and run.'

'Hit an'...er, aye. Aye, yeah.' I got on my arse and had a scan. The barrow were a little ways off, near some bushes.

'What's that smell?' says Mandy. She didn't look too well, looking at her. Pale and a bit scaredy-looking, like she'd had a fright. I ain't sure but I think her hands was shaking.

'Smell? There ain't no smell.'

'Yeah there is. Like...like the grave, it is. The smell of the grave.'

'How'd you know what the grave smells like?'

'I dunno. I think I've always known it, you know? There's some things you just know in life. And sometimes you don't know em at first, but you got to take a while to work em out. And...'

She went on like that for a bit. I took the opportunity to work some things out in me swede. See, this is like I told you just now. I knew the moon would not forsake us, and here's the fucking proof. Not only did I have a motor to drive townward in, but also Mandy Munton: the bird responsible for carking them remains over there in the barrow. I had the whole package tied up and ready to deliver, thereby making the big statement that DI Dave had told us I must do, and thereby—

'So, what d'you say? I mean, I know I'm not the best catch in the world. And I think...I mean, you must know about me, yeah? You do know the things I've been...? I mean, there was that phone call, so of course you know about me. But that's all history. I done summat that...I burned my bridges, Blake. But it's about the future now. So...what'll it be? You and me?'

'Wha?'

'I'm askin' you to come with me, Blake. You and me, in the big city. You look after me and I'll look after you. We'll be a team.'

'But...eh?'

I rubbed my forehead. She were confusing us, sticking a spanner in me train of thought and trying to save her own guilty skin. It's just like before, telling us all that shite and none of it being true, just so she could...could...I dunno what she were trying to do, but I knowed I didn't like it.

'Look, Blakey...' She took me paw in hers and placed it on her cheek, which had a bit more colour to it now and felt nice. Then she kissed it and put in on her left tit. That felt even better.

I knowed what she were up to, with her ways and her wiles. And she weren't getting away with it. Not now I'd come so far. But like I says, it felt nice, so I might as well let her do it for a bit.

'Blakey, I know you're confused. You're confused about everything. I could see it in your eyes when I found you again the other day. This town, it's beatin' you. Don't you see it? It beats everyone. That's why I left, all them years ago. And don't you remember what I said to you then, when I first tried to leave? I asked you to come with us. You said no. And I knew you would. I could see you wasn't ready, see. Not like I was ready. You hadn't seen what I'd seen, you hadn't been…been *fucked* by this place. But you have now, right? You can see it now, right?'

I found it amazing how she could talk and have her tit felt at the same time. Me, I couldn't ever do two things at once. That's the difference between birds and fellers.

'Blake,' she says, moving back. My hand slipped out and started getting cold again straight off. 'You got to listen to me. You got to *think*. The time is *now*, Blake, and we got to…I've done summat that…He…he thought he could give me a poxy ring, and that it would make everything…'

She turned and paced off a little ways, rubbing her head and sniffing. I watched her, appreciating the fine figure that she possessed. And I'll admit to you: I were having me doubts. Doubts about turning her in. Doubts about being a copper. Doubts about staying in Mangel, and…the things she were saying there, I couldn't quite hear em right but…it's like they went into my ears but never reached me brain, instead taking a detour and going south to the guts and making em ache and pine. I knowed she were right, is what I'm trying to say, and that I ought to trust her and go with her, and let her lead us wherever and always look after her, and never let nothing bad ever happen to her.

'Mand,' I says, 'I—'

'What's this?'

She were stood over by the barrow. I'd forgot about that. She put a paw to her gob.

'Oh…' she says, voice turning shrill. 'Oh my…'

I got my monkey wrench out.

It broke my heart, but I had to.

You knows that, right?

30

After a while I noticed the BMW badge on the steering wheel. Funny how you don't notice these things straight off, but I'd had a lot on me mind of late and weren't so observant as normal.

It were a lovely motor, actually, this Beemer. And not too far different from DI Dave's one—right down to the black paintwork. I found that quite amazing, two near-identical posh motors in the same town, and I shook my head at the sheer wonder of it. Mind you, I could see there being three of em in the none-too-distant. I loved the Ferrari but maybe this one here were more of a practical copper's motor. Especially your larger copper, there being lots of room to stretch your pins. Plenty of stowage in the boot as well, which were handy.

I cruised around the outskirts of town, dipping into Barkettle Road and then turning off into Beaver Lane at the last minute, making a Blue Allegro honk at us.

I turned around to give him what for, but left it. I didn't feel like doing all that just now, looking after folks and pointing out the errors of their ways. I were knackered, and I needed a rest summat chronic. But I knew I couldn't have one yet. I had the important bit to do still, the bit whereby I gets me new job and becomes the hero. All the hard graft were behind us and I just had to turn up, hand over the goods, and collect me dues. But...

I turned on the radio, hoping it would set my mind straight and get the bad feelings out of me guts. It's like I had a nest of bugs in em. Mind you, I were a bit peckish, so it could just be pangs along them lines.

Dolly Parton were on the radio, singing 'Stand by Your Man'. I liked Dolly Parton. She had a great voice, all right face, and massive tits. You can't go wrong with them three things in a woman, if you're gonna get her singing songs. I closed my eyes and listened. Then I opened em sharpish, clipping the back end of a parked Jag before pulling the motor straight again. I drove along like that, at about forty mile an hour, until the song stopped.

'And that was Tammy Wynette singing the anthem of downtrodden yet loyal women everywhere: "Stand by Your Man". And let's have that as our thought for the day, shall we? Because, really, where would all you women be without your menfolk? It's nine o'clock and this is Troy Polloy on Mangel FM, bringing you all the news, views, and top tunes this morning and every morning until they sack me. In local news, a policeman has been found brutally murdered in his North Mangel flat. Police are seeking his live-in girlfriend in connection with the murder. She is described as slim, with long dark hair and a nice body. The victim has been named as Detective Inspector David Bor—'

I flicked the radio off, turning the knob a bit too hard and snapping it off. I dunno why they couldn't just play records all the time instead of all that yakking. I drove around bit more, stopping for fags at a filling station up by Muckfield, and then headed townward. There were no putting it off no more. And, to be frank with you, I dunno what I were fretting over anyhow.

• • •

It were the same bird. I went up to her and cleared me throat.

But she got in first with: 'If you've come for one of the "Victims of Crime" leaflets, they've run out. We'll have more next week.'

'No, no,' I says. 'Actually I'm here on an important matter. A very important matter indeed, you might say. I got me motor parked back there and in the boot is—'

Just then her blower went off and she picked it up, saying: 'Hello. Mangel Police Station. We are short-staffed at the moment and can only deal with emergencies. Please call again tomorrow. "Victims of Crime" leaflets have run out, by the way. Thank y... Oh, hiya, Maureen. So did the stain come out all right?'

While she took her emergency call I went over to them posters up by the door and took down the one with the Munton boys on it. I felt like Clint Eastwood in a cowboy film, coming into town to claim his bounty. Only I didn't really want a Bounty cos the bits of coconut gets stuck between me teeth. I'd have a Mars Bar instead, if they had em. And a badge that says I'm a copper.

The bird were still dealing with her Maureen emergency. I felt like I ought to be pissed off about it but I weren't, even though she were going on about getting stains out of carpets and I had three solved murders in the boot of me motor, plus the murderer. I were beginning to relax finally, and found meself thinking ahead to later on, when I'd be celebrating a job well done and a turning point in the life of Royston Blake. I fancied steak and chips down Burt's Caff, followed by a large brandy, nice cigar, and fifteen or twenty pints of strong lager. As I planned the evening I got a fag out and went to light it.

'Hoy, you,' says the bird, holding a paw over the blower. 'No smokin' in here. See that sign? And no more of your chip papers, neither.'

I shook my head and smiled, getting up. She were fucking barmy, that one. I could see me and her getting on all right, having a laugh when I came in each morning and cracking a joke or two. Plus I had a few stains around the house and she might be able to help with them. Especially some of me trolleys, which had gone a bit discoloured in the groin region. And them no more than a dozen or so years old as well.

Outside, I leant against the pillar and lit meself up, watching the passing vehicles. I'd not been stood there a couple of minutes when a feller comes walking towards us across the road, paying scant regard to the traffic and frankly making a nuisance of himself. I were all set to point out the pedestrian crossing just a few short yards up the way when I noticed two uniformed coppers yomping towards us from that direction. Seemed like everyone were coming for us at once, and I found myself drawing straight and getting ready for action. I held steady though and let em pass, engrossed as they was in their conversation and not even noticing us.

'Yeah, they just found it in the car park over there,' the one were saying. 'His Beemer all right, no doubt about it.'

'How come?'

'Cos they checked fuckin' the plates, course.'

'Nah, how come it's there?'

'Well, they reckons his bird put it there. Drove it off after… you know, doing the murder.'

'That's unbelievable.'

'You don't believe us?'

'Eh?'

'You callin' us a liar, John?'

'No, I just—'

'Well shut yer fuckin' cake-hole and listen. Like I was saying…they found the motor and no sign of the bird. But—and this is fuckin' *strange*—the boot of the motor is open and inside it's full of all these animal skeletons and bits of carcasses and that.

There was a couple of rabbit skulls there, apparently, and the better part of a rotted badger.'

'Flippin' hell.'

'Exactly. They're saying she was into all this witchcraft stuff, doing bad spells and that.'

'A fuckin' witch? Blimey.'

'Exactly.'

'Poor old Borstal.'

'Nah, fuck him. He was a wrong un.'

The door swung to behind em, shutting off their yakking. Fucking bastards, ignoring us like that. I'd show em in a day or two, once I became a copper like them. I'd teach em to say hello and call us sir, instead of ignoring us and going on about whatever they was going on about.

'Look, I don't want no trouble.' It were that other feller, the one who'd been jaywalking towards us just now. He looked worried about summat. 'I'm goin' home, OK? Back to Barkettle. I won't bother you no more and I forgive you for what you done, stealin' my satellite dish. I forgive you, all right? Even though it ended up ruinin' my marriage. She loved that dish, you know. It was her favourite pink. And then I lost me job, and the doctor put us on the pills. I just couldn't handle it, you know? That dish getting stolen, it was like…I saw it as a challenge to my manhood. Do you see? Ah, none of it matters now. I just…I need to put this behind me and get my life back on track, and…'

Fuck knew what he were going on about but I recognised him now. I ought to have knowed him sooner but I hadn't ever seen him in daylight before, and he looked a bit different when he weren't raging at us. It were him.

You know, that feller.

The one with the rounders bat, in the park.

The one who'd called us a cunt in the cells.

The one, right, who'd knacked Mandy's face. And you just don't do that. Not to birds. Not even murdering ones.

I went for him.

'Hey...' he says, backing away. 'I'm here to call a truce! I'm here to...'

He couldn't really say no more cos I were after him down the pavement for a bit and then diagonal across the road, zipping in front of motors and causing many a beep and not even caring about that pedestrian crossing back there. I knew the cars would just ping off us, see, if they hit us. I were full up of red-hot metal and nothing could stop us. When my eyes was open I could see the feller there, getting a bit of distance between us but not enough. And when they was closed I saw Mandy's poor busted face, eye all red and closed up and already going black in parts.

'You don't do that to a bird,' I shouts to him as we cut across the carpark, heading for the bridge. 'You just fuckin'...you just...'

I had to stop talking. I'm sharp over hundred yard, but more than that and I ain't sharp. I'm blunt, or summat. Like a blunt instrument, full up of hot and heavy metal, staggering along the road and getting heavier by the second, and just plain flagging like a bastard.

But I weren't flagging this time. I were getting faster, wolfing down the gap between us like it were a long bit of spaghetti and I were hungry. I could hark shouting behind us, someone chasing us perhaps and calling my name. I couldn't look back now though, not with justice in me paws and a villain in me sights.

We was across river now and pegging it up the main road towards Bonehill. It had started pissing down and the ground were wet and slippy, but I didn't care. I had the bust eye of Mandy in my head and I wanted justice for it. All I'd ever wanted were justice. Not for me, but for the world in general. Righting wrongs, steadying the balance, welcoming them what's welcome, sending the others on their way. I just wanted things fair. And…

The feller turned into a back road behind the flats. I knew I had him now. No outsider knows the back roads like I knows em. Not even locals does. All I had to do were cut him off and I'd have him cornered, in a nice quiet spot where no one could see us doling out justice. I were bombing down the back roads meself now. I'd lost sight of the feller but I'd soon find him again. I could smell him and his fear. Just up that road there, by the lock-ups. He were up there and I'd stake my flaming life on it. I reached the corner and looked round it, and there he were.

Just stood there, looking into one of the lock-ups.

I walked towards him, panting hard and smiling to meself, thinking about how I'd do it. I watched him the whole while, in case he got any ideas. He were still looking into that lock-up, and I didn't understand it. Nothing in there could be so interesting that he'd stop running from me. Mind you, that weren't my problem. That were his fucking problem and he were gonna find out about it in ten second flat. I rolled me sleeves up, watching him. While I watched him a load of red stuff sprayed out of the lock-up and splashed all over him.

Summat didn't seem right, and I stopped.

I got moving again, slow now, keeping round the back of him and away from the lock-up. As I rounded it I started getting a view inside it, seeing the thing that had stopped the feller in his tracks. And it were…and…

'Here,' says Nathan, coming out of the lock-up and holding out a dripping axe to the feller. 'You use this on him there, why don't you.' He were addressing the feller and nodding in my direction. 'And make sure you finishes the job right.'

Then he were gone, limping off down an alley. He slipped away into the shadows, holding a big carrier bag with some long dark hair sticking out of it and summat quite heavy inside. The feller hadn't moved. He were still stood there, that red stuff all down him, holding the axe and staring at the headless body inside the lock-up.

Meanwhile the rain pissed down and washed away the blood. But the more it washed away, the more came flowing out of the lock-up.

'Mandy,' I says to her, 'I...I never meant to...'

But I don't think she could hear us.

After a short while, or perhaps a long while, someone came running down the road towards us. It were Jonah and a couple of other coppers. They grabbed the feller and took the axe off him and got him face-down on the hard stuff, clipping on the cuffs and reading him his rights. They looked like they'd been in wars, one of em with a black eye and Jonah with a fat lip.

'We fuckin' got him,' says the one sitting on the feller. 'We fuckin' got the fuckin' Reaper!'

'No,' says Jonah, getting his radio out. 'We never got him. This man here got him.'

'Yeah but—'

'I said *Blakey* caught him, all right? It's only fair.'

They both looked at me. I started coughing. I kept coughing and couldn't stop, and I had to bend over. Summat came up from me guts or me lungs and landed on the wet tarmac. Before the rain washed it away, you could see it had blood in it.

THE END

ACKNOWLEDGMENTS

Thanks go to the many people on Facebook who supported this series and helped to get this book published. All hail the power of social networking, even if it means that people are looking at screens instead of reading books. To Alex Carr who took a chance on something unusual and is responsible for this edition that you are holding. To all the bloggers, journalists and fans who publically stood up for Royston Blake when the chips were down for him. He will repay you in the next life... which is in Mangel. To John Williams and Peter Ayrton who are the ones who got this series going in the first place. It is fair to say that without them I would be on a park bench somewhere, drinking Brasso and shouting at passers-by. This paint stripper is much nicer - cheers for the tip, guys.

ABOUT THE AUTHOR

Charlie Williams was born in Worcester, England, where he still lives with his wife and two children. His novels include *Deadfolk*, *Booze and Burn*, *King of the Road*, and *Stairway to Hell*, and have been translated into French, Spanish, Italian, and Russian.